Praise for Geo

The Secret Poet

"[O]ne of the author's best works and one of the best romances I've read recently...I was so invested in [Morgan and Zoe] I read the book in one sitting."—*Melina Bickard, Librarian, Waterloo Library (UK)*

Hopeless Romantic

"Thank you, Georgia Beers, for this unabashed paean to the pleasure of escaping into romantic comedies...If you want to have a big smile plastered on your face as you read a romance novel, do not hesitate to pick up this one!"—*The Rainbow Bookworm*

Flavor of the Month

"Beers whips up a sweet lesbian romance...brimming with mouth-watering descriptions of foodie indulgences...Both women are well-intentioned and endearing, and it's easy to root for their inevitable reconciliation. But once the couple rediscover their natural ease with one another, Beers throws a challenging emotional hurdle in their path, forcing them to fight through tragedy to earn their happy ending."
—*Publishers Weekly*

"The heartbreak, beauty, and wondrous joy of love are on full display in *Flavor of the Month*. This second chance romance is exceptional. Georgia Beers has outdone herself with this one."—*The Lesbian Book Blog*

One Walk in Winter

"A sweet story to pair with the holidays. There are plenty of 'moment's in this book that make the heart soar. Just what I like in a romance. Situations where sparks fly, hearts fill, and tears fall. This book shined with cute fairy trails and swoon-worthy Christmas gifts...REALLY nice and cozy if read in between Thanksgiving and Christmas. Covered in blankets. By a fire."—*Bookvark*

Fear of Falling

"Enough tension and drama for us to wonder if this can work out—and enough heat to keep the pages turning. I will definitely recommend this to others—Georgia Beers continues to go from strength to strength."
—*Evan Blood, Bookseller (Angus & Robertson, Australia)*

"In *Fear of Falling* Georgia Beers doesn't take the obvious, easy way… romantic, feel-good and beautifully told."—*Kitty Kat's Book Review Blog*

"I was completely invested from the very first chapter, loving the premise and the way the story was written with such vulnerability from both characters' points of view. It was truly beautiful, engaging, and just a lovely story to read."—*LesBIreviewed*

The Do-Over

"You can count on Beers to give you a quality well-paced book each and every time."—*The Romantic Reader Blog*

"*The Do-Over* is a shining example of the brilliance of Georgia Beers as a contemporary romance author."—*Rainbow Reflections*

"[T]he two leads are genuine and likable, their chemistry is palpable… The romance builds up slowly and naturally, and the angst level is just right. The supporting characters are equally well developed. Don't miss this one!"—*Melina Bickard, Librarian, Waterloo Library (UK)*

The Shape of You

"I know I always say this about Georgia Beers's books, but there is no one that writes first kisses like her. They are hot, steamy and all too much!"—*Les Rêveur*

The Shape of You "catches you right in the feels and does not let go. It is a must for every person out there who has struggled with self-esteem, questioned their judgment, and settled for a less than perfect but safe lover. If you've ever been convinced you have to trade passion for emotional safety, this book is for you."—*Writing While Distracted*

Calendar Girl

"*Calendar Girl* by Georgia Beers is a well-written sweet workplace romance. It has all the elements of a good contemporary romance… It even has an ice queen for a major character."—*Rainbow Reflections*

"A sweet, sweet romcom of a story…*Calendar Girl* is a nice read, which you may find yourself returning to when you want a hot-chocolate-and-warm-comfort-hug in your life."—*Best Lesbian Erotica*

Blend

"You know a book is good, first, when you don't want to put it down. Second, you know it's damn good when you're reading it and thinking, I'm totally going to read this one again. Great read and absolutely a 5-star romance."—*The Romantic Reader Blog*

"This is a lovely romantic story with relatable characters that have depth and chemistry. A charming easy story that kept me reading until the end. Very enjoyable."—*Kat Adams, Bookseller, QBD (Australia)*

"*Blend* has that classic Georgia Beers feel to it, while giving us another unique setting to enjoy. The pacing is excellent and the chemistry between Piper and Lindsay is palpable."—*The Lesbian Review*

Right Here, Right Now

"The angst was written well, but not overpoweringly so, just enough for you to have the heart-sinking moment of 'will they make it,' and then you realize they have to because they are made for each other."—*Les Reveur*

"[A] successful and entertaining queer romance novel. The main characters are appealing, and the situations they deal with are realistic and well-managed. I would recommend this book to anyone who enjoys a good queer romance novel, and particularly one grounded in real world situations."—*Books at the End of the Alphabet*

"[A]n engaging odd-couple romance. Beers creates a romance of gentle humor that allows no-nonsense Lacey to relax and easygoing Alicia to find a trusting heart."—*RT Book Reviews*

By the Author

Romances

Turning the Page

Thy Neighbor's Wife

Too Close to Touch

Fresh Tracks

Mine

Finding Home

Starting from Scratch

96 Hours

Slices of Life

Snow Globe

Olive Oil & White Bread

Zero Visibility

A Little Bit of Spice

What Matters Most

Right Here, Right Now

Blend

The Shape of You

Calendar Girl

The Do-Over

Fear of Falling

One Walk in Winter

Flavor of the Month

Hopeless Romantic

16 Steps to Forever

The Secret Poet

The Puppy Love Romances

Rescued Heart

Run to You

Dare to Stay

The Swizzle Stick Romances

Shaken or Stirred

On the Rocks

With a Twist

WITH A TWIST

by

Georgia Beers

2022

WITH A TWIST

ISBN 13: 978-1-63555-987-3

This Trade Paperback Original Is Published By
Bold Strokes Books, Inc.
P.O. Box 249
Valley Falls, NY 12185

First Edition: April 2022

Credits
Editor: Ruth Sternglantz
Production Design: Stacia Seaman
Cover Design by Ann McMan

Acknowledgments

Let me start by saying that I will miss this group of characters. I enjoyed writing this series in ways I can't explain, and Julia, Vanessa, and Amelia feel like my own family. I'm sad to leave them behind, but so, so happy I got to share them with you. I hope they mean as much to you as they do to me. Thanks for coming along on their journey.

Thank you to the usual suspects: Bold Strokes Books and everybody there. Rad and Sandy for keeping things running smoothly. Ruth Sternglantz for making me look like I know how to write a book. My friends—specifically Melissa, Carsen, Rachel, Kris, Ann, Nicole—for checking on me daily. As the only one of us who has been home alone this whole time, your contact meant much more than you know. I love you all so much and consider myself super lucky to have you all in my life.

Thank you to some new folks, who made living in these crazy times just that much more bearable: the creators of Zoom for making it possible to see each other's faces, even when we couldn't fly around the country and actually hug the ones we love. The conference runners, who pivoted with (what looked like) ease and held virtual gatherings rather than canceling things altogether. To Instacart and Door Dash and Amazon and anybody else who risked their health to deliver things to my door so I didn't have to go out into what has become kind of a scary world. To moviemakers who streamed their new releases so those of us who were hesitant to go back to the theater wouldn't miss out. To every single health care worker in this country and around the globe, THANK YOU for all you've done, all you've sacrificed, and all you've put up with. You are all heroes to me.

And to all the writers and the readers: thank you for all of it. To the writers for continuing to write stories and keep us entertained, even though you were stuck in the house, some of you with every single member of your family and no breaks. And to the readers for continuing to support us in what we do. We writers would be nothing without our readers, and now—especially now—thank you just doesn't seem like enough. I send my love and gratitude to each and every one of you.

Chapter One

Seriously, was there anything better than dogs?

The answer to that, of course, was no. Amelia Martini was a hundred percent sure of that. People sucked. Well, many of them. Actually, okay, most of them. Not dogs. Dogs didn't lie. They didn't cheat. They didn't care if you were moody. Or if you put on a few pounds. They didn't alter your entire perception of what your future was going to be.

She gave her head a shake as she waited for Duke to do his business on an unsuspecting maple tree. He was a German shepherd owned by a single guy named Gerard. Gerard was a contractor and usually took Duke to job sites with him, but his current one was in a high-rise downtown. Too dangerous for Duke to be wandering around. So Amelia would be stopping by once a day around lunchtime for the next couple of weeks to spend an hour or two with Duke, walking him, playing in the yard with him. As the owner/operator of Dogz Rule, it was literally her job to do so. And she loved it.

Her super-tiny business, which employed exactly…her, was slowly getting off the ground. Her handful of clients were great at word-of-mouth, and she was picking up a new one or two every couple weeks.

She made a clicking sound with her tongue to coax Duke away from whatever he was smelling so intently. He was a good dog with a gorgeous coat and a nose that wouldn't quit. She was always a bit hesitant to take on dogs that were large—the reason she did a prebooking interview—because she wasn't all that big, and she wasn't twenty-five, and getting dragged around the neighborhood did not sound like a fun time. But Duke was the epitome of gentle giant, and she adored him.

Early summer had come to Northwood on a lovely May breeze, and as June began, the sun shone down on the quiet street. Birds sang their songs from the treetops, and lawns were green and lush. Everything was gorgeous. It was Amelia's favorite season. She felt like she could relax in the summer. No gearing up for the cold of winter. No brown leaves or mud of the fall. No surprise spring snowstorms. Summer was predictable and warm, and she could feel her shoulders relax once the calendar hit Memorial Day.

This summer was a little different, though, because summer meant less clothing, and in her current state, Amelia wanted to wear more. Cover as much of herself as possible, especially her middle.

She sighed heavily just as her phone pinged from the back pocket of her jeans. Rounding the corner on their way back to Duke's house, she peeked at it. Her cousin Vanessa.

Bar Back tonight? Kids driving me insane. Plus, wedding planning. You in?

Amelia smiled, even as she felt a tiny prick of sadness. Her cousins Vanessa and Julia were her best friends in life. Forever and always. They had her back. They had her front. They were her rocks and her mirrors and everything else a woman needed to exist in this world. Julia had proposed to her now-fiancée, Savannah, last Christmas Eve, and they were planning a fall wedding. Amelia had never understood how a person could be so happy and so sad at the same time, but planning a wedding for the cousin she adored while simultaneously trying to make peace with her own divorce had her feeling exactly like that. So very happy. So very sad.

Yep, she typed back as Duke tugged her up the driveway to his house. Because she would be there. She'd always be there. She'd do what she always did: tuck her own crap away and put on a happy face. Julia and Savannah deserved nothing less.

As she was typing, another text popped up. One from Tammy, her ex. She groaned, making Duke's ears perk up.

Need to talk about house, was all it said.

"Well, you can just wait, can't you?" she said out loud at the phone, then slid it back into her pocket and opened the door to Duke's house.

Once inside, Duke went directly to the back door and stood there expectantly. When Amelia made eye contact with him, he looked out the door, then back at her, and she couldn't help but laugh at how clearly he was telling her what he wanted.

"Okay, fine. Just a short game of Kong toss."

As if he totally understood her, his tail began to wag, and he bowed at the door, then stood up. His excitement was plain.

"I mean it. Short."

Outside they went.

❖

Martini's, the bar Amelia's cousin Julia owned, was pretty busy for a Tuesday night. Summer softball leagues had begun, and Julia had sponsored three of them—one men's, one co-ed, one women's. Amelia was proud of the way she'd finally learned that, as a business owner, you had to spend money to make money. Not an easy lesson, especially when there wasn't a ton of extra to spend.

The Bar Back was just that, the back of the bar. When Julia had remodeled, she'd had the back room made into a combination office, practice bar, lounge area where she could work while still chatting with her cousins. And now, her fiancée as well. It was where they met to talk, laugh, and hash out life's problems—and sample new drinks because her cousins were Julia's guinea pigs.

Amelia sat on the couch with her ankles crossed on the coffee table, petting Delilah's big, square head, which was perched on Amelia's thigh. Delilah was Vanessa's rescue dog, but Auntie Amelia was one of her favorite people, so whenever Vanessa brought her along to The Bar Back, Amelia ended up with most of her attention. Which was fine, 'cause remember the whole thing about her liking dogs more than people? So true.

"Do you think you'll make it for two more weeks without killing any of the children?" Savannah asked Vanessa.

"We ask her that every year," Julia said from her spot behind the practice bar. "So far, murder has been avoided."

"Or we just *don't know* about it," Amelia pointed out. "Her kids are small. Easy to hide the bodies."

Savannah looked at her in mock-horror.

"It's been close a few times," said Vanessa, the second-grade teacher. "But I'm happy to report that no blood was shed today."

"How many days left?" Amelia asked.

"Eight with students, ten total," Vanessa answered without even taking a breath to think.

"But who's counting?" Savannah said with a laugh. "Where's Grace tonight?" Grace was Vanessa's girlfriend of about six months.

"She's got a couple weddings coming up this weekend, so she's been working late to get all her ducks in a row. Oliver's with his dad." Grace owned a local flower shop, and Oliver was Grace's son, also Vanessa's student, so they'd been very private about their relationship.

"Oh!" Amelia said as she made the connection. "That means only eight more days of keeping things under wraps, right?"

Vanessa nodded and her smile was adorable. She was crazy about Grace, and it was so nice to see. Amelia was thrilled for them, despite that tiny pang of sadness. It sucked when everybody around you was either paired up or pairing up, and you were the odd girl out. She did her best to buck up, though, because these were her favorite people in the universe, and all she wanted was to be happy for them.

"To no longer lurking in the shadows like creepers," Amelia said and held up her beer.

"Damn, I'll drink to that," Vanessa said, and the four of them touched glasses together. Amelia had a beer, Savannah had a sauvignon blanc, Julia had a Diet Coke, and Vanessa's was a club soda. No drinking on school nights for her. Mostly. And Julia didn't drink when the bar was open. "Next time, I'll have something stronger in my glass."

They sipped, and there was a lull before Savannah asked, "Hey, Meels, how's the dog business? Do Dogz with a Z still rule?"

"Always. And business is not bad at all," Amelia told her, still petting Delilah. "I picked up another new client the other day, and my dad has somebody who may need me to both dog-sit and house-sit. I'm waiting for more details on that."

"You're in a good position to do that," Vanessa said.

"You mean because I am a woman in my forties and I live in my father's house and have no home of my own? Yes, in fact, I am living like I'm fresh out of college. I mean, it's only been what? Twenty-five years since I graduated? Twenty-six?" Immediately she sighed and shook her head. "I'm sorry. Ignore me. I'm in a mood."

Savannah reached over and squeezed her shoulder. "You're just frustrated," she said. "That's allowed."

The other two nodded, gave her smiles, and she sort of grimaced back.

"And it's been twenty-seven years since you graduated college," Julia said, then ducked behind the bar as Amelia frisbeed a cardboard coaster at her.

"Well, with your dad in Florida, it's not like you're actually living *with* him," Vanessa offered up, clearly trying to make her feel better because that's what Vanessa did. "You do live by yourself still."

"I do." Which didn't make it any better. At all. But she appreciated the effort.

"But dog-sitting *and* house-sitting?" Julia asked. "That's a big order."

"The guy's a friend of my dad's, and I guess he's got a long business trip to Japan on tap and is having some work done in his house while he's away. He thought having somebody stay to not only watch the dogs, but keep an eye on the work might be a smart way to go. And my dad offered me up on a plate." Amelia grimaced. "Do I sound less than thrilled?"

Savannah held up her thumb and forefinger a tiny bit apart. "A skosh."

Amelia dropped back against the couch with a sigh of

frustration. "I just need to figure my life out. What do I want to do? Where do I want to live? Do I want a house? An apartment? A town house? A houseboat?"

"If it came down to it," Julia told her as she poured what looked like vodka into a stainless steel shaker, "you could camp out here in The Bar Back. I can tell you from experience that the couch is pretty comfy. I'd rent it to you for cheap." She looked up and winked.

"You're swell," Amelia said as the others chuckled.

"Anything for family," Julia said with a grin.

The topic shifted to other things. Savannah squeezed Amelia's shoulder and gave her a warm smile. She got it. She understood more than the cousins did how Amelia was feeling. It wasn't that she couldn't afford to find her own place. She could. It was that her brain was just…lost.

That was the word. She felt lost.

She just needed to find where she belonged in this new reality of hers. She never planned on being divorced and single at forty-nine. It was nowhere in her grand life plan. Not even close. What she needed to do was scrap that plan and make a new one. Right? That was all.

Which was *so* much easier said than done.

CHAPTER TWO

S eriously, is there anything more beautiful?"
There was a woman nearby, also looking at the paint samples in the Home Depot, and she glanced up, met Kirby's grin. "Um...no?"

Kirby laughed. "No is right. Look at all these colors!"

The woman gave her head a small shake, grinned just a bit, and headed to the counter with her paint chip.

"Good choice," Kirby called after her. "Champagne Toast is a lovely color." She turned back to the wall of color samples, her favorite place in the world. So much variety. So much possibility.

Color was life to Kirby. Color made life better. Cooler or warmer or more inviting or less intimidating. The color of the walls was integral to the mood, the attitude a room portrayed, and she loved everything about it. She could pick out a couple new chips that had been added since her visit last week. Salmon Run was a coral-pink blend. A new soft gray called Morning Mist. A happy yellow named Baby Chick.

"Are you gonna be froufrou hippy color lover all morning, or can we get going?" John Krogorski tilted his bandanna'd head at her, scratched at his graying beard, and waited her out.

She gave him her most dramatic sigh. "First of all, Krog, you're the hippy here, sir. Second, fine. Pull me away from my babies."

"I wouldn't if it wasn't closing in on nine. We gotta be there by nine thirty."

"Fine," Kirby said again before snagging five new color chips off the display. "Come with me, little beauties," she whispered to them.

Twenty minutes later, they pulled the Dupree Paint Design van into the driveway on Marley Lane that ran alongside a cute little Cape. The woman inside wanted her living room painted. Kirby knew she and Krog could knock that off in less than two hours. That afternoon, they had another interior to paint, but that one was a two-story great room, and they were going to need some scaffolding and an extra set of hands.

"Coop meeting us later?" Krog asked, as if reading her mind, which she was beginning to think he could. He'd worked with her father when he'd started the business thirty years ago. Krog had his issues, but he knew paint, and he knew how to paint.

"Yep. He'll meet us there." Jason Cooper—Coop—was one of the part-timers she hired when they had a big job. "Let's get this done. I have to squeeze in a quote before then." Kirby scratched her fingers through her short hair before putting her Dupree Paint Design baseball hat on backward. She'd be rolling today, and she never failed to end up with paint speckles in her hair on rolling days. This was a cake job, though. One color, two coats, easy peasy lemon squeezy. She and Krog gathered their supplies and headed up the walk, where Mrs. Janikowski, a woman in her early seventies, stood in the front door, smiling.

"Good morning, Mrs. J. You ready for a new living room?"

Kirby loved painting. She'd loved it since the first time she went on a job with her dad, and he let her roll part of a wall. There was something about it, something about smoothing a layer of fresh paint, whether it was a bright, bold color or simply white, that spoke of a clean slate. A fresh start. She loved what something as simple as a new color could do for a space. And when she found a customer who let her be creative? Look out.

Business was good, and Kirby was thankful for that but also knew it had to do with her work. It was good. Damn good. Her father had taught her from the beginning, when she was fifteen and he'd actually hired her, taken her on for the summer—never do shoddy work when your name is attached, and always keep the customer happy, no matter what. Invaluable lessons, both of them, given how important reviews were. She checked Yelp and Angi regularly and monitored the comments on the business's social accounts. She had an alert on her phone in case her company was mentioned anywhere online, and she had a list of neighborhood groups she checked at least once a week. Word of mouth kept her schedule full.

Krog laid out the tarp while Kirby moved furniture away from the walls. Mrs. Janikowski brought them each a cup of coffee and offered them blueberry muffins she'd made herself, which were nummy.

They got to work.

Wednesday was softball night, and Kirby looked forward to it each week, looked forward to stretching her legs and working her muscles and seeing her friends.

"How the hell can you say you play softball for the exercise when you do what you do all day long?" Lark Dawson said to her that evening while they warmed up, tossing the ball back and forth. "Your job *is* exercise." She demonstrated her point by miming rolling invisible paint on an invisible wall. "See how my arms are working? My shoulders?" Then she used her imaginary paintbrush and squatted down to paint an invisible bit of trim by her feet. "See me squatting, thereby using my quads and glutes?"

Kirby laughed. "You make a valid point, but I guess I just don't make the connection in my head. One is work, the other is fun."

"Both are exercise," Lark said.

These were her people. And this was her season. Not that Kirby didn't love all the seasons. She totally did. But summer meant softball, and softball was her favorite. She'd loved it since she was old enough to pick up a bat, and her dad had gotten her her very first mitt when she was just five. She also loved volleyball. And golf. And hiking. And swimming. Basically, anything that moved her body moved her.

She hit a double and three singles, stopped a wickedly hit line drive, and turned three double plays before the game was over and she and the team headed off to the bar that sponsored them,

Martini's. By eight o'clock, she had a beer in her hand and was laughing along with her team as they told stories of games past.

"And Kirbs over here," Lark was saying, talking about a game they'd played years ago, "just *crushed* the ball. Right over the fence. Game over."

"I bet that was so cool," said Emma, one of their new teammates this year. She was nice, but a little intense, Kirby thought. She was small and cute, but her eyes always seemed a little bit too wide.

Lark leaned close to Kirby as she signaled for a refill and said under her breath, "Crushing hard on you, that one."

Kirby snorted as the conversation continued and Emma's attention was pulled away.

"Nothing there?" Lark asked quietly. "She's nice, and she clearly likes you."

"What is she, twelve?" Kirby asked on a scoff.

Lark shook her head. "I forget you prefer to date the elderly."

Kirby gave her a playful punch. "Hey. Shut up. I do not." Before they could get into it, though, they were interrupted by Julia Martini, owner of the bar and one of the bartenders that night.

"You guys win?" she asked, her thick, dark hair pulled back in a low ponytail.

"We did," Kirby said. "Eight to three. We're undefeated so far."

"Nice. Bring me home a trophy, will you? I'll put up a shelf."

Kirby loved this place, and it made her happy to patronize a client. She'd painted the interior when Julia was remodeling. She'd talked her into the cool, but inviting gray—which was called Serene Cliffs, but Kirby would've named Don't Slate Me Because I'm Beautiful—that was on the main wall, and every time she walked in, she congratulated herself on choosing an impeccable color. It worked perfectly in the setting, accenting two walls of windows and one of exposed brick.

"Admiring your handiwork?" Julia asked her, pulling her back to the present.

Kirby felt her cheeks heat up as she laughed. "Yes, sorry. It's just a really perfect color." As she drained her beer, she recognized the attractive woman sitting at the far corner of the bar and grinned to herself. "Unless we ask her." She gestured with her chin.

"Who's that?" Lark asked, even as Julia chuckled.

"That's my cousin Amelia. She and Kirby disagreed on the color of that wall when I first opened." Turning her dark eyes to Kirby, she added, "I'm surprised you even remember her. That was last year, wasn't it? When we first opened?"

Kirby shrugged. "Just stuck in my head, I guess." What she did not say was, *Of course I remember her because she's freaking hot. I thought so then, and I think so now.* No, she'd keep that to herself.

But Lark didn't miss it, and as Julia left to help another customer, she said, "Now *she* is just your type."

"Totally."

"Does she drive on our side of the street?"

Kirby shrugged. "No idea."

"Want me to find out?"

Kirby turned wide eyes to her friend, then realized she was kidding, even as she stage-whispered, "Don't you dare."

"Isn't it time you started thinking about dating again?" Lark's brown eyes were the exact color of a Hershey bar, and they softened as Kirby met them. "It's been a while. Time to get back on the horse, you know?"

A sigh. A gulp of Bud Light. A nod. "I know. You're right. I've been...thinking about it." And that was true. Her last relationship had ended almost two years ago. It was for the best, and she'd thrown herself even more into her work than her ex had accused her of doing. And there hadn't been anybody new since. Maybe Lark was right.

"You're a catch, Kirbs. Reactivate your profile."

❖

It was almost midnight, and Kirby really should've been off to Snoozeville by then. Tomorrow was a busy day—she had a really cool design project as well as a meeting with a very high-end client—and she really needed to make an attempt to sleep. Instead of turning off the lights, though, she was lying in bed, phone in hand, squinting at her dating profile and trying to decide if she should reactivate it like Lark said.

So many of her friends had met each other online. It was how things were done, right? Who had time to meet people when you had work and family and life taking up your time?

"I don't have time for a dog," she said out loud to her dark bedroom. "When would I have time to date?"

It was a super weak excuse, and she knew it.

With a groan, she clicked the phone off and set it on her nightstand. The fan in the corner of the room was on low, and the soft breeze felt nice, cooling the room and her skin, and she snuggled down into the covers. In another month, she'd be sweltering—the AC unit would be shoved in her window and humming like crazy. She really needed to find a place with central air, but for now, her parents' house was just fine.

Sleep hadn't been Kirby's friend for a long time now. Years, in fact. She could be exhausted beyond belief, going through life like a zombie, but the second she hit the mattress, her brain began to whir, her thoughts decided it was time for a show, and sleep ran away and hid someplace where she often couldn't find it at all.

As she lay there, staring up at the ceiling, she tried her deep-breathing exercises. The ones the therapist had given her so long ago.

Breathe in for a count of four...

Hold it for a count of seven...

Exhale for a count of eight...

Slowly, so very slowly, she felt her heart rate begin to calm. Her limbs relaxed. She imagined her body melting into the mattress...

A car horn honked outside, and her eyes flew open.

"Goddamn it," she grumbled.

Yeah, it was going to be one of those nights.

CHAPTER THREE

This is the kind of thing you do now, right?" Amelia's father asked over the phone. His hesitation was clear in his deep voice. "This is your job, yeah?"

"Yes, Dad, this is what I do now." It really was cute that he was checking, like he didn't want to screw it up. "I walk dogs, I check in on dogs, I dog-sit. That sometimes includes house-sitting, if the dog is more comfortable staying home than being boarded."

"Okay, good," her dad said, and she could hear his grin. "Well, Vic's a good guy. I've known him for years. He's a straight shooter." That was the highest compliment a person could get from Tony Martini. If he called you a straight shooter, you were in. "You'll meet with him today?"

"We've got an appointment for later this morning."

"Good. Ask questions. Take notes."

"Yes, Dad." Amelia shook her head. Sometimes, to her father, she was still sixteen and new to jobs, to the world, to life in general. "I got this."

"Vic knows a lot of people. If he's happy with you, his word alone will probably get you more business.

She liked that idea. A lot. "Okay. Great."

"Let me know how it goes."

"I will. How's Florida life? See any bugs the size of my fist today?"

"Not today, but there was an iguana on my back fence yesterday."

A shudder ran through her. "How sad that you have to move now."

Her father's laugh was deep, a sound she loved more than anything. "They're not so bad."

"They're dinosaurs, Dad. In your backyard."

He and her mother had started out going to Florida for a couple weeks each winter. That gradually increased to a month, then two. When they'd retired, it had stretched into a four-month stint, and now that Amelia's mom had passed away, she sometimes thought her father might never come back. He was down south for more of the year than he was home. And he was happy down there. Happier. He had a nice place. He had friends. His arthritis was easier to handle when the weather was rarely colder than fifty degrees.

Amelia missed him terribly.

They chatted a little more, and she hung up with the promise to call him later and let him know what she thought.

A text had come through while she was on the phone, and a glance told her it was Vanessa in the group text that included her, Julia, Savannah, and Grace.

LAST WEEK WITH KIDS was all it said, followed by many smiling emoji, firecracker emoji, and any other random emoji that slightly resembled any kind of celebration. She laughed out loud alone in the house because it was like this every June. The others had all responded, so she added her own text to the group.

Only five more days to not murder kids. You can do this!

She took a few minutes then to scan her day's schedule and, as she started to sweat, pulled off the hoodie she'd layered over her outfit. She sighed and scrolled on her phone while she waited it out. She was going to hit Junebug Farms for an hour or two and walk some dogs before her meeting with Victor Renwick. After that, she had three midday dog walks to do. And it was Monday, so Sarah Peterson had her yoga class right after work, which meant her Scottie, Reggie, would need dinner and a walk. Not a full day, but she was getting there.

Once the hot flash had passed, she grabbed a paper towel and wiped the sweat from under her bra with a sigh, wondering for about the hundred and fiftieth time when this would ever end. She rinsed her coffee mug and put it in the drainer, then stood at her mother's sink and stared out the window at the bright June morning. The bird feeder swung in a light breeze, empty, and it occurred to her how bummed her mom would be about that.

"Better get some birdseed," she said softly and made a mental note. Then she inhaled slowly and let it out. No, this was not where she'd expected to be in her late forties. Single, perimenopausal, and living in her parents' house. A scoff shot from her nose. No. Not even close. But she was doing her best, and she had no choice but to be okay with that. What else was there, right?

Phone in her pocket, she grabbed her bag and headed out for her first stop of the day.

❖

Victor Renwick didn't live in an actual mansion, but his house was stunning just the same. At least that's what Amelia thought as she pulled her Toyota Corolla along the circular driveway and stopped behind a silver Mercedes parked in front of a huge garage door made of reddish-brown wood. It was a gorgeous light brick building with a lawn so lush and green, and landscaping so perfect, she wouldn't have been at all surprised to find everything made of plastic. Grass, flowers, all of it.

"Oh wow," she muttered as she turned the car off. Her father had said Victor Renwick was successful, but he did not mention that Victor Renwick might've had money coming out his ears. She gave herself a second or two to get it together and put on her mask of professionalism before she got out of her car and walked up to the house. She wasn't a person who was floored by the appearance of wealth, but class? Yeah, she liked classy, and Victor Renwick's house was gorgeously classy.

The double front door had to be eight feet tall and was painted a deep brick red, though, as she got closer, she noticed some chips and bubbles on its surface. She pushed a button, and the doorbell could be heard inside, an elegant series of soft low notes that sounded cheerfully musical, but not obnoxious, and it was followed by the muffled sound of barking. Amelia tried to keep herself from craning her neck at different angles to take in all the features of the exterior: wrought iron lights, stone steps, arched window frames…

"Hello there," a voice boomed as the door swung open, and Amelia felt herself jump a little in surprise. The frantic barking was louder now, coming from somewhere deep in the house. "You must be Amelia."

"I am," she said.

"Your father has told me so much about you." Victor Renwick held out his hand and Amelia shook it. Warm, firm but not too firm. She'd met enough men in her professional life who asserted their authority by crushing all the bones in your hand during the handshake. That was not Victor. His eyes were kind and crinkled in the corners when he smiled. Amelia put him in his mid- to late-sixties, slightly younger than her father, and very handsome, dressed in black slacks and a light blue Oxford, his salt-and-pepper hair neatly styled. He was clean-shaven and smelled of a subtly spicy aftershave. Everything about him was inviting. "Come in, come in." He stepped back and held out an arm in invitation.

She had to make a conscious effort not to be obvious about looking around the impressive house. The foyer soared two stories with a marble floor and an enormous window above the door, the wide sill draped with artificial tree boughs and vines. She absently wondered how the hell somebody was supposed to dust that.

"How is a person supposed to keep that from catching dust?" Victor asked her as if reading her mind.

"Right?" She smiled, liking this man already.

"Before you meet the boys, let me point out the work that'll be done." When he gestured toward the wall, she noticed the paint—or lack thereof, rather. The walls all seemed to be white, but the coat was very thin, and she realized it must simply be primer. "I had some work done." Victor scrunched his mouth to one side and amended, "I had a *lot* of work done. The place was a mess."

Amelia looked around, but other than the walls, the place was beautiful.

"Trust me," he said with a laugh. "It was a mess."

"I believe you."

"Anyway." He began to walk down a hallway toward what she assumed was the heart of the house, and she fell in step with him. "My reason for telling you that is I'll have some painters in and out while I'm away. That's a big part of why I want you to stay here." They reached the enormous expanse of a kitchen-great room combination, and the barking grew louder. Off the kitchen was a large three season room, a wall of windows separating it from the house. Two dogs bounced around on the other side of the glass, tails wagging, barks growing.

Amelia grinned. "Hi, guys."

The dogs were nothing alike. A springer spaniel, brown and white, with long legs and gorgeous curly ears stood next to a French bulldog, who was basically a third the size of the springer, all stubby legs and enormous ears. Amelia's fingers itched to pet them.

Victor reached for the door handle and met her gaze. "Ready?" He was smiling, and it was super clear how much he adored his dogs. His excitement to introduce her was written all over him.

"Ready."

He tugged, and the door didn't move. He fiddled with the handle. "Sometimes this latch sticks, and sometimes, it doesn't latch at all. I have a baby gate I use when I get irritated enough." He pointed at it on the other side of the door, leaning against the wall. "Good Lord." He tsked as he yanked, but then the door slid open, and the lovefest began.

"Meet Stevie," Victor said, gesturing to the springer, "and Calvin."

"Omigosh, omigosh, omigosh," she said in a playful voice as the dogs tried to get as close to her as they could. "Look at these handsome guys. Look at them." Tails wagged. Hell, entire dog bodies wagged. She sat on the floor. It was her favorite way to get to know dogs, getting down to their level. Talking to them like she was talking to toddlers. When she glanced up at Victor, his grin was huge.

"I don't think they like you," he said, teasing.

"I don't really like them either," she replied as Calvin made himself comfortable in her lap and Stevie rolled onto his back, clearly asking for belly rubs. "They're so mean. Standoffish, even." Her voice went up three octaves as she scratched Stevie. "And not at all friendly. No, they're not. No, they're not."

Victor leaned his back against the kitchen island and folded his arms across his chest with what looked to be a satisfied smile. "You have no idea how much better this makes me feel about going away."

"I'm glad," Amelia said as Calvin licked her face. "Dogs are my favorite. We don't deserve them."

"We really don't."

"I promise you, I'll take good care of your boys. Where are you off to?"

"Tokyo."

"So just a short flight."

A snort. "Yeah. Blink of an eye. I'll be gone the better part of a month. Possibly longer, which is part of why I didn't want to board these guys, why I wanted somebody to stay here instead. I was afraid they'd start to think I'd abandoned them."

Amelia could tell by the dark shadow that passed over his face that it had been a real fear for him, and she liked him so much just for that. She nodded her understanding, knowing she'd feel the same way. But then he went on.

"Since my husband died, I can't bear the thought of them thinking I left, too, you know?"

"Oh, I'm so sorry." Amelia's heart squeezed in her chest.

Victor seemed to give himself a shake. "Anyway. That's part of it. It's better for them to be in their own house."

"What's the other part?"

He furrowed his brow. "Hm?"

"You said the length of your trip and wanting them to stay in their own house was one part of why you wanted somebody here. What's the other part?"

"Oh, right. The workers I mentioned on the way in."

"Right, right," Amelia said, now remembering he'd said workers would be in and out. "Painters. Is there a set schedule for them?"

Victor lifted one shoulder in a half shrug. "I mean, they have a schedule, but my experience with people in construction and design means who knows what their schedule will be? I'll be touching base with them from Japan, but you're going to be living here, so make sure they work with your schedule, okay? They know what they're doing, so you shouldn't have to make any decisions, but if they ask you to, just go ahead and do what you think will work. If it's crazy complicated, you can text me. Just remember the time difference, so I may not reply right away."

For the next hour, Victor showed Amelia around the house, the dogs following along, and she did her best to keep her jaw from hanging open. She knew she'd have plenty of time to explore more slowly once she was here alone, so she nodded and listened and jotted notes on her phone if she thought she might forget something. It was a stunning house, a gorgeous five bedroom, four-and-half bath place, and he was obviously pouring—and had already poured—a lot of money into updating it. She wanted to point out that it seemed like a lot of house for one man but didn't know him well enough to mention it. Maybe he had somebody new. She'd have to see what her dad knew.

By the time she was back in her car and headed to her first client for the day, she was excited to be living in such a nice place, a little overwhelmed about all it would entail, given there would be dogs and painters to handle, and stunned by the ridiculously generous amount of money Victor insisted on paying her. He'd waved away her protests, telling her his dogs were worth the best care, and he insisted that she treat the place like her own while she was there. That included having her friends over, using the pool, the Jacuzzi, and the theater room in the basement. She'd shaken his hand, loved on the dogs a little more, and waited until she'd driven out of his driveway and around a corner to the next street before she'd let loose a high-pitched squeal of delight.

Yeah, she was *really* looking forward to the next month or so, and it had been a long, long time since she'd looked forward to anything.

❖

"I love that you're so excited about this," Savannah said as Amelia finished talking about Victor Renwick's house, his dogs, his pool. She smiled warmly. "It's nice to see you this way." Her voice had gone soft, and Amelia smiled back at her, then snorted.

"You mean, not miserable with my life, crying over my marriage ending, or ripping off layers of clothing? Give me time." But she let herself smile to let Savannah know she was just teasing. Sort of. "Anyway, Victor said to make myself at home, to have my friends over, to use the backyard and the Jacuzzi and the pool. So we'll definitely be having a night or two there."

"Swimming in a pool or floating in a Jacuzzi sounds fabulous." Savannah turned to Julia behind the practice bar. "We could use some downtime, huh, babe?"

"Damn right, we could." Julia continued to work on whatever concoction she was creating, but when she looked up, she indicated Savannah with her chin. "You definitely could."

"Work? Your dad? Your brother?" Amelia asked, familiar with Savannah's life since she'd been with Julia for over a year now.

"Yes, yes, and yes," Savannah said and took a swig from the white wine she was drinking. Savannah had just begun working as a nurse since getting her degree not long ago. Her father was suffering from early-onset dementia, and her brother was a recovering addict. There was a lot on her plate and always had been.

"You wanna talk about it?" Amelia asked her.

"Nope." There was a beat, then they both burst into laughter.

"I will drink to that," Amelia said, and clinked her beer bottle with Savannah's glass. "Hey, when do we start wedding planning? Soon?"

Savannah nodded and Julia said, "Yeah, we've got to set up a time. We've been making lists of things that we need to do, but not actually doing any of them."

"I keep telling her we should hire a wedding planner, but she says we don't need one." Savannah arched an eyebrow.

"I mean, you have me and Ness and Grace," Amelia pointed out. "We can manage. And if we need help, we can ask Aunt Anna—" The name of Julia's mother was barely out of her mouth before Julia barked a very sharp no at her, eyes wide, which made Amelia laugh. "As I was saying, we do *not* need any help from Julia's mom. No, we do not, thank you very much."

The door opened then, cutting off further conversation as Vanessa entered The Bar Back in a burst. She looked from one to the next of them, then flopped down on the couch and blew out a breath as if she'd just run there. The room stayed quiet until she finally said breathlessly, "One. More. Day."

"And we trust the children are all still breathing?" Julia asked.

"Yes. Barely. But yes." She lifted a hand to take the Diet Coke Julia brought to her.

"You sure you don't want something stronger?" Savannah asked with a laugh, knowing the answer.

"Tomorrow," Vanessa said, then sipped the soda. "Tomorrow, I will drink all the alcohol. Grace will be here, and I'll make her drive."

The conversation circled around, catching Vanessa up on things she'd missed. They talked about wedding planning and school and how the bar business was doing. Vanessa caught Amelia's eye.

"Any bites on the house?" she asked.

Amelia shrugged. "A few nibbles. Slightly below asking. Tammy wants to wait." She did her best to fake being nonchalant.

"And what do you want?" Vanessa asked.

Amelia took a deep breath and blew it out loudly. "I'd like to take any offer at all just to have it done and over with, so I can sever the last tie with her." Okay, that was mostly true. She did want the house gone. She hated that it was a thing with both their names on it. Tammy was with Nina now. *Nina.* What a stupid name. She sneered it in her head whenever she thought about her. *Nina.* How could you not sneer that name? It sounded like something a baby who couldn't talk would say. A made-up word.

"You're saying *Nina* in your head, aren't you?" Julia asked, and it made Vanessa laugh.

"She is making the Nina face." Vanessa pointed at her.

"I am!" And Amelia couldn't help but laugh with them as she wiped a hand over her face, literally trying to wipe off the expression she was making—the Nina face—and just like that, she was yanked away from the chasm that she so often got so close to. The chasm of divorce and blame and infidelity and all the things that had weighed on Amelia for the past two years. If she wasn't careful, she'd get super close to the edge, peer over, sometimes fall in and be trapped for an entire weekend, watching sad movies and eating crap and drinking too much. But more and more often, her cousins rescued her, dragged her away from the edge and made her laugh. Thank fucking God.

"When do you start your fancy-schmancy house-sitting gig?" Savannah asked when the laughter finally died down.

"Victor flies out Sunday morning, so I'll head over around lunchtime."

"You missed it, Ness, but we're all gonna go have a pool party and pretend to be Real Housewives at the place Amelia's sitting." Savannah slid her empty wineglass across the bar to Julia, then returned to the couch.

"Awesome," Vanessa said. "I'm in."

"I'll let you guys know how it goes after my first night." And then they were back on the topic of the gorgeous house, and Amelia felt better again. You'd think she'd be used to the up and down of her emotions lately, but they still took her by surprise the majority of the time.

But her cousins. They grounded her. She sat back in her chair and listened as they talked, a soft smile on her face that she could feel. Her life might not be what she wanted or what she expected, but she had these women, and for that, she'd be eternally grateful.

"I love you guys," she said quietly in the midst of their conversation. There was a beat of silence when the other three exchanged glances.

"Group hug!" Vanessa shouted, and the three of them ran to Amelia, wrapped her up until they were one, big eight-legged, four-headed hugging body. And for just a moment, in the midst of the hug and her muffled warnings of how they were going to trigger a hot flash, and she'd spontaneously combust, and then they'd be sorry, for just a moment, Amelia was happy.

CHAPTER FOUR

Kirby stood at the van door, scanning over her equipment, paint cans, tarps, pointing with a finger, counting, making sure she had what she needed. Krog stood next to her, waiting. He knew her process, knew she was a weirdo with superstitions, and they wouldn't officially start their day until she finished counting, finished pointing, and said *go*. Her dad had been the same way.

"Okay, I think we're ready." She turned to him and raised her brows. "See anything I'm missing?"

Krog shook his head. Today's bandanna was black. He wore a Harley-Davidson T-shirt with the sleeves cut off that was probably older than she was. Jeans and biker boots finished his outfit, and Kirby would never understand how he didn't swelter to death in those things. He was imposing to look at, but she knew he was a big softie with a heart of gold, and she trusted him with her life.

"Looks good to me," he said.

"And you're all set?" He was using his own pickup truck today, as he'd be at another site while she got set up at the big one. He gave one nod and sipped his coffee.

"Okay. Good." She shook out her arms like a boxer readying for a bout. Nerves.

"Whatsamatter with you?" Krog asked her, a half grin on his bearded face. "You got the jitters?"

"I do," she said with a weird laugh. "What the hell?"

"Big job." He closed the van door. "No reason to be nervous. You got this." He gave her shoulder a squeeze, a clear sign of affection from him, a man who was not a toucher. "Plus, he's not even gonna be there. Bonus."

Kirby told him to keep in touch and give her a shout if he ran into any problems. She wasn't worried, though. He was better at exteriors than she was, anyway. And he loved them. He loved being left alone to do his job. Not like interiors, where the homeowners liked to hover, scrutinize, comment.

Not today, though.

Kirby started up the van and pulled out into traffic. Nope, today began a big job in a really nice house with the owner not just away, but out of the country. She planned on sending photos every step of the way to make sure she was doing things to the client's liking. The last thing she wanted was to have to do things over again. That didn't happen often, but it did happen. She never argued. Never told a client they were wrong. She would just do a job again and again until it was met with approval. Something she'd learned from her father. The customer was always right. The only way to stay in business. If you wanted word-of-mouth referrals, the customer was always right.

A quick stop at Dunkin' was next. She wanted a doughnut. She needed some coffee. Okay, maybe she *needed* a doughnut, too. One with sprinkles felt celebratory, so she picked that one. Seriously, sprinkles were happy. Fun. And that was Kirby that morning, especially given this job was paying her very well.

It would also be one of her more creative jobs, and that was what she was really looking forward to. Painting could be simple. Roll color onto a wall. Sure. But getting creative with patterns and textures? That was where the real joy lived for Kirby. It didn't happen often, those types of jobs, but when one came along, she got this excitement, this heat in her core, this anticipation. Butterflies. All of it. And this was one of those jobs. Seven rooms to paint. Three of them with added elements of creativity. She always did this type of job on her own, sending Krog and Coop to handle the more straightforward ones in the meantime, and this one would take her a good three to four weeks, possibly longer. She was looking forward to the alone time, just her and her music, and she couldn't wait to get started.

She popped the last bite of the doughnut into her mouth and dusted her hand on her thigh as she turned into the driveway where she'd spend the next several weeks. A black Toyota was parked in the driveway, and Kirby remembered her client telling her that he had a house-sitter to take care of his house and dogs while he was away. Must be their car. Kirby didn't care. She'd stay out of their way. As long as they stayed out of hers, everything would be fine. Simple and easy.

❖

The first night in Victor Renwick's house had gone off without a hitch. Amelia'd had to mess with the thermostat a bit to get the AC set right so she didn't spontaneously combust at three in the morning, but she'd gotten a good four hours of sleep. She rarely expected more than that, not since her perimenopause symptoms had kicked into high gear. Four hours was a full night for her now. It just took her a little longer to find her footing in the morning. She sipped her coffee, courtesy of the fancy coffee maker it had taken her nearly fifteen minutes to figure out.

"But, God, so worth it," she said quietly and took another sip of the richest, most decadent coffee she'd ever had. Maybe she needed one of these.

She was staying in Victor's bedroom, not because he'd had it all cleaned and had the bed made up for her—he had—but because of the elegant, spa-quality bathroom, beautifully appointed with terrazzo tile, a shower with multiple heads to knead out any and all tension from her body, a garden tub big enough for three people, and windows that looked out onto the backyard and the woods beyond. It was stunning, and she almost wanted to live in it. *Almost* because the one bad aspect was all the damn mirrors. This change of life, as her Grandma Martini would call it, was wreaking havoc on her body. She avoided looking at herself naked as much as possible, as if the view would sear her eyeballs in her head. It probably would. The extra weight? The shifting of things? She'd never been so uncomfortable in her own skin, and if she looked too carefully, she'd burst into tears—another thing that was happening way more often than normal. Amelia was not a crier. Well. She didn't used to be. Now? She got teary at least once a day. It was ridiculous. *She* was ridiculous.

She sighed and sipped the delicious coffee. Stevie and Calvin were bounding around the backyard, and she watched them from the kitchen window. They were understandably a little confused by her presence. Probably missing their dad. But the night before, they'd eventually cuddled in the corner of the enormous leather sectional, one dog on either side of her, and watched *The Great British Baking Show* together. She'd explained the rules and the judges to the dogs, pointing out how nice everybody was to each other, that Paul Hollywood actually *was* his real name, and he could be tough, but was also kind of a teddy bear. Stevie had dozed off, but Calvin seemed to listen to every word, his giant ears at attention, his huge eyes watching her as she spoke.

Yeah, she might be a little in love with that boy already.

As she watched them, they started barking and ran toward the part of their yard where the gate was, and Amelia heard a car door slam. Victor had said the painters might arrive this morning. Good thing she'd gotten herself up and dressed right away.

The doorbell rang—no. Victor's doorbell didn't ring. It chimed. It sang. It broadcast a sweet aria throughout the entire house. Amelia carried her coffee to the front door and opened it.

And blinked.

"Oh," said the familiar young woman who stood on the stoop with a white stained tarp under one arm and a cup of Dunkin' coffee in the other hand. She wore paint-stained jeans, cute pink-and-black Nikes, a long-sleeved white T-shirt, and a baseball cap on backward. She stood an inch or two shorter than Amelia and wore an uncertain smile on her pretty face. "I know you."

"You do?" Definitely familiar, but Amelia couldn't place her.

"Yeah, you thought the color I chose for Martini's was— lemme see if I can remember…" She scrunched up her face and rubbed her chin in mock thought. "Oh, right. Cold and uninviting."

Amelia wasn't sure what to make of this person, even as recognition finally dawned. Was she joking around? Serious? She shrugged. "Well, I mean, slate gray? It's right there in the name."

"The name is Serene Cliffs."

"Yeah, not really helping your case." They stood there and a beat passed. Finally, Amelia stepped aside. "I assume you're here to paint."

"No, just to cover something with my tarp. Then I'll be on my way."

Ah, so biting humor it is. Not unlike her own, Amelia thought, impressed, but ignoring it.

The woman stepped into the grand foyer, her eyes scanning over the marble floor, then up the staircase and around, taking in the whole area. "Man, this place is beautiful," she said softly, and Amelia wasn't sure if she was talking to her or to herself, but she studied her anyway. Blond hair cut above her shoulders peeked out from under the cap, and Amelia couldn't tell if her eyes were deep green or more hazel like her own. She had a round, pleasant face, cute little freckles across her nose, and Amelia was just scanning her shape when she realized the woman had turned back to her. She snapped her gaze back to her face. "Anyway. Hi." The woman held out her hand. "Kirby Dupree."

"Amelia Martini." Amelia shook her hand, met her eyes, and felt instantly ensnared by them. What the hell was that? She took her hand back, hoping she hadn't yanked it like she'd been burned. Because it felt like she had.

"Oh, right. The cousin."

"One of them. There are lots. Italian and all that."

"Mm-hmm." Kirby nodded and Amelia watched her take in the space, probably much like she had on her first visit.

"You've been here before, yes?"

"Yeah, when I gave the estimate. But I just can't get over how gorgeous this foyer is."

Amelia nodded and they stood there together like two strangers in a museum, admiring the artwork. The dogs' barking tugged Amelia back to the present. "I need to let them in."

"Sure. I'll just..." Kirby gestured toward the stairs with her chin. "I'm gonna start with one of the bedrooms. Mind if I go up?"

Amelia held her arm out with a flourish, then watched for a second or two or seven too long. *That ass in those jeans...* She shook her head hard. "Oh my God, stop it," she whispered to herself, then hurried to the back of the house to let the dogs in.

Of course, she'd forgotten to put the gate up, and they both immediately bolted through the kitchen toward the front door, then up the stairs.

"Damn it," she muttered as she hustled after them.

The upstairs of Victor Renwick's house had five bedrooms and four bathrooms, each room with its own except for two smaller rooms that shared a Jack-and-Jill bath. The dogs found Kirby in one of those bedrooms, and by the time Amelia got there, all three of them were on the floor, Kirby talking to them in much the same baby talk Amelia used.

"Oh, you're so handsome. Yes, you are." Kirby kissed Stevie on his brown-and-white head and ruffled his ears as Calvin pushed against her thigh with his whole face. "Am I ignoring you, Mr. Calvin? I'm so sorry. You're handsome, too. Yes, you are."

Amelia folded her arms and leaned against the doorjamb, watching the love pile on the floor for a moment. There were dog people and there were not dog people, and Amelia had grown to recognize them in a snap. Kirby was definitely a dog person, and Amelia grudgingly gave her a few points in her head before Kirby looked up and saw her. She hurried to her feet, as if worried she'd be seen as screwing around, which Amelia found amusing. "Which rooms are you painting?" she asked.

"Four of the bedrooms. The main was done already. Then the dining room, the three season room, the half bath, and the front living room."

Amelia felt her eyes go wide. "That's a lot."

"It is. Afraid I'm gonna be in your hair quite a bit. Sorry about that." She didn't really sound all that sorry.

One shoulder went up. "I'm just the sitter. Doesn't matter to me. Not my call." She glanced around the room. "What color are you painting this one? Axe Murderer Red? Hang Myself Beige?" She meant it to come off light and teasing but realized by the shuttering of Kirby's face that it fell short, came off a little snarky instead.

"You'll have to wait and see," she said, and her tone was clipped.

And I thought I was the one with no patience for people. She watched as Kirby set down her tarp—which the dogs took to sniffing every millimeter of—and began to carefully slide the furniture away from the walls. There wasn't a lot in the room, as it was a guest room and, Amelia suspected, not used very often. Just a bed, a couple nightstands, a dresser. "Do you need help?" she asked.

"Nope," Kirby answered almost before Amelia finished the question. "I got it." And it was clear she did. She probably did it all the time. Amelia watched the ease with which she slid things, all toward the center of the room, clearing a path along the walls like a moat. The muscles in her shoulders flexed as she pushed and...

"Okay then," she said, clearing her throat, wanting to get out of that room. Fast. She clapped her hands. "Come on, boys." To the surprise of no one, the tarp and all its smells were way more interesting than Amelia's clapping. She was pretty sure she saw a tiny smug smile on Kirby's face as the dogs continued to ignore her. With a quiet sigh, she grabbed each by the collar and directed them out of the room and toward the stairs. "I'll be downstairs if you need anything."

"I won't."

❖

What the hell was it about that woman?

Kirby couldn't figure it out, but she tried as she went out to her van and grabbed more stuff. They didn't know each other. They'd barely met. Each time Kirby had seen her—twice, if she remembered correctly—had lasted a whole twelve seconds. Both times, Amelia Martini was frowning or scowling. Miserable, clearly. Mad at something? Someone? Annoyed with life? She had no idea. All she knew was that Amelia made her nervous. And people didn't make Kirby nervous.

So what the hell was it about that woman?

"I mean, she doesn't respect my job," she said as she pulled out roller covers and the roller and its telescoping handle. She shouldered the aluminum ladder and headed back to the front door. Kirby did not handle that well, people who had no respect for what she did. It was so much more than slapping paint on walls, but lots of people didn't get that. She shook her head. *Lots* of people didn't get that, so why did it matter what this chick thought?

Another trip down the stairs, this time for the can of primer. The downstairs had been primed already, though she didn't know by whom. Maybe the guys who replaced the drywall? The upstairs needed it, though. Every room. So she hauled the five-gallon pail into the house and up the stairs, and once in the room, she took a minute to catch her breath. 'Cause damn, that sucker was heavy.

The first time she'd met Amelia, her initial thought was that she was hot. And that hadn't changed, unfortunately. Amelia was slightly taller than her. Quite a bit older than her, maybe in her mid- to late forties. Light brown hair with gold highlights that glimmered when the light caught them just right. Her eyes were a unique shade of hazel, and the few glimpses of grins she'd seen flashed the promise of dimples. Maybe she could make her laugh so she'd get a good look…

"Aw, what the actual hell, Kirbs?" she asked herself quietly in the empty room. "You and your damn crushes. Just stop it."

From the back pocket of her jeans, her phone beeped a text, and she pulled it out, wondering if Krog needed her for something. She trusted him to do exemplary work, but he wasn't always the smoothest or most genial with the clients.

But no. Not Krog. It was Katie. Katie Kim, one of her bffs. She, Kirby, and Shelby Mitchell were an inseparable trio and had been since high school. They had a group text, and it lit up at least once a day. Sometimes, all day.

S'up, bitches! Katie's standard morning greeting.

Yo, yo, yo, Shelby responded before Kirby had a chance. *You in town, KK?* Katie was a sales rep for a medical equipment company, and the job required her to travel pretty often.

Yup. Till Thursday. Then off to NYC. Back Friday night. Katie added a plane emoji and then an Empire State Building.

We can only wish to be as VIP as you, Kirby typed, a smile on her face.

Keep trying. And three laughing emoji.

Katie and Shelby were her people. Her rocks. Her mirrors. Her voices of reason. They'd met playing volleyball their senior year of high school. Shelby and Kirby hadn't really moved in the same circles and Katie was new to the school, thanks to her parents' divorce. But when they'd been grouped together in practice, they'd just…clicked. Kirby had no other way to describe it. They had the same sense of humor, the same intensity about sports, and it turned out they'd lived within a five-block radius of each other.

Out tonight? Was Shelby's next text.

On a Monday? Kirby typed.

I miss ur stupid faces. Shelby wasn't the only one. It had been over a week since they'd gotten together, and they rarely went longer than that between visits. *Martini's at 8.*

CU then bitches, Kirby typed.

And now she had something to look forward to. She silenced the convo because she knew Shelby and Katie would chat for a bit longer. They both had office jobs and could text during work. It was harder for Kirby, who needed both hands and some focus when she painted. She set her mini Bluetooth speaker on a dresser, picked a new music station on her phone, and Billie Eilish suddenly filled the room. She kept the volume to a reasonable level, knowing Amelia was downstairs. It was a very big house, and she was pretty sure her music couldn't be heard everywhere, but pissing off Amelia wasn't something Kirby was in a hurry to do.

Though, she does get that sexy divot above her nose when she scowls…

"Stop it," she quietly commanded her brain once again. But this time, she could feel the corners of her mouth pulling upward into a soft grin. *Just* a bit.

CHAPTER FIVE

I can't stay long," Amelia said as she slid onto a barstool at the practice bar in The Bar Back.

"Oh, you started your new gig, right?" Savannah asked from the couch. "The mansion."

"I may have exaggerated." Amelia grinned and took the mysterious cocktail in a martini glass Julia set in front of her.

"Not a mansion then?" Vanessa this time. "Well, that's disappointing."

"It's not, but it's beautiful," Amelia said, then sipped. "Ooh, this is lovely…oh, wait." Her lips puckered. "A little tart."

"Too tart?" Julia asked.

Amelia held her thumb and forefinger scant millimeters apart.

Julia nodded, took the glass back, and started again.

"The house is gorgeous. Huge. I'm planning on swimming in the tub. Alone. But in the pool with you guys."

"There's a pool?" Vanessa was known throughout the family for her inability to tolerate humidity. "'Cause it's summer, almost, and I'm gonna need to swim. Are you allowed to have company?"

With a nod, Amelia said, "I told you there is. Maybe if you listen to me once in a while…" She grinned at Vanessa to take away the edge her voice always seemed to have these days. "I was actually gonna see if you guys wanted to come over for dinner Saturday. We can cook on the grill. And by we, I mean Savannah. You can swim."

"Hey. I can cook." Vanessa pouted.

"You swim better," Amelia said.

Vanessa tipped her head from one side to the other. "Truth."

"The water'll be chilly," Savannah said.

"Heated," was Amelia's reply.

"Let me check with Grace, but I think Oliver's with his dad this weekend, so we're in."

"Is it weird, being in a strange house alone?" Savannah asked. "I mean, I've house-sat, but never for a complete stranger."

Julia slid another martini glass in front of Amelia, who dutifully sipped. "Better," she said. "Still a bit heavy on the lemon aspect."

"Crap," Julia muttered, but gave a determined nod and took the glass again.

"The weird part is that there's work being done on the house," Amelia said.

Vanessa wrinkled her nose. "So you've got guys tromping in and out?"

"Not guys. One guy. Who's not a guy. One girl. Painting." Amelia's grimace was all it took for Julia to catch on.

"Is it Kirby? It's Kirby, isn't it."

"It's Kirby."

"Who's Kirby?" Vanessa asked. "And why are you making those faces? You guys never tell me anything."

"You've met Kirby," Julia said. "Dupree. She owns the paint company her dad started."

"Wait, the one who painted out there?" Vanessa used her chin to gesture to the door to the main bar. When Julia nodded, she added, "Oh, she's adorable. All bubbly and cute with a great ass."

"How do you know she's got a great ass?" Amelia asked.

"Through the magic of sight," Vanessa replied, waving a hand in front of her eyes and making both Julia and Savannah snort with laughter. "Seriously, she's super cute." It took about four seconds of blinking at Amelia before she jumped in and said, "Oh my God, you should ask her out."

"What?" Amelia felt the expression of horror bloom across her face, and her brain started to shout its stream of consciousness at her: *What why what a ridiculous idea why would she suggest that so stupid and dumb and stupid and why would she say that...*

"I can tell by the way your eyes have gone wider than my ring light that you love the idea," Vanessa said with a laugh.

"She's, like, fifteen." Amelia scoffed.

"She's *my* age." Vanessa was thirty-five. Amelia's eyes bugged wider. How come Vanessa felt so much older than Kirby did? It was weird.

"I rest my case," Amelia said. At Savannah's puzzled expression, she sighed and explained. "That's fourteen years younger than me. *Fourteen.* Besides, I don't need to ask anybody out right now."

"You *exactly* need to ask somebody out right now," Julia muttered, loud enough for them all to hear.

"Is that your not-so-subtle way of saying I need to get laid?" Amelia asked.

"It's *exactly* my not-so-subtle way of saying you need to get laid." Julia popped the stainless steel half of the martini shaker on and gave it a slap with her hand. Then she shook the drink over her shoulder, her eyes on Amelia's the whole time.

She wanted to be angry about it. Tried hard. But the truth? Getting laid wouldn't be the worst thing in the world. Lord knew it had been a long time. Her divorce was final. Tammy had left almost two years ago. They hadn't had sex for two years before that. Holy hell, had it actually been four years since she'd had sex?

"I'm not exactly feeling sexy lately," she said, and that was as honest as she could be. She didn't go into detail then because she had in the past. Talked about her perimenopause, how it was wreaking havoc on her body and her mind. But her thirtysomething cousins didn't really understand, and after a while, they made her feel silly, like she had no tolerance and complained too much. Like she was being ridiculous. And she knew they didn't really think that and she was projecting, but still. It sucked. So she shut up and suffered in silence. With a sigh, she took the drink Julia gave her and sipped. Gave a thumbs-up. "Third time's the charm," she said, then sipped again.

"Excellent." Julia glanced up at the door to the bar when Clea, her bar manager, popped her head in and summoned her out front.

"I bet this is one of those times when you miss your mom a

lot," Savannah said, and her tone was sympathetic. Julia could be sharp, abrupt, but Savannah never was. She softened Julia's edges. Like Amelia, she'd also lost her mother, so she got it.

"God, it really would help to talk to her about it."

When Julia came back in, her smile was almost comically big, her eyes dancing.

"What's that face?" Vanessa asked, moving her finger in a circle in front of Julia's head. "Tell us. Right now."

"I'll give you three guesses who's sitting at the bar right now with her friends."

Amelia and Vanessa looked at each other blankly and shrugged. Amelia shook her head.

Savannah, on the other hand, said simply, "Kirby the painter."

"That." Julia pointed at her fiancée. "That right there is why I'm marrying you."

"Oh my God, that's so weird," Vanessa said, her eyes wide as she looked at Amelia. "Did we conjure her?"

"I think we might have," Julia said. She gave Amelia a playful shove as she walked by. "You should go talk to her."

"What? Why? Why? Why would I do that?" Amelia asked.

"Why did your voice just go up about three octaves?" Julia asked.

"It did not." It totally had. Amelia cleared her throat and tried again. "No, it didn't."

"So did," Vanessa agreed, then took a sip from her water bottle. Amelia shot her a look of death and Vanessa shrugged. "What? I just call 'em like I see 'em."

Amelia hated this. All of it. The attempts to fix her up. Her own nerves. The teasing. And most of all, the utter and complete discomfort she felt with herself, her situation, her life. When the prick of tears hit her eyes, she looked down at her drink and prayed for them to go away before any of the others noticed. As the seconds ticked by, she knew there was only one way to get these bitches—said lovingly—off her back about it. She stood up.

"Fine. I'll go talk to her." And before any of them could say a thing—to support or to stop her—she hurried out into the main bar area.

Mondays weren't super busy, but there was a decent crowd of people around the bar and taking up some of the tables. She spotted Kirby at a high top with two other women. One had sleek black hair and the cutest yellow summer dress Amelia had ever seen. The other was a redhead with wide-set eyes and a seriously hourglass figure. Kirby had lost the baseball cap and her blond hair was shiny, even in the dim bar lighting. Her paint-stained clothes had been traded for a clean pair of jeans, a cute navy-blue top, and sandals. Amelia was surprised to see purple-polished toenails. Kirby faced her, and when their eyes met, a line of emotions shot across her face so clearly, Amelia almost laughed. Obvious surprise, followed by what looked a lot like happiness, quickly replaced by dread. One, two, three.

Amelia made her feet do their job and approached the table.

"Amelia," Kirby said. "What a surprise. Hi."

"I was about to say the same thing. What are you doing here?" She meant it to be an honest, conversation-starting question, but it came out the tiniest bit bitchy, and she swallowed her own wince.

"I'm having a drink with my friends. How about you?" If Kirby was offended, she hid it well.

Amelia jerked a thumb over her shoulder. "Just hanging in the back with my cousins."

By this point, the other two at the table looked like they were watching a tennis match, their eyes moving from one to the other and back. Kirby indicated the dark-haired woman. "This is my friend Katie. And this is Shelby. Guys, this is Amelia Martini."

Amelia nodded to each of them.

"So, you're staying at the house Kirby's painting?" Katie asked, which made it clear to Amelia that she'd already been talked about. She swallowed hard.

"I am, yes. House-sitting and dog-sitting."

"You should see these dogs," Kirby said, and her eyes—which looked more green tonight—lit up. "A springer and a Frenchie. Super sweet boys." She looked up at Amelia then, meeting her gaze as if waiting for her approval.

Amelia nodded. Smiled.

"Adorable. I said hi to them and then they have to stay

downstairs while I paint, but then I say good-bye before I go."
Kirby's cheeks had pink blossoms on them as she spoke. It was
clear she'd had a drink or two. She wasn't drunk, but she seemed
happy. Lotta smiling going on.

"Well," Amelia said, feeling the sudden, super urgent need to
be anywhere but caught in Kirby Dupree's semi-intoxicated gaze.
"I won't interrupt any longer. I just wanted to say hi."

"It was nice to meet you," said the one named Shelby, and
Amelia swore she could feel her eyes on her, looking her over,
taking mental notes.

"Same here."

"See you in the morning," Kirby said as she lifted one hand
and wiggled her fingers in a little wave.

Amelia hurried away toward The Bar Back, but if somebody
had asked her why, she'd have had no idea.

"See?" Vanessa said when Amelia had retaken her stool.
"That wasn't so bad."

"She's single, you know," Julia said. She would know. She
was a bartender. She knew everything about everybody. It was
awesome for gossip. Unless the gossip involved you.

"That's nice," Amelia said and finished off her drink in one
slug.

"What is wrong with you?" Julia asked with a slight edge to
her voice. That's how Julia talked to her a lot lately. Like she had
little patience left for her cousin, and Amelia felt it.

"Nothing's wrong. I'm just tired." She left her glass and
grabbed her bag. "I need to go take care of the dogs now."

"Meels," Savannah said softly and reached a hand out toward
her from the couch.

"I'm fine." She gave her a weak smile and squeezed her
hand. "Really." With a glance around the room in which she didn't
actually look at any of them, she said, "I'll talk to you guys later,"
and pushed out the side door. She knew they probably thought she
was being ridiculous. She knew they might've been rolling their
eyes right now and talking about her. She didn't care.

No. Lies. She *did* care. She cared too much. But she was
going through stuff that she couldn't explain to herself, so how

could she expect other people to understand? No, the best thing for her to do in situations like that one, where she felt like everybody was against her—even though they probably weren't and it was all her and not them at all—was to remove herself. So she did.

Anyway, she had to take care of Victor Renwick's dogs. Stevie and Calvin would be happy to see her. She knew that. She needed that.

Not for the first time, she cried her way home.

CHAPTER SIX

Kirby had to do a couple of estimates that Tuesday, so she needed to get as much done at the Renwick house as she could before two. Rather than meet with Krog and Coop, she texted with them, made sure they were set with the job they were doing—and they were, Krog was an old hand at this—and then headed right to Renwick's.

Amelia's appearance at the bar last night had tickled her mind all the way until she'd fallen asleep. And then she'd dreamed about her. The details faded away in the morning the way dreams tended to do, a clear picture that went gradually fuzzy until you could no longer make out any of the crisp edges. But Amelia had been there, in her head, all night. It was that underlying sadness she had. Kirby wondered if it was there all the time or if she was just going through something in the moment. She also wondered if anybody else saw it. Kirby's mother had always told her she was intuitive, that she had the gift of being able to read things, to see emotions and feelings in people that others maybe missed. She'd grown used to it as she got older, and she was rarely wrong.

Amelia Martini was sad.

Kirby didn't want to know that.

With a sigh, she parked her van in Victor Renwick's driveway and hopped out. Pretty much everything she needed was already here, so she grabbed her small Yeti cooler with her water, a Diet Coke, and lunch, and headed up the front steps. She'd gotten two of the upstairs bedrooms primed yesterday. Today's plan was to prime one more room, then start back at the first room. The fun stuff. The creative part that she loved so much. She and Victor had talked about doing some textures, some patterns, and Kirby was excited. It was the part of her job she loved most.

She rang the bell, heard the barking, and waited until the door was pulled open.

Amelia wore jeans with ripped knees and a navy-blue tank top. Her feet were bare, her toes polished a surprisingly cheerful red. Her hair was in a ponytail. She held a mug with a smiley face on it, ironic given how she rarely smiled, and the coffee in it smelled decadent.

"Morning," Amelia said, and only when the exhaustion in her voice registered did Kirby notice the slight darkening under each eye. Amelia Martini was clearly not sleeping well.

"Hi there." Kirby stepped in as Amelia moved aside. "It was nice to see you last night."

Amelia nodded, and if she intended to say anything, it was cut off by the cacophony of barking dogs. She tipped her head backward, indicating the direction behind her. "I remembered to gate them in the three season room today, so they don't swarm you."

Kirby smiled and headed for the stairs. "Aww, I'll miss those furballs."

"Feel free to come down and say hi if you want."

That was new.

"I might do that," Kirby said over her shoulder as she took the steps. Four up, she turned. Amelia was still standing there, her mug held in both hands, apparently watching her go up the stairs. "Will you be here?" she asked, then had to force herself not to wince at having actually asked the stupid question out loud. *What the fuck, Kirby? Where did that come from?*

Also seemingly surprised by the question, Amelia took a beat or two before she inclined her head once. "For a while. I'm not going to Junebug Farms today. I have a dog to walk at lunchtime but should be here the rest of the day."

"Okay. Good." Kirby gave one nod, then hurried up the rest of the stairs before she could do or say something else stupid. God.

Why did she have a voice? She didn't deserve one. She clearly didn't know how to use it. *Just shut up, go upstairs, do your job.*

She worked steadily upstairs for the next four hours, music playing, humming along, getting both remaining bedrooms primed rather than just the one she'd expected to. Proud of herself and feeling jazzed about it, she cracked open her bottle of water and glanced out the bedroom window. The view was of the backyard. Specifically, the pool, all shimmering blue in the sunshine.

And there, floating on a bright green inflatable raft—and wearing a black one-piece bathing suit—lay Amelia Martini. Eyes closed, skin slick and bronzing, glittering almost as much as the water. One arm above her head, one at her side, fingers trailing lazily through the water. One knee bent, the other leg straight. Despite the water she'd just slugged, Kirby felt her mouth go dry.

"Wow," she said quietly, surprised to hear her own voice. She hadn't heard Amelia leave or come back, but she'd primed through lunch, and it was now after one, so she must have. Her eyes were glued to the sight, her attention riveted. Amelia still sparked the same response as the first time Kirby had ever laid eyes on her—she was freaking hot.

Before she knew what she was doing, before she could even entertain the idea of stopping herself, Kirby turned and headed down the stairs, through the house, through the gourmet kitchen with its cherry cabinets and granite counters and ceramic tile floors, through the three season room. She tried to stop herself, but Amelia looked up from her raft, and if Kirby stopped moving then, it would look like she'd been standing there staring like some kind of creepy weirdo, so she forced her body to keep moving, to slide the door open and step out, to squat down and give the dogs love when they ran to her.

"Hi," she said with a quick wave to Amelia, then turned her attention back to the dogs. *No, of course I wasn't ogling you like some stalker. I'm just here to see the dogs. That's it. That's all. I'm a very normal not at all creepy person, see? Look at me loving these dogs.* Her brain went on a litany in her head. Wouldn't stop.

Amelia uttered a greeting and began paddling herself to the edge of the pool where she'd left a towel.

"Don't get out on my account," Kirby said. "I just needed a break and wanted to say hi to the dogs." She jerked a thumb over her shoulder. "Going right back inside." Something about the way Amelia seemed to be hurrying to cover herself up bothered Kirby. She felt guilty. "Seriously. Sorry if I disturbed you." She watched as Amelia wrapped the towel around her body. She stifled a sigh and pushed herself to stand, the dogs circling her feet. "It's a great day to be in the pool."

Amelia nodded, picked up a bottle of water and took a sip. "It is."

Okay, not so much with the talking. "Well, I'll get back to it." Kirby didn't know what else to do to stop the awkward, aside from removing herself, so that's what she did. She shook her head all the way back through the house, the entire way up the stairs, and back into the bedroom where her lunch waited for her. She grabbed her cooler and took it out the front door.

If having her around was so horrible for Amelia, Kirby would eat in her van. "It's whatever…" She sighed to herself and bit in to her turkey sandwich.

❖

"Oh my God, I am officially ridiculous." Amelia muttered the words to herself as she scanned the windows of the Renwick house. Ashamed to admit she was looking for signs that Kirby was gawking at her out one of them, she squinted against the sun, shaded her eyes with a hand, until she was sure all windows were free of spies.

It wasn't about Kirby, though. At all. At least she knew that part of it, and admitting it to herself was a pretty big step, if she said so herself and thank you very much. She unwrapped her body and draped the wet towel across the back of a lounge chair to dry in the sun. Then she lowered herself back into the water and dog-paddled to the raft, now floating in the center of the kidney-shaped pool. Once back on it, she sighed. Not in relief, but in frustration. With herself.

Her dash for the towel had been all about her because she

didn't want anybody—especially Kirby Dupree—seeing her body in its current state. Bloated. Uncomfortable. Just...not pretty. That being said, she was pretty sure she'd made Kirby feel awful, made her feel like Amelia thought she'd been inappropriate.

She owed her an apology.

This wasn't her. This wasn't who she was. Amelia was so tired of that fact—she just did not feel like herself lately. God, how she wished her mother was still around so she could ask her questions. Yes, she had aunts. Yes, she had the internet. But she'd always felt safe and—dare she say it?—less crazy about medical or physical things relating to her body when she could talk to her mother about them. She'd been gone almost four years now, and there were days when Amelia would still pick up her phone and begin dialing her mom's number. Not nearly as often anymore, but it did still happen, and it crushed her heart a little bit every single time.

Let it go. Just relax and let it go.

Good advice from Savannah a few months ago. Of course, it also conjured up visions of an ice princess singing with the perfect voice of Idina Menzel, but that was way better than dwelling on the other thoughts in her head. She hummed quietly and let the warmth of the sun and the soft rocking of the water lull her into relaxation. The dogs were both lying in the shade, and the hedges and privacy fence around the entire backyard made her feel like she was in her own private little haven.

Yeah, she could get used to this.

When Stevie barked, it startled her so much that Amelia realized she must've dozed. She was now on the opposite side of the pool, and the sun had shifted a little bit. She needed to turn over, or she was going to be unevenly tanned, and Vanessa would never let her hear the end of it. Like that time they'd gone away to the beach together and Amelia had gotten so absorbed in her book, she'd completely forgotten to flip over. She looked like two different people from the front and the back, and Vanessa called her Half Moon, like the cookie, for the rest of the summer, even after Amelia had managed to even things out.

She paddled to the edge and hauled herself out of the pool,

her eyes with that slightly swollen feeling that came with napping in the sun. She stretched her arms over her head and woke up her muscles as both dogs came to inspect her. She squatted down, gave them love, and let them kiss her face and her legs, likely more about sunscreen, sweat, and pool water than her. Then she stepped into the shorts and T-shirt she'd left on a chair, slugged some water, and headed inside.

She had some music to face.

Remembering to gate the dogs in the three season room, she set her empty water bottle on the counter for refilling and grabbed another from the fridge before heading for the stairs. About halfway up, she could make out music. Something upbeat and poppy. She followed it to one of the guest rooms with its door ajar. She pushed it and it opened silently.

Kirby was working on the far wall, her back to Amelia. The room was sparsely furnished, and with everything shoved to the middle, she could clearly see Kirby's work. Which was impressive, to say the least. While the color was a deep burgundy, it seemed to have actual texture. Like it would if it was made of stone or concrete. Rough. Bumpy. So very interesting. It was all Amelia could do to stand still and not cross the room to run her palm over the wall. She stared, tipped her head to one side, squinted.

Kirby stood, pushed the hat off her head, and scratched the light blond hair before repositioning the hat. Then she put both hands on her hips and tipped her head, much the way Amelia just had.

"It looks amazing," Amelia said, immediately sorry when Kirby nearly jumped out of her skin.

"Jesus, Mary, and Joseph, you scared the crap out of me," Kirby said, hand pressed to her chest. But she laughed, and Amelia liked it, a throaty sound that seemed to come from deep within her.

"Sorry," Amelia said, joining her laughter. And then they both stood there, sort of staring at each other, and Amelia actually toed the floor. "Listen, I wanted to say I'm sorry for being a weirdo down there earlier."

"For floating in the pool on a gorgeous summer day?" Kirby asked, then shook her head. "So weird." Then she busied herself with brushes and rollers and paint things, and Amelia was pretty sure she wasn't doing anything but touching them randomly.

"For jumping out of the pool and glaring at you."

"*Oh*, that part."

"Yeah. That part." Amelia felt her face flush, actually felt the heat crawl up her neck and settle in her cheeks.

Kirby gave a shrug that was just a little bit too nonchalant. "S'okay."

"No. It's not. I'm just..." She cleared her throat and took a few steps into the room, then focused her gaze on the beautiful new wall so she didn't have to look at Kirby as she spoke. "I'm not used to anybody seeing me so...not dressed."

"Well, that's too bad."

"It is?"

Kirby blinked at her once. Twice. "Are there no mirrors where you live?" Then her eyes widened just a bit, and she quickly went back to fiddling with her equipment.

"How did you do this?" Amelia asked, eyes on the wall again, desperate to change the subject. "It looks like rough stone."

"Doesn't it? It's a special paint. Kind of hard to work with, but looks super cool."

"I wanna touch it." Amelia snapped her gaze to Kirby and quickly added, "I won't. But I want to."

"You can tomorrow. Or even later tonight. Give it a good six hours to dry." Kirby slid her focus to Amelia. "You like it, huh?"

"It's like nothing I've ever seen."

"Mr. Renwick picked it. It can be kind of much in a bedroom, so I was surprised he chose it, but he definitely has an eye."

Amelia grinned as she said, "Well, stereotypes would say it's in his genes to be good at interior design."

Kirby shrugged. "Yeah, he did ping my gaydar a bit."

"Mine, too," Amelia said. "And then he mentioned his late husband, so..."

Kirby took a second. To absorb what she'd said? Maybe. She recovered quickly, though. Then she grinned and returned her attention to the wall. And so, yeah, that was all cleared up now. "I don't know a lot of straight men willing to experiment with color and texture in their guest room." They looked at the wall together. "Plus, dude, the guy is *stylin'*."

"Oh my God, right?" Amelia asked immediately, agreeing. They laughed together and quieted as the conversation faltered a little bit.

"Well, I'd better get back to work," Kirby said.

"Right. Right. Sorry." Amelia turned to go, then turned back to her. "If you, you know, want to bring your suit sometime, I don't see why you couldn't jump in the pool to cool off. If you wanted."

Kirby held her gaze, and Amelia noticed her eyes were more hazel than green today. "I'll remember that," she said. "Thanks."

Amelia nodded and left the bedroom, heading downstairs to where she'd left the dogs lounging in the three season room. As she passed the fridge, she pulled it open and grabbed a yogurt. She really wanted the chocolate fudge brownie ice cream she knew was in the freezer, because she'd put it there, but a glance down at the sudden extra weight that made her so self-conscious lately forced her to stick to the fridge. And the yogurt.

A heavy sigh whooshed out of her as she sat in a lounge chair near the pool and spooned yogurt into her mouth. Her mother would be frustrated with her right now. She could almost hear her saying, *So, you're divorced. So, this isn't what you planned on. Life doesn't often go the way we plan. Look around you. Look at what a nice life you have. You've retired early and have a pension—do you know how many people would kill for that? You're getting paid to sit next to a shimmering blue pool and watch a couple of pretty well-behaved dogs. You've got family and friends who love you. Why are you so glum? What's there to be glum about?*

Knowing her mom was right didn't help the way it should've, though. The problem was that Amelia couldn't help the way she felt. Couldn't fight it. She was frustrated and uncomfortable, and it felt like she would feel this way for the rest of her life, and no matter what she did, she couldn't pull herself out of it.

Deciding she couldn't sit there and wallow any longer, she finished her yogurt and decided to take the dogs for a walk.

A change of scenery might do her some good.

CHAPTER SEVEN

"And how are my boys doing?" Victor Renwick's voice was cheerful as he spoke to Amelia on the phone that Friday. It was going on six in the evening for her, which meant it was Saturday morning for him.

"They're great," she told him as she opened the refrigerator with one hand and pulled out the blocks of cheese she'd purchased earlier. "I think Calvin misses you more. He can seem a little low-key at times." *Yeah, good job, Amelia, make the guy feel like his dog is depressed.* She quickly added, "But we've been playing lots of ball and tug and going for walks. Stevie helps a lot." She clenched her teeth and grimaced, hoping she hadn't made him sad.

"He's a pretty emotional guy. I knew that when I got him. I'm glad I decided to hire you instead of boarding him. How's the painting looking?"

His topic shift startled Amelia, and it took her a second to catch up. "It looks really great so far." And it did. Kirby had been working steadily all week and had two of the bedrooms almost finished. In fact, she was still upstairs as they spoke, wanting to finish the room she was on before the weekend.

"That company does good work, huh? Your dad recommended them, and I got a good vibe during the estimate."

Her dad knew Kirby? That was news to her. She made a mental note to ask him about it when she talked to him next.

"She's been texting me photos," Victor went on. "And they look great, from what I can see. But you're right there and can see the work in person. So, you like it? It looks okay?"

There was no hesitation in her praise of Kirby's work, and she reassured him as best she could. "I think you're gonna be really happy."

They spoke for a few more minutes before hanging up. Amelia liked Victor a lot. She hoped he was a client she kept.

She'd had a busy day, and she could say now that, much as she enjoyed a good, lazy afternoon by the pool, it was nice to have her brain occupied all day. She'd been at Junebug Farms all morning, helping get them set up for tomorrow's adoption day. Then she'd had to visit Duke, Chip, and Rascal, three different dogs at three different homes that all needed lunchtime walks. Then she'd hit the store for munchies for tonight, then had come back to the house to do some invoicing and scheduling before heading back out to two clients' homes where dogs needed dinner and walks.

Now? Now she was exhausted, but happy. Stevie and Calvin were crashed out on the other side of the gate, at least until Kirby was done and they could have free rein again. Savannah, Vanessa, and Grace were coming over so they could work on some wedding planning. Julia didn't like to leave the bar on Fridays, so she'd bowed out for tonight.

She stood at the gorgeous counter and slid one of Victor's gleaming knives out of the sleek knife block, so she could cut up some raw veggies for the veggie tray. Ranch dip was chilling in the fridge. Music was playing at an easy volume, Katy Perry singing about it never really being over, and Amelia rolled her eyes at the sentiment. Then, of course, she sang along. 'Cause Katy Perry.

"I'm gonna head out."

Kirby's voice startled her, the knife jerked, and she couldn't stop her slicing momentum fast enough to keep from slicing into her finger. She cried out and dropped the knife as blood dripped onto the counter.

"Oh my God, I'm so sorry." Kirby dropped her things to the floor with a crash and rushed to Amelia's side. "Oh my God. Lemme see." She grabbed Amelia's hand in both of hers and tugged her to the sink. "Brace," she said just before turning the water on. Amelia sucked in a breath as it hit, the pain making her hand throb. "I just want to see how deep it is, see if you need stitches."

They were close, their heads nearly touching, Kirby's hands warm and strong as they held hers. She smelled like paint and baby powder, a weirdly comforting mix. Heat came off her body, Amelia could feel it, and she found herself wondering if Kirby was a person who slept hot, as her mom called it.

"It's not that deep, thank God," Kirby said then. "You just sliced into the skin pretty good. I think if we stop the bleeding and bandage it up tight, you'll be okay." She yanked a paper towel off the roll on the counter and wrapped it around Amelia's hand. Then there was eye contact. Definitely hazel today, those eyes of hers, and this close, Amelia could see gold flecks in the irises, see the surprisingly dark shade of her eyebrows, much darker than her light hair. Dark lashes. Full lips. It occurred to her that if she just leaned the smallest bit, their mouths would meet... "Hey, you okay?"

Amelia blinked rapidly, yanked out of her reverie, thank freaking God. "Yeah. Yeah. Fine." Nodding. Lots of nodding. Blinking and nodding. Jesus.

"I have a first aid kit in my van with some good bandages and stuff. I'll go grab it. Stay here."

"Not going anywhere," she called as she watched Kirby hurry out of the kitchen.

When was the last time she'd cut herself while cooking? She couldn't remember. Of course, she also couldn't remember the last time she'd worked with knives that sharp. She picked up the culprit and was studying the blade when Kirby returned. Their eyes met, and Amelia shrugged. "Suckers are sharp."

"I'm not surprised," Kirby said as she set a red case with a white cross on it on the counter and popped it open. "I don't think Victor Renwick skimps on much. It makes sense he'd have super expensive, disturbingly sharp knives, you know?"

Amelia agreed with more nodding. "Plus, I should pay more attention when I'm using dangerous utensils."

"Ha. That, too." Kirby sidled up next to her. "Okay, let me see." Again with the closeness. A repeat of the warmth. Amelia felt her own body heat increasing with the proximity, traitor that it was. She swallowed and wondered if Kirby felt it.

Three things happened all at once right then. The dogs began to bark from where they were still gated. Noise sounded from the hallway. A loud, familiar voice called out, "The party can start now, we're here!"

And before Amelia could comprehend what was happening, Vanessa, Grace, and Savannah were suddenly there, arms full of things like grocery bags and bottles of wine and beach totes.

"The front door was open, so we just came in...Oh my God, what happened?" asked Savannah, the first to notice the first aid kit.

"Stab wound," Kirby said without looking up from the medical care she was giving, raising her voice to be heard over the barking. Savannah was a nurse now, but Kirby must've been doing a good job because she didn't take over. Amelia was surprised. And impressed with Kirby's work, as the bleeding had stopped, and the bandage felt snug and secure.

"What?" Vanessa's eyes went wide at Kirby's words, and Amelia couldn't help but laugh.

"Crudité injury," she said as explanation, indicating the partially chopped veggies with her chin. "My client has alarmingly sharp knives."

"Looks like things are under control," Vanessa said. Her eyes met Amelia's across the island counter, and she raised her eyebrows in question.

"It's the least I could do," Kirby said, not looking up from Amelia's hand as she wrapped one last piece of medical tape around the bandage. "It was my fault."

"It was not," Amelia said and ignored the speed with which she defended Kirby. Then to Vanessa, "Can you give the dogs some attention so they stop barking?"

"It was. I scared her by popping into the kitchen while she was chopping. My bad."

"Well, looks like you made up for it with some stellar bandaging," Savannah said.

"Yeah?" Kirby asked.

"Savannah's a nurse," Amelia told her. Then her manners kicked in. "Do you all know each other?"

"We do," Vanessa said from the other side of the gate where she sat on the floor with Stevie and Calvin. She moved a finger between herself and Kirby. Then she pointed. "That is my girlfriend, Grace, and our friend Savannah."

Kirby shook hands with the two women she didn't know and then took a subtle step back from Amelia. "All set. Maybe have the nurse look at it"—she shot a look toward Savannah—"but I think it'll hold for a while."

Amelia held her hand up, bent her finger slowly. "It has a heartbeat."

"It will for a while," Savannah said with a smile. Then to Kirby, "You didn't think it needed stitches?"

Kirby shook her head. "It's more of a surface slice than a deep cut."

Grace had moved near the cutting board. "Well, at least you were considerate enough to bleed on the celery and not the peppers. Now we know what to throw out."

They laughed and then Kirby held her arms out to her sides and let them fall. "Okay. I'll get out of your hair now." To Amelia she said, "I'm so sorry again."

"You're welcome to stay," Amelia heard herself say then tried to keep her eyes from going wide and giving away her own surprise.

"Yeah," said Vanessa. "We're just going to eat, drink, and talk wedding plans."

"Who's getting married?" Kirby asked.

"You know my cousin Julia at the bar? She and this lovely woman right here." Amelia indicated Savannah, who gave a little wave. "They're getting married next Valentine's Day."

Savannah bugged her eyes out in mock-horror and Kirby laughed.

"Congratulations to you." Kirby moved around Grace and backed toward the doorway where she'd dropped her cooler and bag. "Thanks for the invite, but I'm playing Frisbee golf tonight, so I need to bounce." She pointed at Amelia. "Don't get that wet."

"Yes, ma'am." Amelia smiled at Kirby, and she smiled back, and for a second or two, there wasn't anybody else in the room.

Then, of course, Kirby's footsteps sounded down the hall, and the front door shut, and suddenly there were three other people in the room again. Three very large, very loud people. And they all had opinions.

"Well, wasn't that cozy." Vanessa.

"She's adorable—you should ask her out." Grace.

"Are you okay?" Savannah. Then, "And Grace is right."

"Shut up, all of you, and somebody pour me some wine. I'm injured."

"I will happily do that," Savannah said, "but you will need to spill some details for us."

"The details we're here to discuss have to do with your wedding." Amelia took the glass of wine Savannah handed to her.

"I'm perfectly willing to put a pin in that and talk about the sexy painter and how well she took care of you just now."

And then Vanessa was there, and Grace came closer, and they both put their elbows on the counter and their chins in their hands and stared at her, and Amelia wanted to crack up and also scream at them to leave her the hell alone.

"I hate all of you."

"Lies." Savannah began unpacking one of the grocery bags, setting out cheese, crackers, chips and dip, cookies. "You love us."

"I do." She sighed.

"And do you *luuuuuv* Kirby, too?" Vanessa asked, then popped a baby carrot into her mouth.

And the frustration started to bubble. Amelia felt it simmering, stirring in her gut, and couldn't stop it. This was how it had been since Tammy announced she was leaving, and Amelia's entire life had changed in an instant. Her patience with people was nonexistent. Even people she loved.

"Look, just stop, okay?" Her tone was sharper than she'd meant it to be. She could tell by the quick flinch that zipped across Vanessa's face. "She's too young for me. I doubt we have much in common. And I don't want to date anybody right now. I keep telling you guys that. I feel completely undatable." She grabbed the cheese board Savannah had arranged and headed for the door. "We'll eat out back."

Without looking behind her, she moved the gate with her foot, went through the three season room and out onto the back patio, the dogs following her—or, more likely, following the cheese—closely. Once outside, she set the board down, took a deep breath, and did her best to swallow down the emotion that, as usual, appeared out of nowhere and threatened to swamp her.

Vanessa hadn't deserved that. Nobody did. She hated that she got like this, but it happened more and more often lately. The snark. The short fuse. *Oh, and let's not forget the tears*, she thought as her eyes welled up. Thank God her cousins were giving her a few moments of space, and she used them to pull herself together.

God, I hate this.

She hated feeling this way, hated that she felt this way almost more often than not, hated this person she'd become. She missed her father. She missed her mother. She missed feeling like herself. And God help her, she missed her old life. She knew she was never getting that back, that she needed to let go and embrace the new her, the new life of Amelia Martini, middle-aged single woman, which sounded like a terrible sitcom beginning this fall. She had to let go and move forward.

She just wished she knew how.

A deep breath in, she steadied herself, then turned and headed back inside. She owed her family an apology. Again.

CHAPTER EIGHT

By the following Wednesday, Kirby had finished three of the bedrooms and was starting on the fourth, the last one she had to do upstairs before moving to the first floor, where she was well-aware she'd be in closer proximity to Amelia Martini.

Why was that on her mind? What did it matter? She worked around clients all the time. This wasn't anything new, and she needed to chillax about it. She mixed her paint, humming along to Lizzo on the radio. This room was going to take some concentration on her part. Victor Renwick had very specific taste, and he'd liked some of her more complex designs. This room was going to be a light lavender gray, and on one wall, she'd do a very faint diamond pattern. She'd practiced it at home a few times, and it had come out beautifully.

"Hi."

Her hand jerked and paint sloshed a bit and dripped over the side of the bucket. Good thing her body was between the paint and Amelia, and she didn't see that she'd startled her.

"Hey," Kirby said as she stood and turned to see her. They'd developed a bit of a routine, whereby Amelia unlocked the front door when she got up and gated the dogs as soon as they'd eaten, so by the time Kirby arrived at nine, she could just let herself in and get to work.

Amelia stood in the doorway in denim shorts and a black tank, super simple clothes that somehow made her look super sexy. Maybe it was the bare feet. Maybe it was the messy bun. Maybe it was all the skin she could see. Kirby stuffed down her surprise because she had no idea when she'd started thinking of Amelia as sexy. Hot, yes. Attractive, definitely. Sexy was new, but she didn't know when that had happened. She tried to pinpoint it. The pool last week? Maybe. But it just suddenly *was* now. Amelia Martini was sexy as hell. Fact.

"It's, um, gonna be a hot one today, and I made myself some iced coffee this morning," Amelia said, holding out a tall glass. She shifted her weight from one foot to the other. "Thought you might like one, too."

Well. This was new.

"Thanks." She crossed the room and took the glass. It was filled with ice and creamy, delicious-looking coffee. A red straw poked out, and Kirby took a sip. It tasted as good as it looked, and she made a humming sound of approval. "Wow."

"Yeah, seems Victor knows his coffee," Amelia said and gave Kirby a peek at those dimples. "I've been grinding the beans every morning, and it took me an hour to figure out his coffee maker. I think NASA invented it."

"Well, you clearly broke the code. This is fantastic. Thank you."

Instead of turning to go, which was what Kirby expected Amelia to do, she wandered into the room, looking around. It was another guest room that was sparsely furnished, and Kirby had as usual pushed what was there into the center, so she had access to the walls. She looked at the primed walls, then down at the open can of paint.

"See, now *this* gray, I like." And when Amelia looked up, Kirby caught the tiny sparkle in her eye that said she was teasing.

"Spring Showers," Kirby said.

"Even the name is nice."

"I'm *so* glad you approve." She made a show of wiping her brow, but there was no snark. Just a gentle teasing, and Amelia took it as it was meant, judging from the small smile that appeared.

"Are you a one-woman operation?" Amelia asked, still wandering the room.

"I have a couple of employees. They're taking care of other

jobs. I do the more complicated ones." She watched as Amelia moved, tried not to stare.

"And this one qualifies as complicated?"

Kirby nodded and felt herself shift slightly into business mode. "The last room had the textured paint, and this room will have a wall pattern. I do those things. My guys do straightforward jobs and big jobs. I also do all the estimates, the billing, that kind of thing."

"So you're a one-woman operation with a little bit of help."

A nod. That was about it, yeah. She was about to ask Amelia a little bit about herself when a barking frenzy started downstairs.

"I'd better go see what that's about." Amelia headed for the doorway.

"Thanks for the coffee," Kirby said to her retreating form. And yeah, she watched her go, of course she did, because those denim shorts did wonders for Amelia. And for Kirby. "Wow," she muttered to herself.

She took a big breath and gave herself a handful of moments to haul her brain back into work mode after that, but while she was there, she let herself wonder. Because there was a lot to wonder about Amelia Martini, and Kirby didn't want to be fascinated by her, but for whatever reason, she absolutely was.

Why didn't Amelia smile more?

That was the big question. As she stirred the paint some more, she thought about that. And she didn't mean it in the same way men meant it when they told a woman to smile more. Rather, she wanted to know why Amelia was so serious all the time. Why was she sad? Because Kirby was convinced that she was, a little bit. What was it that kept that divot above her nose, not quite a scowl, but a very serious expression? Even the tiny glimpses of smiles she'd seen completely transformed Amelia's face, made her even more beautiful than she was when she was serious.

And Amelia was seriously beautiful. There was no denying that. She could never, ever smile and Kirby would still think so.

She got to painting, began all the cutting in. She actually enjoyed this part much more than the rolling. For bigger areas, they'd spray, but for smaller rooms, Kirby liked to go old-school, the way her dad always did it. Paintbrushes. Rollers. Trays. Blue painter's tape. Tarps. There was something really satisfying about doing a room fully by hand. And once she got into the pattern, she really felt like an artist.

She'd been painting since she was a kid and she was good at it, which also meant she was fast. Before long, she was cutting around the windows that looked onto the backyard. There was Amelia, tossing a tennis ball for Stevie while Calvin lay near her feet. She grinned, and before she could stop herself, she slid the window open.

"Calvin seems to think chasing a ball is beneath him," she called down.

Amelia shaded her eyes with a hand as she turned to look up. "I think you're right." A beat went by before she added. "How's it going up there?"

"Steady." Their gazes held, which was weird because Kirby wasn't a person who liked silence or stillness. She liked to talk. To move. She liked action. But the moment drew on until finally Stevie nudged Amelia with his tennis ball mouth, and she pulled her eyes away.

Kirby watched as she threw the ball, a line drive with power. "Nice arm. You know, my softball team is always looking for subs. I think we need one tonight, actually."

Amelia snorted a laugh. "Been a long time since I played."

"Well, from up here, you've still got it." Kirby grinned down at her. Was she being creepy and weird, staring out the window? A tickle of panic crawled up her spine. "Anyway." She reached up to close the window, but Amelia spoke before she could, made a sweeping gesture with her arm, à la Vanna White, encompassing the pool.

"Remember. Any time you want."

It took Kirby a minute to realize she was referring to the pool. Swimming. *Swimming, Kirby.*

"I'll keep that in mind." Then she shut the window and got back to work.

❖

A lot of people would consider Amelia super lucky. And she was. She knew that, tried to remind herself. She had retired before fifty and had a government pension. She now ran her own small business, which didn't make her a ton of money, but that didn't matter because…government pension. It did give her some extra play money, though. Now that she lived in her parents' house, she had little debt aside from her car payment. And she hung around dogs all day.

Yeah, it was a life worth envying.

Amelia had trouble grasping that, though, because the majority of the time, all she felt was lost.

It was after lunch now, and she'd walked Duke and stopped in on another dog to give her some meds and attention. Now, she could relax. She cranked open one of the umbrellas on the patio around the pool. It was getting hot out, June signing off for the year with a blast of heat and humidity that rivaled late August. Stevie was happy to crash under her lounge chair in the shade, but Calvin clearly didn't like the heat and scratched at the back door until she let him into the three season room where he collapsed dramatically onto the cool tile floor and lay there like a rug.

She'd grabbed herself a Diet Coke on ice and three of the stack of nine books she'd brought with her and settled on a towel on the lounge chair. She opened a book and had only read for a few moments before she heard the back door open. She turned in her chair to see Kirby, looking slightly unsure.

"Um, is it okay if I stick my feet in?" Kirby asked as she gestured toward the cool blue water of the pool.

"Absolutely. Have at it."

Kirby Dupree was fun to look at. There was no denying that. And Amelia could scold herself. Scoff internally. Roll her eyes. But she was looking. She was definitely looking. She couldn't not. It was impossible.

Great shoulders. That was the first thing Amelia noticed. Kirby wore a tank top today, and she imagined all the lifting and reaching and rolling she did every day had toned her, created her shape, almost that of a swimmer—her torso a very subtle triangle, wider at the shoulders and tapering to a slim waist. Of course, the curve of her hips made her physique very feminine, and for a quick blip, Amelia flashed on what it might feel like to grasp those hips, right where they flared out, to pull them closer to her…

"You okay?"

Kirby's voice yanked her almost violently from her vision, and Amelia blinked rapidly, swallowed hard, had to clear her throat before she found her voice. "Yeah. Yeah, fine. You?"

Kirby studied her with an amused smile on her face. "I'm good, yeah." Their gazes held for a beat. "Whatcha readin'?" she asked as she left her work boots on the edge of the pool and dunked her feet. With her head, she indicated the book in Amelia's hand, which she now wished was something by Lisa Scottoline or Harlan Coben.

"Um…" She held the book up for Kirby to see the title.

"*The New Hot*. What's it about?"

"Menopause." Amelia sighed and closed the book, embarrassed now.

"You hit it early?" Kirby asked, unfazed.

"Early? No, I'm pretty much on time."

"You don't seem old enough."

"Oh, I am definitely that. Forty-nine," Amelia said, surprised to have offered that info so readily.

Kirby made a *pfft* sound as she waved a hand. "That's young."

"Says the thirty-year-old."

"Thirty-five, thank you very much." Kirby grinned at her, must've noticed Amelia not grinning back. "Seriously. Forty-nine is way far from old."

"I could almost be your mother," Amelia said, which made Kirby bark a laugh.

"Yeah, if you'd been really careless in junior high!"

Amelia watched as Kirby's eyes traveled to the table next to her lounge chair and took in the other books before she had time to do something like…shove them to the ground or toss them into the pool, maybe?

"So, you're reading about menopause and divorce and—what does that one say?—*Starting Over at Fifty?*"

Where was a giant black hole when you needed one? Couldn't

the earth just swallow her up now? Sinkhole? Alien ship? Anything? Please? She closed her eyes, her embarrassment heating her skin from a source that had nothing to do with the summer sun.

"What happened?" Kirby asked, and her voice was surprisingly soft, almost tender.

"What do you mean?"

Kirby poked her chin in the direction of the books. "Seems like you're trying to find something. Or figure things out. I was just wondering what happened."

"I have never wished harder for my Kindle than I am right now." She saw the flash of—was it disappointment?—zip across Kirby's face before she turned back to the pool and quietly kicked her feet. Amelia took a deep breath and let it out slowly. "I'm sorry. That was snarky." Kirby looked back at her. "Seems to be one of about nine kazillion symptoms of menopause, unprovoked snark. It just pops out sometimes. I apologize."

"No worries. Not my business anyway." Kirby waved her off, but Amelia knew she'd hurt her feelings, and it bothered her. More than she cared to dwell on.

After only another moment, Kirby pulled her feet out and stood up. Amelia's guilt deepened.

"Well, I've got an estimate to do, so I'm gonna jet." She picked up her boots and socks and then stood in front of Amelia, looking like she was trying to decide something. After a moment, she said, "Listen, we play softball at Krieger Park, off of Bay. If you're bored, you should come check it out. I promise not to rope you into subbing." She smiled, and her entire face softened. It was kind of an amazing thing to see, the way her forehead smoothed, and Amelia had a sudden weird, inexplicable urge to rest her palm against Kirby's cheek. Yeah, so what the hell was that about?

"So noted," Amelia said with a smile of her own, 'cause that was nice, right? She'd been a bitch, and still Kirby had invited her to watch softball.

Kirby squatted and gave Stevie a few pets, then stood and looked down at Amelia. "See you maybe later." She grabbed Amelia's bare toe and gave her foot a little jiggle before heading into the house.

Amelia stared at the pool water, listened to the gentle gurgle of the filter, and sighed. Feeling eyes on her, she glanced to her left where Stevie sat, staring at her with definite accusation in his eyes.

"I *know*," she said. The dog made a snorfling sound and lay back down, as if he'd had enough of her and her bullshit. "Yeah, join the club," she muttered back to him.

CHAPTER NINE

G od, it was hot.

Kirby swung the bat a few times as she waited on deck for her turn in the bottom of the fifth inning. Her shoulders were a little stiff, and she could feel a bead of sweat roll down the center of her back. Both Katie and Shelby sat on the bottom bleacher, their game having finished a few minutes ago. They'd wandered over from the other field to catch the end of hers before they all went out.

Kirby wiped her hand across the back of her neck. Sweat. For a quick zap of time, she wished she was back at Victor Renwick's house sitting on the edge of the pool—Calmly Azure is what she'd name the color of the water—with her feet gently moving in it. Just relaxing. Surprisingly, in this fantasy she was creating, Amelia Martini still lounged in her chair, reading a book, looking delectable. Big sunglasses on her face. Olive skin bronzing. Smiling at her on occasion.

"Earth to Kirby! You're up!"

Lark's voice yanked her out of that lovely place, and she let go of a scoff as she approached the batter's box, because it was truly a fantasy. Amelia didn't smile at her. Amelia barely looked at her.

It's whatever. She shook her head, tried to place it back in the game where it belonged. She dug her toe into the dirt—a holdover from her high school softball days—took a couple swings, and waited for the first pitch. Let it go by. Always. *Never take the first pitch.* Her father had taught her that.

The second pitch was perfect. She swung hard, pulled the bat, and fired a base hit right between third and short. Once she was safe at first, she adjusted her hat and glanced at the stands.

And her breath caught.

Amelia Martini sat alone on the top bench of the small set of bleachers. They made eye contact. Amelia lifted one hand, wiggled her fingers in a tiny wave, and gave her a small smile, and Kirby was so shocked to see her that she forgot to lead off. It was only when the bat connected with a solid thwack that she was jerked back to the present and ordered her legs to move.

She was thrown out at second.

"What the hell was that?" Lark asked her as she returned to the bench. Her tone was more surprised than annoyed. After all, this was rec ball. Not high-stakes. "If I didn't know better, I'd say the very attractive woman in the bleachers distracted you."

Kirby looked away because of course Lark was right, and her eyes said she knew it.

Lark leaned closer. "Who is she?"

"Who's who?" Emma was suddenly next to Kirby. And *next to her* was actually *standing in her personal space*, so yeah, Emma's crush was apparently still alive and well. Kirby tried to be subtle about stepping away a bit.

"That woman in the white tank top sitting at the top of the bleachers," Lark said, not moving her lips as if they were talking in code.

Kirby shot her a look.

"What about her?" Emma asked, eyes scanning, then clearly finding Amelia.

"Likely the reason Kirbs here forgot to lead off of first." Lark pulled a face at Kirby, who glared at her.

Emma's eyes clouded. "Oh." Then she busied herself with her glove, and then needed to tie her shoe, and then muttered something about her water bottle and hurried off.

"That was unnecessary," Kirby hissed at Lark. "And kinda mean."

"Yeah? Do you want to go out with her?"

"Who?"

"Emma, weirdo."

"No."

"Okay then. It *was* necessary." Lark lifted one shoulder. "You're welcome." The third out was made, and they grabbed their gloves. "I want to hear all about this chick later."

It almost sounded like a warning to Kirby, who couldn't help but chuckle even as she shot Lark an exaggerated eye roll. Lark loved nothing more than knowing all the details all the time about everything. And she wouldn't let up until she had them. It was something admirable about her, and also could be kind of annoying. Kirby was used to it—it was just who Lark was. Being the subject of her probing, though, that was new. And not exactly comfortable.

Besides, what was there to tell?

Kirby glanced up at the bleachers again from her place between second and third. Amelia was in the same spot, her phone in her hand, but her attention on the game, and aside from being happy to see Amelia in the crowd—something she'd have to analyze later—she was surprised. She'd stepped in it with Amelia earlier. Unintentionally, but still. Amelia had snapped at her instantly.

Yet there Amelia was. Sitting in the bleachers, watching her game.

What to do with that…

She decided as the next batter took her place in the batter's box that she was going to just take it. Stop analyzing. Stop wondering. Amelia was here, watching her game, because Kirby had invited her. She'd come. That was awesome.

Focusing on the game was easier after that.

They won, 7–5, and as players gathered their equipment to make way for the next game, Kirby glanced up at the bleachers. Amelia was gone, her seat now empty, and the disappointment that fell over her like a weighted blanket shocked her. She'd really wanted to talk to Amelia, to thank her, to find out—

"Nice game." And there she was. Standing behind her. Kirby turned to face her, smiled at the slight glimmer in those hazel eyes. "Well, except for that whole getting thrown out at second. You didn't even lead off." She was teasing her. Flirting with her? Well. This was new.

"It's possible I was distracted." Oh God, did she say that out loud? Seriously?

"Really? Interesting."

And then their gazes held, and there was a heat Kirby could feel between them like some kind of sexy electricity. Could anybody else see it? Was it, like, yellow currents of lightning zipping between them, there for others to witness? What exactly was happening? Had Amelia been visited by body snatchers? Was this even her? So very different from the earlier version of Amelia. Confusing, and very much preferable.

"Hi, I'm Lark. Friend of Kirby." Leave it to Lark to notice an intense moment and interrupt it. She stuck out her hand toward Amelia.

"Amelia." She glanced at Kirby before adding, "Also friend of Kirby."

"Mm-hmm. I see. Are you going to join us for drinks?" Lark wasted no time.

Amelia blinked, then turned to Kirby. "Where?" At Kirby's grin and head tilt, Amelia's dimples made an appearance. "Right. Martini's." Kirby nodded, and they both laughed.

"What's funny?" Lark asked.

"This is my friend Amelia," Kirby said. "Amelia *Martini*. Her cousin owns the bar."

"I *knew* you looked familiar," Lark said, pointing at her. "We've probably seen you there before."

"I practically live there, so I'm sure you have." Amelia turned back to Kirby. "Yeah, I'll go for one. Meet you there?"

Kirby nodded then tried to dim her smile a bit, but failed. Which she knew as soon as Amelia was out of earshot and Lark leaned into her.

"Uh-huh. I see. Nice. Very nice."

"You see what?" Kirby asked, feeling her own blush no matter how hard she tried to fight it.

"Mm-hmm," was all the explanation Lark gave, but her smile was wide, her eyes knowing. "Let's go drink."

❖

Amelia had probably driven too fast to the bar. Nerves? Maybe. Which was silly, really. What was there to be nervous about? She'd beaten the team to Martini's, found her usual stool at the end of the bar, and ordered a drink from Julia, who liked to tend bar a bit on nights when one of her sponsored teams played.

"You're twitchy," Julia said as she slid a gin and tonic to her. "What's the matter?"

"Twitchy? I'm twitchy?" Amelia made a face. "Odd choice of words."

"I stand by it. You're twitchy."

She took a sip of the drink, perfectly mixed, as usual. "This is good."

"Okay, don't answer me." Julia pointed two fingers of one hand at her own eyes, then flipped them toward Amelia. "But I'm watching you."

"I stepped out of my comfort zone," she blurted before Julia could walk away.

Her cousin squinted at her. "Okay. Explain."

"I went to watch a softball game tonight." She picked up her drink, took another sip.

Julia continued to look at her with narrowed eyes. "Okay," she said, and drew the word out as she waited for some kind of elaboration. Any kind, probably.

"The team that's coming here. I watched their game."

Julia scratched at her forehead. "All right. I see this is a puzzle you want me to figure out. Lemme see…" She wrinkled her nose. "The team that's coming here…" Clearly, she was running through information in her head. When recognition flashed in her eyes and she snapped her fingers, Amelia knew she'd hit on it. "Kirby's team." Amelia nodded. "Did she invite you to come watch?" Another nod. "And you did?" That question came with a huge dose of disbelief in the tone.

"I did."

"Wow. Meels." Julia grinned. Grinned big. "You *did* step

out of your comfort zone." She reached across and squeezed her forearm. "I'm proud of you."

Any more conversation was cut off as the team in question arrived, laughing and talking, and Julia shot her a wink before moving to take drink orders.

Amelia's eyes found Kirby without her even consciously scanning for her. Kirby wasn't tall. Maybe five four? Five five? She had an athletic build, and Amelia remembered her shoulders from earlier, almost disappointed now that she wore a T-shirt that covered them. She'd turned her hat backward, blond hair peeking out in different spots and through the fastener now above her forehead. Her gaze landed on Amelia from way across the bar, and did her smile grow? Seemed like it might have...

"Hey, you made it," Kirby said when she'd made her way to Amelia's seat. "You've surprised me twice now today."

"Yeah? How so?" Amelia sipped her cocktail.

"First, by showing up to the game and second, by coming here." Kirby caught Julia's eye, and they did some kind of sign language thing Amelia didn't understand, but suddenly there was a beer in front of Kirby.

"Okay, first of all, wow." Amelia indicated the beer. "I'm family and don't get served that fast. Two, you invited me to the game, so why are you surprised I came?"

Kirby swigged from the bottle, and Amelia tried not to stare at the long column of her throat as she did. "You weren't exactly happy with my prying this afternoon."

In that moment, the thing that Amelia grabbed on to was the fact that, despite Kirby being right and Amelia having been kind of bitchy earlier, she was there. She was talking to her. She hadn't tucked tail and hid. Amelia decided right then that Kirby Dupree had confidence and assertion and wasn't easily scared off. Points to her. Big ones.

"I'm sorry about that." Amelia spun her glass between her hands slowly. "I've been kind of struggling lately, and it's shortened my fuse in a big way." She laughed because what else could she do?

Kirby studied her for a moment, holding eye contact, which

was another thing Amelia wasn't hugely familiar with. Tammy had been terrible at actually looking at her when they talked. Probably because she didn't think Amelia was worth the effort it took. "I've been told more than once that I'm a really good listener," Kirby finally said. "So if you ever want to talk about these struggles you're having…" She shrugged. "I'm gonna be around for a while. Like, literally around. 'Cause painting." Her smile was beautiful. How had Amelia not noticed that before?

"Thank you for not making air quotes around the word *struggles*. I appreciate that more than you know."

"Listen, air quotes are awesome when used correctly. But nobody else gets to judge your struggles, right?" Kirby raised her bottle. "To the proper use of air quotes."

"I'll drink to that," Amelia said and laughed through her nose as she touched her almost-empty glass to the bottle. She wanted to talk to Kirby more, was kind of surprised at that. But before they could continue their conversation, Kirby's two friends from a week or two ago made their way over. The tall, thin one with a sleek, dark ponytail. The other was curvier and super cute, her baseball hat working hard to contain her mass of red curls. Amelia struggled to remember their names. Didn't one start with a *K*?

"We play each other next week, I think," the taller one said as she bumped Kirby with a hip.

"Allow me to apologize in advance for tromping you." Kirby grinned. Then she turned to Amelia. "Amelia, you remember my friends Katie and Shelby?"

"I do. Nice to see you both again. Did you win?"

"Ugh. No. We suck," said the redhead, then laughed like it made no difference. "You play?"

"I did in high school," Amelia said. "But I wasn't very good." She inclined her head toward Julia, who was shaking a martini shaker and laughing at something a customer said. "My cousin there is the real athlete in the family." Then she let her gaze fall on Kirby. "So, you play softball. You mentioned Frisbee golf the other day. What else do you play?"

"Oh my God, what *doesn't* she play?" Katie said with a super dramatic eye roll that made them all laugh.

"Kirby is one of *those* people," Shelby told her. "She can play anything and she's good at every sport or game she tries."

"No lie," Katie confirmed.

Kirby's cheeks started to pinken, which Amelia found cuter than she even wanted to think about. "Well, that's an exaggeration," Kirby said.

"Is it?" Katie asked, then leaned close to Kirby and repeated more intensely, "Is. It?" She looked to Shelby. "Remember when your dad took us all golfing?"

"She got a hole in one." Shelby shook her head, eyes wide. "And when we taught her poker?"

"She left with all our money." Katie groaned.

"You threw that party, and Ricky brought his cornhole game," Shelby said and pointed at Katie.

"Oh my God, and Kirby played for, like, three hours, 'cause her team never lost, even though she kept rotating partners." Katie turned to Amelia. "She's good at *everything*. It's disgusting, really. We actually kind of hate her."

"It's true," Shelby said with a serious nod. "We do. Deeply. Deep hate."

They were all laughing, Amelia included, surprised by how much she was enjoying herself. A new drink appeared before her, and when she glanced up at Julia, her cousin winked at her. She sat there for the next hour listening to stories of the three women—who she'd learned knew each other from high school—and laughed more than she had in a very, very long time.

"What do you do, Amelia?" Shelby asked when they'd gotten on the subject of work.

"I've recently started my own small company called Dogz Rule. I basically take care of other people's dogs." She gave a small shrug.

"Like, if I have to work late and my poor dog has been home with his legs crossed for a million hours?" Katie asked. "You go over and let him out?"

"Exactly. And walk him. Play with him. Or if you have a dog that needs meds during the day."

"Oh my God, what a great job," Shelby said. "You get to play with dogs all day long. Jelly over here."

"Do you have cards?" Katie asked. "I have some coworkers who travel a lot. They could probably use somebody like you."

"They're on order," Amelia told her with a frown. "Should be here any day. I can give a handful to Kirby to pass along to you, if that's okay."

"Perfect."

Kirby met her eyes, and that zing passed between them again as Kirby smiled at her.

"Speaking of dogs," Amelia said as she slid off the stool, deciding this was exactly the right time to take her leave, "I'm watching a couple, as Kirby knows, and I need to get back to them."

"I told you guys about them, remember?" Kirby said, her cheeks still pink, but probably from the beer at this point. "Stevie's a springer and so super soft and playful. And Calvin is…" She glanced at Amelia. "A Frenchie?" At Amelia's nod, she went on. "He's got these enormous ears and walks around like he owns the place. Which, I guess he kinda does." She shook her head. "They're super cool dogs."

"They like you," Amelia added as she signaled Julia and dropped a twenty on the bar.

"You off?" Julia asked.

"She's got dogs," Shelby told her with a grin.

"Ah, that's right." Julia shoved the twenty back at her. "You're family. Your money's no good here."

"Then put it in the tip jar," Amelia told her and slid it back. To Kirby, she said, "I'll see you in the morning?"

"You will," Kirby said with a nod.

"I'll have the good coffee on." Amelia smiled at her, waved to the other two, and headed for the door. She was sure she could feel eyes on her as she left, and she grudgingly admitted to herself that she hoped they were Kirby's.

Of course, once she got to her car, slammed the door, and

glanced at her own eyes in the rearview mirror, all her worries and insecurities came tumbling down on her, crushing her where she sat. "What are you thinking?" she whispered to her reflection. "You're not in your thirties anymore. You won't even be in your forties for much longer. Going to a softball game and hanging out at a bar with people more than a decade younger than you?" She shook her head as she started the car. No, she was supposed to be home with her wife, working on their house, planning vacations they couldn't afford when they had been Kirby's age, figuring out what warm place they wanted to retire to.

Back at Victor's house, she let the dogs out, grabbed herself a glass of water, and sat out in the backyard by the pool while they sniffed and wandered and checked every inch of their space. The night was beautiful, warm but no longer sticky, tons of stars visible in the dark sky. And all Amelia could think about was that she was there alone. Tammy had always loved this kind of night, just sitting and *being*. The hard realization for Amelia now was that Tammy just didn't want to sit and be with *her*.

Later, as she got ready for bed, she studied herself in the giant mirror in Victor's spa-like bath. She took off all her clothes and stared, picked out every flaw, every blemish, everything that was bigger than she thought it should be, every bulge that hadn't been there a year ago, every bit of new pudge that showed up out of nowhere. Her eyes filled with tears because what she saw looking back at her was an old, sad, lost, lonely woman.

She sucked in a breath, clenched her teeth until her jaw began to ache, and did her best to swallow down the emotion that so often threatened to swamp her. Some nights, it did. Hit her like a wave of pain and anguish. Other nights, she fought it off.

Tonight, she prepared for swamping, but much to her surprise, the wave dissipated. Receded. She swallowed hard and pulled her super soft T-shirt over her head. Switched off the lights before she could critique herself again. Headed for the enormous king-size bed where both dogs sat, waiting for her like this was what they had done their whole lives.

As she slipped under the covers and wondered why she'd been able to avoid the levels of emotional basket case she'd been expecting, Kirby's face drifted into her head. The blond hair, those kind eyes—more hazel again tonight—the infectious smile. And that smolder. That was the word she'd been searching for when she thought about the way Kirby looked at her sometimes. She *smoldered*. It was hot and flirty and sexy as hell. Most importantly, what it had done was remind Amelia that she was alive.

She slipped between the sheets with the enormously high thread count—crazy soft, but they also held the heat, which was brutal given her night sweats. As soon as she settled on her side, Stevie stretched himself out along her back, like a bookend keeping her propped up. Calvin curled up in a ball against her stomach, and it was like they'd always slept this way. Amelia didn't have her own dog—Tammy had never wanted one—and she liked to think this new career of hers gave her the dog fix she craved. But sleeping like this with the dogs close? There was nothing like it, even as she realized she was completely pinned in. She inhaled a big breath and let it out slowly and willed herself to relax. As she started to drift off, Kirby's face, her smile, floated into Amelia's mind once again. This time, she didn't chase it away.

CHAPTER TEN

"Come on," Amelia muttered at the coffee maker. "Come *on*." For the amount of money the thing probably cost, not only should it make the coffee faster, it should bring it to her in bed.

She needed caffeine. Badly. Rough night did not begin to cover it, and you'd think she'd be used to it by now, but no. Every time she woke up drenched in her own sweat, unable to get back to sleep, topped out at a total of maybe four hours of sleep—maybe—she acted surprised. *How could this happen? What a weird occurrence! What's going on with me?*

"What's going on with me?" she asked nobody as the coffee trickled into her cup at a rate that seemed so slow, she actually wondered if the machine was purposely messing with her. "Menopause. That's what's going on." Just as she finally finished doctoring the coffee and lifted the cup to take a sip, her phone rang. She had no intention of answering it—clients could leave a message. Or better yet, text, like normal people. But her dad's face popped up on the screen, and she always answered him. It was their agreement since her mother had passed away—always, always to answer one another's calls, if at all possible.

"Hi, Dad," she said, trying—and failing—to inject some cheer into her voice so he wouldn't worry.

"Good morning, sweetheart. How are things?"

"Things are fine. How is Florida? Any dinosaurs in your yard lately?" Just hearing his voice covered her in a blanket of calm, and she could feel some of her muscles relax.

"Ha ha, no. Not today. It's a little cool, though," he told her, and she could hear him sip his coffee.

"Oh yeah? What, like, sixty-five? Brr."

His laugh was a deep rumble. "That's about right."

"Well, it's been hot here, but I gotta tell you, Victor's pool is amazing, and I could get used to living like this."

"He's a good guy."

"And thanks for putting me in touch with another gay person. That'll help with word of mouth among my own people." She chuckled to herself, as that's how her dad referred to LGBTQ+ folks, *her people*.

"Not sure how much he told you, but he was with the same guy for a long time. Nearly twenty years, I think. Then Jeff had a stroke a year or two ago and passed away just after they bought the house."

Amelia felt her heart squeeze in her chest. "He mentioned that his husband had passed away, but not how long they'd been together. Ugh. That's awful."

"Yeah, he vowed to go ahead and do all the things they'd planned on doing to the house when Jeff was still alive." His tone had changed, his sympathy clear. Her father knew what it was like to lose your partner in life that way. "He struggles, so I think working on the house helps him cope."

"I would've never known," Amelia mused. "He seemed very happy and friendly. And he loves his dogs so much."

"Like I said, really good guy."

A beat of silence passed between them, and Amelia tried to lighten it up a tad. "Well, I adore his pups. And they're really well-behaved." She glanced out the back window into the yard where Calvin was lying in a spot of sun near the pool and Stevie had his nose to the ground, sniffing the perimeter like he did every morning. "Anyway. Enough about here. What are you up to today?"

"I'm taking it easy today. I haven't been feeling great the past couple of days."

Amelia was instantly on alert. "Why? What's wrong? Have you called the doctor? Do you want me to do it? Should I come down there?"

He had to say her name three times before she stopped with the questions. His tone was amused as he said, "Sweetheart. I'm fine. I'm just old. When you're old, you get aches and pains, and sometimes, you need a day to just take it easy. I'm fine."

"Promise?"

"I pinkie swear." That made Amelia laugh, because she'd taught him pinkie swearing when she was just a little girl, and he'd never forgotten it. They pinkie swore all the time.

"Okay. Just…please call me if you need anything. I can hop a plane and be down there in a couple of hours." She didn't even try to hide her worry. She knew she'd become overprotective of her father since her mother's death. She knew that but didn't care. Overprotective was fine with her.

"I will."

They chatted about a few more mundane things and finished the call. Amelia stood there, long after they'd hung up, and stared at his profile pic on the screen. There was a niggling in the back of her mind. Annoying, yes, but probably nothing. Menopause had changed so much of her, had made it so she barely recognized her own body, her own signals, and she'd become used to shrugging off pains and ignoring aches and weird feelings. Her dad was likely doing the same thing. He was right. It was part of aging.

She let the dogs in, showered, drank more coffee, and started to feel…well, not normal. She still felt large, sluggish, and irritated by every single thing except the dogs. But a little less old and useless, and that was probably as good as it was going to get today.

It wasn't until the dogs started barking at the sound of a car engine that Amelia remembered the previous night. Her venturing to the game, then out to the bar. The closeness to Kirby. How good she'd felt. Confident. Almost sexy. And then she took a quick glance in the mirror and saw the darkness under her eyes, the extra weight around her middle, and just felt…God, the opposite of confident and definitely not sexy. How she wished for somebody to get it. To understand and not make her feel like she was crazy.

She pulled the front door open just as Kirby was coming up the steps, and the dogs greeted her with the same level of excitement they'd have if they were just meeting her for the first time. True to her nature, Kirby set down all her stuff and dropped down to her knees to lavish them with attention. It was super sweet. And Amelia clenched her jaw.

Kirby glanced up at her from her place on the floor. "Hi to you, too." She smiled and Amelia could've sworn the room lit up just a bit. Ugh.

"Hey."

"Rough night?" Kirby's eyes went instantly wide as her words hit the air. "Not that you look it. That's not what I meant. You just seem…subdued, is all. And I know you've had trouble sleeping…" She grimaced, likely knowing she'd dug herself a hole.

"Yeah, it was a rough night. Come on, boys. Let's let Kirby get to work." She tugged the boys along, away from Kirby and toward the back of the house so she could get to work.

It was rude.

She knew it.

She did it anyway.

And when she heard Kirby gather her things and head upstairs, she stood in the kitchen and cried silently.

❖

Well.

"Back to the old Amelia, I see," Kirby whispered to herself as she hauled her supplies upstairs. She honestly wasn't surprised. More than anything, she felt bad for Amelia, because it had to be crazy-making to shift and change so often. Happy one minute, miserable the next. She wondered how menopause would affect *her* when the time came.

As she reached the room she was working on today, she recalled the books Amelia had been reading. Divorce books. Starting-over books. Books on self-improvement. She was clearly unhappy in her own skin, and that made Kirby sad. Because she could see through the moodiness and the irritation. No idea why, but she could. She'd seen flashes of who Amelia really was. She was in there. And she was worth knowing.

Maybe she just needed to understand that somebody saw her.

"And why does that have to be you?" she asked herself. "You don't have to see her. It's not your job." She stood with her hands parked on her hips and stared at the wall she was about to work on. Visualized how she wanted it to look, how she and Victor had discussed it. "This. *This* is your job."

As she prepared the paint and the tape and the stencil, she thought back to the bar after Amelia had left.

"So?" Shelby had asked. "When will you be taking that girl out on a proper date?"

Kirby had blinked at her in surprise. "What?"

"Oh, come on," Katie had continued. "You two have more chemistry than Bill Nye the Science Guy. Ask her out."

They'd teased her for a while, and she could admit it had crossed her mind once or twice. She was wildly attracted to Amelia, that wasn't in question. But Amelia was, well, hung up. On a lot of things, it seemed. Their age difference. Her body. Her life situation in general, which—admittedly—Kirby would like to know more about. Her new business.

But there was something else there. A draw. A pull. Kirby believed in signs. She believed in fate and in destiny, and there was something about Amelia that just would not let Kirby write her off. Even when she wanted to. Even when she thought it was probably the best thing to do.

Driving herself insane with this circular train of thought did not sound like a fun time, so she gave her head a literal shake and did her best to focus on her work. She turned on the music, hoping some fun and bouncy pop might take her mind off deep things and help her concentrate on her craft, on doing the thing she loved more than anything in the world. Deep breath in to steady herself, to visualize, and she got to work.

As usually happened when her project was extra creative or took more concentration, the time flew by. She completely lost track of it, squinting and focusing and taking care with every stroke, and when a voice sounded in the room, she flinched in surprise.

"Wow. That's...wow."

Amelia stood in the doorway, leaning against one side with her arms folded over her chest. Kirby had no idea how long she'd been there, but she looked pretty comfortable, like she might've been watching for a while. Her eyes were big, and she stepped into the room slowly, her gaze never leaving the wall Kirby had spent the day on.

"This is…" Amelia paused in front of the wall, scanning, then staring. "I've never seen anything like this. It's so…" She shook her head. "It's beautiful. It doesn't even look like paint."

Kirby tried to see the wall through Amelia's eyes. The background color was a light blueish gray, more gray, but with a barely discernible tint of sky blue. There was a pattern on it now. Large diamonds. Even and symmetrical. Covering one entire wall—the accent wall. They were delineated by a very slightly lighter color, and the effect was that the lines looked almost like satin, smooth with a tiny shine, as if it wasn't paint at all, but thin ribbons crisscrossing the wall.

Amelia lifted her hand as if to reach out and touch the pattern, but she didn't, and her hand floated in the air for a moment before she turned to Kirby. "You're an artist," she said, her voice quiet and soft. "This is artistry."

She couldn't have chosen a better compliment, and Kirby felt herself blush to the roots of her hair. "Thank you," she said and had to clear her throat. "That means a lot."

"It's just gorgeous. I've never seen anything like it." The awe, the reverence in Amelia's voice, did things to Kirby. Swelled up her pride. Made her lift her chin.

Turned her on.

She swallowed. Cleared her throat. Finally found her voice. "Thank you."

"How…how do you do this? Like, how did you come up with the idea? It's so uncommon."

It was hard to explain where her ideas came from. She'd tried more than once. "I guess, Victor and I were just kind of on the same wavelength." She lifted one shoulder. "I mean, he didn't say, *Paint me some diamonds on my wall*, but we talked about pattern and texture and color. We went through some websites together, some examples of other houses I've done, and I sort of got a feel for what he likes."

"And ran with it?"

"And ran with it, yes."

Amelia stared and shook her head in obvious wonder. "It's beautiful."

"Thanks."

There was silence then. Not uncomfortable. Companionable. Amelia tilted her head this way and that, seemed to just be taking in the wall. Kirby slowly began putting her things away. Her eyes were scratchy from concentrating, so she decided to allow herself to leave a little early. She was squatting down over the paint tray when Amelia spoke.

"I'm sorry."

Kirby looked up. Amelia was still looking at the wall, her back to her. "For what?"

This time when she spoke, Amelia did turn to face her. "For being a bitch earlier." She sighed, looked around the room in a way that told Kirby she was embarrassed to make eye contact. "I don't know what happens to me, what gets into me." Were those tears in her eyes? "I just…I feel unattractive and angry and confused and so freaking old and sad and God, I'm starving. Like, all the time. I want to eat everything. And I—" It was like she caught herself then, like she suddenly realized she'd blurted out so much personal information and was mortified by it. She shook her head again, brought her fingers to her lips, and when she blinked, one single tear escaped. Just the one. Like it had been orchestrated to grab Kirby by the heart and squeeze it.

Because all she wanted was to wipe it away and make Amelia feel better. Somehow. Some way. She stood up and brushed her hands on her jeans.

"Okay, first of all, you are not old, and you are *certainly* not unattractive. Not by a long shot. My God, woman, have you looked in the mirror lately? You're, like, stupidly sexy. It's really not fair to other women." When she saw Amelia blush, she knew it was okay to push on, and an idea hit. "Hey, what are you doing for the rest of the day?"

Amelia blinked, sniffed, and wiped her hand over her cheek. "Like, now?"

"Yeah, like now." She glanced at her watch. "It's almost two. You have plans for the rest of the day?" She expected to be blown off. Or at least offered a weak excuse. To her surprise, though, Amelia answered her in what felt like honesty.

"I was just going to wander over to Junebug to see if they needed any dogs walked, but I'm a volunteer, so I don't have to. So, no, no plans. Why?"

"Let's go do something."

"Who? Us? Like, you and me?" The shock on Amelia's face was almost comical, and Kirby couldn't help but laugh.

"Yeah, like you and me. Is that so crazy?"

"Do something…like what?"

"I don't know. Anything." She met Amelia's hazel eyes, held her gaze as she said, "Let's go to the zoo."

Amelia didn't say anything. She didn't balk or protest. She didn't jump up and down in celebration. She simply kept looking Kirby in the eye, tilted her head to one side, then nodded. And then she laughed and shrugged and said, "Okay. What the hell? Let's go to the zoo."

Kirby felt her own grin widen and hoped she didn't look like some lovesick schoolboy, 'cause that's what she felt a little like. But she shook it off. "Yes! Great. Okay, give me half an hour to clean up and change clothes and then we'll go. We'll stroll. We'll look at animals. We'll eat crap. Yeah?"

Amelia laughed and shook her head, the complete opposite of the mood she'd given off just five minutes earlier. Then Amelia stopped and looked at her. Just looked at her for several seconds before she finally spoke. "I don't know what it is about you, Kirby Dupree," she said softly. After another beat, she seemed to force herself into gear. "I'm gonna go change, too."

Kirby watched her walk out of the room, heard her footsteps retreat down the hallway, and then a soft click sounded as she closed the door to the main bedroom.

She didn't let herself dwell on what she'd done, what she was about to do. No, instead, she focused on cleaning up. She hauled her stuff down to the basement, used the big laundry tub down there to clean off brushes and rollers, the whole time not letting her mind wander, start to question. All she wanted to do was make Amelia happy. See those dimples. Be the cause of their appearance. There was nothing wrong with that, and there was no reason to wonder why. Was there? And animals made people happy, right? So the zoo made sense for somebody who was unhappy. Yes, she was maybe nursing a little crush, and she knew it, but that was allowed. It didn't go deeper than that. Nothing deeper than wanting to help out somebody who was feeling down.

It was nothing deeper than that.

Nothing at all.

A snort burst up through her nose.

"Yeah, keep telling yourself that, Kirby," she muttered to herself. "Whatever you say."

CHAPTER ELEVEN

The Northwood Zoo was not big by any measure, and it didn't garner a ton of attention. But it had animals. Giraffes and elephants and red pandas and otters and that was good enough for Amelia.

It was also fairly quiet because they'd hit the perfect time of year. School had just ended the week before, so parents weren't yet scrambling to find things to do with their kids. Plus, it was a Thursday afternoon. Amelia couldn't help but think how amused Vanessa would be, knowing she was spending time at the zoo.

She'd driven so they didn't have to take Kirby's van, and Amelia enjoyed how well she'd cleaned up. Not that she hadn't noticed Kirby before, because of course she had. But Kirby not in paint-stained clothes and a baseball hat was…well, pleasing was an understatement.

"Do you always carry extra clothes with you?" she asked as they headed for the gate entrance.

Kirby nodded. "A lesson I learned from my dad, and one I didn't take seriously until I dropped a can of paint all over myself and had to work in those pants all day."

Amelia wrinkled her nose. "Sounds uncomfortable."

"It was. After that day, I've always kept a bag in the van with two changes of clothes. One for working and one for playing."

"Are we playing?" Amelia asked, shocked when the words came out of her own mouth. What the actual hell?

"We're relaxing," Kirby said as she gently nudged Amelia out of the way and paid their entry fee. "My idea, my treat."

Wristbands in place, they headed in.

"God, I haven't been here in forever," Amelia said as she stood and just looked around. Yes, it was small, but she remembered coming there as a kid with her mom, the memories flooding her.

"My mom used to bring me here when I was little," Kirby said, as if reading her mind, and her voice was so soft, Amelia wondered if she'd meant to say it out loud.

"Yeah? Mine, too. Does she live nearby?"

"No. She passed away."

Amelia stopped and put a hand on Kirby's arm until she looked at her. "I'm so sorry, Kirby. When? Mine's been gone for almost four years now."

"Really? Well, I'm sorry, too. My mom died when I was twelve."

"Oh no. That's so hard."

"It was." Kirby sighed, and then her face lit up. "I'm starving. Can we grab some food and then wander?"

While Amelia kind of wanted to talk more about Kirby's background, she also didn't want to dwell on a painful subject. After all, they were here to relax and take their minds off shitty things. "I am all for food. What should we get?"

Fifteen minutes later, they were wandering with hot dogs in hand, sharing a Diet Coke and heading for the elephants.

"How can you eat that without mustard?" Amelia asked, gesturing with her chin at Kirby's condiment-lacking hot dog. "Or ketchup. Or relish. Or anything at all?"

"I am enjoying the actual taste of the hot dog, thank you very much."

"You're weird."

"So I've been told." Kirby took a bite of her hot dog as she watched the elephants and Amelia watched her. "Do you ever wonder what they think, being here?"

Amelia turned to the animals in question, so enormous, their feet huge, their trunks impossibly thick and strong. "Like, being in the zoo?"

"No, being in upstate New York. In a place with cold and snow. They're used to the desert."

"That's a good point. Maybe they have sweaters." Kirby grinned and Amelia liked the sight so much, it startled her. She pointed at the elephant. "What color would you call that shade of gray?"

Kirby tipped her head as if really thinking about it before pronouncing, "Elephant Skin."

A laugh burst out of Amelia. "You know, I was gonna call cop-out on that, but it's kind of perfect."

"Right?"

They laughed together and moved on. "That's a game we're gonna play now."

"What game?" Kirby asked, finishing off her hot dog and taking the Diet Coke from Amelia's hand.

"Name that color." To demonstrate, she pointed at the gray wolves in their pen. "What about them?"

"Okay, first of all, holy shit they're big! And second, can we do something that's not gray?"

"Gray is in. You said so yourself."

"This is true. All right, fine. Let me think."

They stood there at the barrier, watching the male wolf stalk around, his shoulders as high as Amelia's hip. Kirby wasn't kidding about the size of him.

"Don't Be An Ash," Kirby said finally.

Amelia thought about it, then gave a nod. "Works."

"On to the zebras," Kirby announced, pointing.

They wandered through the zoo slowly, aimlessly, and Amelia couldn't remember the last time she'd felt so...*un*stressed. She didn't think about work or Tammy or her body. She simply existed with this other person. Laughed with her. Put her concerns in a little box, closed the lid, and set it aside, at least for a little while. And when was the last time she'd done that?

"Hey." Kirby pulled her out of her head. "Smell that?"

Amelia sniffed. "Cinnamon?"

"Yes! Cinnamon almonds. Over there." She pointed at the little cart. "We need those."

"We do?"

"Absolutely. Come on." Kirby grabbed her hand. Kirby's

was warm and strong and solid in hers, and she tried hard not to squeeze it. But she wanted to. Oh, she wanted to. She let herself be tugged to the almonds.

This day. God, this day. Amelia felt the corners of her mouth slowly begin to turn upward. It was sunny and warm. It was the middle of a weekday afternoon, and they were at the zoo. This woman with her…She inhaled quietly, let it out slowly. This woman with her was…honestly, she was just what Amelia needed in that moment. Not a fact she wanted to think about. No. She had so much baggage. So many issues. And Kirby Dupree was fun and cheerful and a definite free spirit and—

"Here you go." Kirby's grin was wide and infectious as she handed Amelia some almonds. They were warm in her hand and the smell was divine. "Where to next, boss?" Kirby asked.

"Penguins," Amelia said without missing a beat.

"Penguins it is." And as if she did it without thinking, Kirby took her hand and led her to the penguin exhibit.

And Amelia let herself be led.

❖

Kirby wasn't at all surprised by the great time she was having. She was the queen of spontaneity. Katie and Shelby could both attest to that. Katie was a super planner, needed her day—her week, her month, her life—mapped out in detail, and Kirby loved to come along and toss in a wrench by taking her someplace unexpected at the very last minute. Katie always kicked and screamed and always ended up having a fantastic time.

Amelia was not as easy to read as Katie, though she was much more vocal in most cases. She blurted out whatever she was feeling, and Kirby wondered if that was normal Amelia behavior or if it had been affected by the recent changes in her life.

Also, how good did Amelia's hand feel in hers? Yikes. So good. Too good. It wouldn't be hard for Kirby to find herself pulled in. She wasn't exactly fighting it. And God knew Amelia was just her type. She liked older women. Established women.

Women like Amelia. When they found their spot and Amelia let go, Kirby almost whined in protest.

"God, I love penguins," Amelia said softly, and Kirby wasn't sure if she was talking to her or herself.

"They're the coolest looking things, aren't they?" The penguin display wasn't large and there was a rope barrier that kept them from getting too close, but the birds were super cute with their tuxedo coloring and round bellies. "I just want to hug one."

"I wonder what they feel like. Are they slimy? Slick? Feathery?"

"We could ask if they'd let us take one and adopt it. I mean, they have, what? Six? They won't miss one."

"We should adopt two, so they don't get lonely."

"Good call."

And then they were quiet and just stood close together and watched as the penguins played and dived and swam. Kirby couldn't remember the last time she was so comfortable in the presence of somebody who also turned her on in such a big way. Butterflies in her stomach. Throbbing between her legs. A lump in her throat. She did her best to shake it off, and after several minutes, they turned together and began walking again as if they'd telepathically discussed it.

"Why the zoo?" Amelia asked, seemingly out of nowhere, as they strolled.

"What do you mean?"

"I mean, you could have chosen to take me anyplace. A bar. A movie. A hiking trail with cliffs where you could shove me off and never be bothered by my snark again."

Kirby made a show of seriously thinking about the suggestions. Keeping her expression completely deadpan, she responded to each. "Well, your family owns a bar and you're there a lot, so taking you to a bar would've been horribly unoriginal on my part. You can't really talk during a movie, so maybe I didn't give that one enough thought." She tapped her finger against her lips for a beat, then continued. "As for the cliff idea, I've watched enough *Dateline* to know I'd never get away with hurling you off one and claiming it was an accident. The people who try that always, always get caught. So the zoo was the only logical option."

Amelia looked at her as they walked. Blinked a few times. Clearly struggled to decide whether Kirby was serious or not.

Finally, Kirby bumped her with a shoulder. "My mom brought me to the zoo all the time when I was a kid, I told you. And after she was gone, my dad did. It always made me feel better to be around the animals. That's why."

"You and your dad must be close," Amelia said, opening her cinnamon almonds up again.

"We were. Very. He died when I was twenty-one."

Amelia's gasp was soft. "Oh, Kirby, I'm so sorry."

"Thanks. Long time ago. But the zoo always makes me think of my parents and the good times we had here."

"It doesn't make you sad?"

Kirby honestly thought about the question, then shook her head. "No, not at all. I mean, I'd love it if they were here with me like old times, but no. I don't really get sad anymore when I think about my parents. I used to. When I was younger, it nearly crippled me." What was she doing? She didn't talk about this stuff. Ever. With anyone. But there was something in Amelia's eyes that made her feel...safe. Was that it? Was that even possible? "Like I said, my mom died when I was twelve, so it was just me and my dad for a long time."

"Kirby, I'm so sorry. That's so young."

"Yeah. Fuck cancer."

"Seriously."

And then they reached the next exhibit, and the world righted again for the moment. Kirby laughed. "But really, how can you be sad when there are monkeys, am I right?"

As if on cue, one of them swung on a branch so close to them it was almost like they could reach out and touch him.

"You are so right," Amelia said as she laughed at his antics.

Had anything ever felt as perfect as standing in front of the monkey exhibit, crunching on cinnamon almonds and feeling Amelia's body heat? If anything had, Kirby couldn't think of it.

"What about you? Are you tight with your dad?" she asked, now curious and wanting to know as much as she could.

"Very," Amelia said, and her eyes seemed to get a faraway look to them. "I lost my mom three—almost four—years ago. Car accident."

"That sucks."

"It does. My extended family is very large, but I don't have siblings, so after that, it was kind of just me and my dad. Like you and yours."

Kirby nodded, watched Amelia's face. Jesus, she was pretty. Her skin smooth, those hazel eyes much wiser than she'd initially understood.

"Three years isn't that long ago. Is he okay? Are you?"

Amelia inhaled slowly, as if she was really thinking about the question. "I think so. I mean, it's been hard on him. He's in his seventies. He's made it clear that my mom was the love of his life, and he has no desire to date again."

Kirby nodded, remembering how her dad said something similar, even though he was only in his forties at the time.

"That being said, he's in Florida in a retirement development right now, and he's been labeled the most eligible bachelor by lots of the widows there." Amelia's laugh was genuine. Kirby could tell by the way it bubbled up from deep in her lungs, and how it made those gorgeous dimples pop.

"That's awesome."

Again, without saying a word, they turned away from the monkey display and headed toward a building that housed the reptiles.

"I've been living in my parents' house since my divorce," Amelia went on, and Kirby hid her surprise at learning more.

"I can see positive and negative to that," she said.

"*Thank* you," Amelia said, and her eyes widened like nobody had ever said that. "My cousins see only that I'm not paying rent."

"Which is great. And frees you up to work for Victor. The positive aspects."

"Exactly. And the negative ones are?"

This was a little bit of a test, and Kirby knew it. Felt it. She wasn't even sure if Amelia realized it, but it was. "You don't have your own space anymore. You're a grown woman living in your parents' house, and you hate it. But you're not sure what you want for yourself yet, so you don't want to rush into buying the next thing. But *also*, there's an element of safety being at home, which I would think helps with the pain of a divorce. I would also think people who haven't gone through a divorce might not understand that..." She let her thoughts trail off and made a slight grimace, hoping she hadn't gone too far. Worrying that she had. When Amelia stopped walking and looked at her, Kirby scrunched up her nose and braced.

Instead of unloading on her, Amelia's eyes watered. She rolled her lips in for a moment, as if collecting herself. "Do you know that you're the first person I've talked to about this, about any of these aspects of my life, who actually seems to get them?" She blinked. Kirby saw her throat move as she swallowed. And her voice dropped to a whisper as she said, very simply, "Thank you for that."

"I live in my parents' house, too," Kirby said with a shrug.

"So you really do get it."

"I do."

They stood there for a moment, their gazes locked, and it was like they were the only two people in the entire zoo. Everything else faded away for a few seconds.

"Let's go look at snakes," Kirby finally said with a grin, and they headed into the reptile house.

CHAPTER TWELVE

Fridays tended to be busy for Amelia. People went away for long weekends or left work early to hit happy hours and asked her if she could let their dogs out at lunch or stop by and feed them dinner. She was also going to pay a visit to her father's house to change out some clothes and stop by Junebug Farms, since she'd bailed out of her volunteering duties the previous day. She and Kirby would be ships passing in the night today.

Kirby.

Amelia shook her head as she stepped into the shower and let the water from Victor's six different shower heads run over her body. Jets combined with gentle sprays to slowly wake her up, ease her into the day.

Even many hours later, she was still surprised by what a good time she'd had with Kirby. At the zoo, no less. The zoo! Who'd have thought?

It had been a long time since she'd felt listened to. And it made her feel guilty even thinking that, because her cousins loved her and her father loved her, but she'd become kind of repetitive over the past six months or so, and she knew it. Chances were, six months from now, Kirby would tune her out as well.

And then she was shaking her head and whispering, "No, I don't think so," into the water spray, a smile blossoming as she thought back to their return to the house last night, Kirby going directly to her van.

"You want to come in?" Amelia had asked, shocking herself.

Kirby had hesitated, and Amelia was sure she wanted to say

yes. Instead, she'd shaken her head, but with a very wide, very sexy smile. "Not tonight. Not yet." And she'd left it at that. Cryptic. But Amelia somehow knew there was some sort of plan in that blond head of hers, and she was good with that. It didn't freak her out, didn't tick her off. Just left her feeling...calm. Happy. Anticipatory.

When was the last time she'd felt that way?

The hot water sprayed her face as she tried to remember. Even considering her marriage to Tammy, she had to go back pretty far. Years. Years and years.

God, had she really been that unhappy for that long?

But her marriage had ended almost two years ago and hadn't been great for a couple years before that. Her mom had been killed almost four years ago.

"So, yeah," she said aloud, her voice echoing against the terrazzo. "Wow."

That's a long damn time to be unhappy.

Not that she suddenly wasn't. One fun afternoon with Kirby didn't negate how awful she felt in her own skin, how miserably she slept thanks to the hot flashes, how unattractive and unconfident she felt thanks to both being left for another woman and the extra weight menopause had deposited around her waist.

"Ugh." So much for feeling better.

Why did she do this to herself?

That was the big question. The one she failed to find an answer to, no matter how often she asked it. Which was every single fucking day.

She finished her shower, dressed, dried her hair, and was fixing her coffee when she heard Kirby's van pull into the driveway, the dogs barking their welcome.

"Good morning," Kirby said with her usual cheer as Amelia pulled the door open for her. There was something else on her face, though. Something different. Relaxed. Easy. Her eyes definitely leaned toward green today, influenced by the green T-shirt she wore. "Sleep well?"

"Not bad," Amelia said, and it was the truth. Only two hot flashes had woken her up, down from five the night before. "I'm on my way out in a few minutes." The disappointment on Kirby's face was clear, and something about it warmed Amelia's blood, made her quickly add, "But I might be back before you finish." She honestly didn't think she would be, but wanting to bring back Kirby's smile took precedence.

The smile didn't come back, though. Instead, a grimace took its place. "I'm just gonna paint the downstairs half bath today because I need to go help my guys with a job they're working. So I probably won't see you."

Well, that was a bummer. Truly. But it felt weird to admit it. "That's too bad," she said anyway.

"I mean, it's not like I'm done yet," Kirby said with a shrug, and the smile was back. "I've got two more rooms after the bathroom."

And there was relief. So weird. Amelia didn't want to think about it, but she couldn't help herself. It flooded her body with warmth. Two more rooms to do. Kirby wasn't leaving yet. Amelia cleared her throat.

"The dogs are gated in the three season room and can get outside through their dog door if need be, so they'll be fine while I'm gone."

"Can I give them a little love before I get started?" Kirby asked, and her voice was soft and cute and how the hell would Amelia ever say no if she wanted to?

"Of course you can. And I made coffee and left some for you."

"You did? That was nice of you. Thank you." Was that a blush she saw on Kirby's cheeks? Pretty sure it was, and Amelia felt a weird little surge of power when it happened, a little shot of *I did that*. She liked it, liked that feeling, that satisfaction. It had been too long since she'd made another woman feel good and had known it.

"You're welcome." They stood there for a few moments, smiling at each other like a couple of idiots, before Amelia said, "Well, I'm off."

"Is it…" Kirby began, then stopped, then nibbled on her bottom lip. Which did things to Amelia. "Is it weird if I say I'll miss you? That's weird, right?" Kirby frowned and looked so uncertain, like Amelia might scoff or roll her eyes or laugh at her. Instead, she simply shrugged.

"We can be weird together then." And she could hardly believe she'd said the words. In a rush, she added, "Have a great day, and just lock up when you go." And she hurried out the door and didn't allow herself to look back because, holy hell, what had she been thinking, saying that? But then, as she got into her car and started the engine, she smiled and her shoulders relaxed a bit. And it was okay. Totally fine that she'd said that. Because who *didn't* want to be told they'll be missed?

She shifted the car into gear and pulled out of the driveway. She slid her sunglasses on and plugged in her phone, hit a fun, happy playlist.

Yeah. It was gonna be a good day.

❖

The job Krog and Coop were on was an enormous living room-dining room combo with two-story ceilings, and Coop needed to bail out at one o'clock. So Kirby showed up to relieve him and help Krog finish up. The classic rock radio station was on, and she was up on the scaffolding doing the cutting in along the ceiling, lost in her own thoughts, when Krog turned down Aerosmith.

"What's up with you?" he asked.

She glanced down at him, surprised by the question. "What do you mean?"

"I mean you're quiet, you're not singing along to the music, and you've been working on the same three feet of wall for half an hour. What's up with you?"

She flushed. She could feel it, feel the heat crawl up her neck and settle in her cheeks. Krog had known her since she was a kid, so having him notice a change in behavior wasn't unheard of, but it still caught her off guard. A shrug was the best she could offer. "I'm good."

"No, no. Don't do that. I know you. You only get quiet when you're stuck on a chick."

She blinked in surprise and again turned to look down at him, eyebrows raised.

"In the beginning," he clarified. "You get quiet in the beginning when you're thinking about whether or not she's a good idea. Once you've made up your mind about her, you sing more. You're extra."

"I'm extra?" She grinned at him. "Your niece teach you that?"

"Maybe."

"I might have a little crush," she said on a sigh, knowing she couldn't hide anything from Krog. And maybe she needed to talk it out. He knew her. Knew her habits, knew her past relationships.

"On…?" He went back to painting, like he'd broken through and now they could talk. Which was true.

"At the Renwick job there's a house-sitter. This gorgeous woman who's staying there watching the dogs and…" She shook her head. How to describe what was going on in her head?

"She hot?" Such a guy, Krog was.

"Super hot."

"Under forty?"

He knew her well, and she laughed before answering, "No."

"'Course not. She like you back?"

"I think so?"

He stopped working to look up at her. "Don't you think you should find out for sure?"

"I mean, yeah, but…how? Just ask her?"

Krog's shrug meant yes, and really, he wasn't wrong. She could literally ask. Couldn't she? Would that be ridiculous?

"I took her to the zoo yesterday. She was having a rough day, and I had time."

"You loved the zoo when you were a kid. Your dad took you all the time."

"That's what I told her. And it worked. Pretty sure I cheered her up. She was smiling when I brought her home."

"Kiss her?"

"No." That made Krog stop all activity and lift his gaze so he could see her. She could feel his eyes on her, and she lasted all of four seconds before saying, "What?" in an annoyed tone.

"You like her. More than a crush."

She scoffed. Silly. Ridiculous. "How do you know?"

"Because if you didn't, you'd have made a move already."

Goddamn him. Why did he have to know her so well? Why did he have to point out the one fact she'd been so careful not to think about? "What do you think I should do?" she asked, her voice low and uncertain. Because she honestly wasn't sure what her next move should be. She'd realized that morning when Amelia said they likely wouldn't see each other the rest of the day that she wanted nothing more than to see her. Every day, if possible.

"You're asking a guy with three ex-wives for relationship advice? Man, you're hurtin'."

That got a small laugh from her.

"I can tell you what all three exes told me I didn't do enough," he offered, refilling his roller.

"What's that?"

"Talk."

"You *are* more of the grunting type."

He grunted in response. She laughed. He turned the music back up, and they worked. But Kirby's brain didn't stop. Rather, it kicked into overdrive. Talk. Was it really that simple? Maybe she'd run it by Katie. Or Shelby. A woman, just to be sure. Krog *was* a guy and he *did* have three exes, but he'd never steered her wrong in all the time she'd known him.

Feeling the tiniest bit better about things in general, she refocused her energy on the paintbrush in her hand and got back to work, though a gorgeous pair of hazel eyes still hung out in the back of her mind.

❖

"Anybody going to see the fireworks tonight?" Vanessa asked as she opened her laptop. "Grace and I are taking Oliver over to the park. He's stupidly excited. Like, bouncing off walls excited."

"Kids love fireworks," Julia said with a nod. "I might see if I can scoot out of here for a short time and meet Savannah there. She's going with you, if I'm not mistaken."

Vanessa shrugged with a laugh. "Could be. I have no idea. I just show up where I'm told."

Amelia smiled at her cousins as they sat in The Bar Back on Saturday afternoon. They'd met to polish up the final guest list for Julia and Savannah's wedding. Grace was at the flower shop, but Savannah should arrive soon.

"I hear that," Julia said. "I'm the same."

Was it wrong that Amelia felt a twinge of jealousy when her cousins talked about their relationships, how wonderful it was to have a partner to take care of the daily schedules for them? She was happy for them. Absolutely, that was never in question. She loved them with all her heart, and their happiness made her happy. But conversations like the current one always reminded her how alone she was. She didn't miss Tammy, but she missed *somebody*, having a person to do stuff with or to tell her where to be and when because she'd made plans for them. She smiled and nodded along, and sometimes, she'd even joke, but the whole time, there was an ache in her chest, a vast feeling of loneliness she just couldn't shake, that she worried would swallow her whole one day. Would it ever go away?

She was on the couch next to Vanessa, so she leaned over to see the spreadsheet so far, the guests divided into Julia's side and Savannah's side.

"Wow, Jules, your guests outnumber hers, like, three-to-one," she said with a laugh. "Damn Italians."

"She said the same thing." Julia set down the bottle in her hand and leaned on the practice bar. "Is it my fault that half the family members I'm inviting because I have to, in order to keep them from getting mad at my parents?" She shook her head and went back to mixology. "I wanted a small wedding. Mom and Pop nixed that immediately."

"It's not every day their only daughter gets married," Amelia said, remembering how she'd wanted a traditional wedding and Tammy had insisted she didn't want to be the center of attention and that getting married at the courthouse was just as meaningful. She snorted, then realized her cousins were looking at her. "Nothing.

Sorry." A shrug. Vanessa studied her. Amelia hated that. Vanessa saw everything, like she was looking into your soul. It creeped her out, made her feel fidgety and uncomfortable and so *exposed*. And she was doing it now, and Amelia couldn't help herself. "Stop it," she whined. "I hate when you do that."

"That's why I do it," Vanessa said. "What's up with you? Why are you weird today?"

"Lemme guess," Julia said. "Menopause? Wreaking havoc?"

"You know what?" Amelia snapped, pointing at Julia, then at Vanessa, and back. "I cannot wait until you two hit it. I'm going to make your lives miserable. I'm going to make fun of you. I'm going to tell you you're crazy when you start feeling not like yourself. I'm gonna laugh and tell you that you can't blame menopause for everything."

Vanessa, at least, had the good sense to look the tiniest bit ashamed. "Sorry, Meels. But you seem...different today. Everything okay?" Then, as if remembering, she sat up straight with a gasp. "Oh! How are things with the painter?"

And Amelia flushed. Hard and hot. Her damn body betrayed her by making her blush like a schoolgirl, and she didn't have a prayer of hiding it. Vanessa barked a laugh and Julia pointed at her.

"Oh my God, I can see your red ears from over here," she said. "Aw, Meels, you're so cute when you blush."

"I'm going to take that as *Things are going quite well with the painter, Vanessa, thank you so much for asking*." Vanessa's grin was wide and satisfied.

"Nothing is happening with the painter," Amelia said. Which was a lie. Of course. But only because she wasn't sure what was happening with the painter.

"Your blush says otherwise," Julia pointed out.

"Fine. She took me to the zoo yesterday." Amelia blurted it out before she could second-guess herself. She hadn't intended to tell anybody because she was still analyzing how she felt. But despite her irritation with Vanessa and Julia, they were her people. If she was going to tell anybody, it was them.

"What?" Vanessa managed to sound excited, shocked, and

betrayed all at the same time. "Is that where you were when your texts got so short? I hate that, by the way. Just tell me you can't talk."

"Maybe take a hint," Amelia snarked back. "I have a life, you know." A flinch of pain zipped across Vanessa's face, and Amelia reached for her arm immediately. "I'm sorry. I'm sorry. I didn't mean that."

Vanessa softened instantly. Because that was Vanessa. "It's okay. And I'm sorry if we're pushing too much. We just..." She tipped her head to one side and gave Amelia a lopsided smile. "We want you to be happy, and—honestly?—I hate seeing you so..." She glanced Julia's way. "What's the right word, Jules? What is she?"

Cranky. Snarky. Bitchy. Amelia was waiting for any or all of those descriptors, but Julia surprised her when she said softly, "Sad."

Vanessa nodded her agreement.

Amelia's eyes filled with tears. "Oh my God, I'm such a fucking mess." And then Vanessa's arms were around her, and she was crying mascara all over Vanessa's shoulder, and then Julia was there, too, and they were three people making up one blob of human when Savannah came in and found them.

"Oh no, why are we crying? And hugging? I wanna hug, too. I'm coming in." And then her arms were around them, and Amelia couldn't help but laugh. She hadn't felt so loved in a long time, and she told them so.

Several moments later, they were all laughing softly and wiping their eyes. Savannah looked at Julia with wide eyes and said, "I'm so glad I got here when I did."

"As always, impeccable timing, my love," Julia said and kissed her mouth.

"Just in time for a group hug." Vanessa's expression was still a bit worried when she glanced at Amelia.

"I'm fine. I'm good." Amelia ran her fingertips under her eyes to wipe away the smeared makeup. "I promise. This happens all the time now. No worries."

"Okay. Good." Vanessa sat and signaled to Julia across the room just like she would to any bartender.

"Me, too," Amelia said, because it was time to talk to her family. She waited until Julia delivered glasses of a new rosé she was selling before she finally blew out a large breath and said, "I think I like this girl."

Savannah grinned. Vanessa squealed. Julia nodded as if she'd known all along.

"But I'm a fucking mess, and I haven't dated in more than ten years, and she's *so* much younger than me and…" She let her voice trail off because wasn't that enough? Jesus Christ on a cracker, what was she thinking?

"Stop." Vanessa held up a hand. Savannah nodded her agreement. Amelia blinked at them both, surprised by the vehemence in that one word. "Listen, I get that you've been having a tough time. Nobody's denying that. It's sucked. Breakups suck. Tammy sucks. And throw menopause in there…" Amelia opened her mouth to speak, but the hand went up again. "I know. I watched my mom go through it. I know we pick on you, but I also know it can be awful, and I'm really sorry if you've felt unsupported through it." She shot a look Julia's way. Julia grimaced and looked at her hands. Vanessa continued. "But we love you so much, and it's really, *really* difficult to watch you be so hard on yourself."

"Part of me is glad I came along after Tammy was gone," Savannah said. "But another part wishes I knew her because she and I would have *words*."

Amelia laughed through her nose. God, she loved these women. "You guys are the best."

"Damn right, we are," Julia said.

"But we're here to work on the guest list." Amelia was taking the focus, and she felt guilty about that.

Savannah snorted. "You mean Julia's guest list and my four family members and three friends?" But her grin was genuine, and the look she shot at Julia was filled with affection.

Could Amelia have something like that again? Could she have it with somebody else? With Kirby? She watched as the conversation shifted into lighter territory. Jokes about family members. Friends. Who should—or more importantly, should not—be seated together for the wedding reception. She knew these women so well. Even Savannah, who'd only been part of the family for less than two years. Even Grace, a missing piece this evening, whose absence was felt even after less than a year. There was one more space in this family puzzle, and it was right next to Amelia.

I need to get to know her.

She had that thought about Kirby right then. Clear. Loud. "I *want* to get to know her." She didn't realize she'd said it out loud until Vanessa turned to her. Julia and Savannah were having their own conversation, but she had Vanessa's attention. Her cousin smiled at her, gave one nod, and put a hand on her thigh. Squeezed.

"Then do that."

Amelia blinked at her. "Is it that simple?"

"It really is, Meels. It really is. Chances are, she wants to get to know you, too." She lowered her voice and added, "I mean, she took you to the zoo, for God's sake."

Amelia grinned. "True."

"You know what else?" Vanessa waited until Amelia met her gaze. "You're worth getting to know."

CHAPTER THIRTEEN

Rain had moved in Saturday afternoon, had dumped on them, then had moved out just in time for the fireworks that night. Now, on Sunday morning, Amelia sat in Victor Renwick's backyard with a cup of tea, both dogs lounging nearby, and watched the sunrise.

It was barely five thirty, but a super intense hot flash made it impossible for her to stay in bed, and the morning temperatures in the sixties called to her. Not yet ready for her morning blast of caffeine, she opted for a cup of chamomile and a chaise lounge.

She'd been able to make the shift yesterday, putting her own stuff on a shelf so the focus could move back to Julia and Savannah's wedding, where it should've been all along. She'd helped with the guest list, the menu options were enormous, and once Grace had arrived, together they'd decided on the invitation design. It was a lot, though. So much to do and choose, and she knew Julia was feeling a bit overwhelmed. Talk of maybe hiring a wedding planner was batted around, but they'd left it up in the air. Afterward, she'd even gone to see the fireworks with Vanessa, Grace, and Oliver. And she'd smiled. Had fun. Listened intently as Oliver painstakingly explained which superheroes were Marvel and which were from the DC Universe.

And the whole time, all day, all night, and into that lovely Sunday sunrise, Kirby Dupree stayed parked in the back of her mind. Out of sight maybe, but not forgotten. Far, far from forgotten.

So far from forgotten, in fact, that she found herself pulling out her phone. Before she could stop herself, or second-guess herself, or talk herself out of it, she typed and sent a text.

Hi there. You busy on this gorgeous Sunday? Dogs and I spending the day by the pool. Join us if you want.

Was that too impersonal? Too personal? Too casual and flighty? Did it say she didn't really care if Kirby showed up or not?

"Oh my God, stop it," she whispered to herself, and Stevie lifted his head from the ground to look at her. "I know," she told him. "Believe me. I know."

❖

Son of a bitch, who the hell was texting her before six on a Sunday morning?

Kirby slapped at the nightstand until she found her phone. Since her father had passed away, she'd vowed to always check her texts, no matter what time of day or night. She didn't necessarily have to respond, but she'd never forgive herself if somebody she loved needed her in a time of crisis, and she blew them off in favor of not losing a little sleep.

Her room was dark as midnight—those blackout curtains she'd bought didn't mess around—and the phone was disturbing in its brightness. It was funny, though, how quickly her irritation could fade, given the right medicine.

That morning, the medicine came in the form of an invitation from one Amelia Martini.

"Well, what do you know?" she said quietly to the darkness of the room.

It wasn't *exactly* an invitation. Amelia had been careful not to word it like one. It was more of an *If you don't have anything to do, I'm gonna be here anyway and I suppose it wouldn't make much difference if you were here too* kind of text. But Kirby was getting to know Amelia, was beginning to understand her better. And this noninvitation? Was a big freaking deal. A huge step. Kirby was strangely proud of her.

Not so proud that she was going to play games, though. No. Games weren't her thing. Kirby was a tell-it-like-it-is kind of girl, and she took that seriously. Life was too fucking short to—as her father would say—pussyfoot around. She could easily tell Amelia *maybe*. Play Amelia's game. She could wait for a few hours before responding. Say that she had some things to do, but if she found herself with the time, perhaps she'd pop by. But Kirby much preferred being a straight shooter. She was interested in Amelia. She'd made that clear, but it looked like she was going to have to continue to do that for a while.

Love to. Time? What can I bring?

She added an emoji with sunglasses and sent the text, then rolled over and closed her eyes, completely aware of her goofy grin.

Oh, yeah. Today was going to be a good day.

❖

How was it possible to be completely relaxed and also a total bag of nerves?

Amelia had no idea, but she fit the bill, because Kirby would be there in an hour, and her brain vacillated between *I can't wait to see her* and *Holy good God, what have I done?*

She almost texted Vanessa. Then she almost called her. Had her number up on the phone and her finger hovering over the green button before changing her mind and closing up her contacts.

No. She was going to do this on her own. She didn't need a pep talk. She didn't need encouragement or reassurance. Why? Because this was Kirby, and she wanted to spend time with her.

She *wanted* to.

It didn't mean anything, right? Nothing other than she wanted a chance to get to know this woman a bit more. It wasn't a date. Just like the zoo wasn't a date. They were simply two people, two friends, who had spent time together looking at animals.

"And one of those people gave the other one weird fluttery feelings in her stomach and stared at her lips a lot." Calvin lifted his head from his spot on the cool ceramic tile of the kitchen. His ears were so big it was comical, but his eyes seemed to be waiting her out. "I know," she finally sighed at him, and he put his head back down, clearly satisfied that she at least understood her own ridiculousness.

She gave the counter a scan. She had a veggie tray with hummus. Some cheese and crackers on a slate tray she'd found in Victor's cabinet. A rosé chilled in an ice bucket. She'd cranked the umbrella open on the patio near the pool, so they could take the food out there and not melt—she had a feeling Kirby would want to get in the pool. She herself was in her bathing suit under her shorts and T-shirt and completely self-conscious about that, but maybe she could avoid swimming...

In the fridge was a bowl with chicken sitting in a lemon dill marinade, just in case they decided to throw something on the grill. After all, that's what July was for, right? Swimming and grilling and sipping rosé by the pool?

With a bolstering breath, she carried the food out to the table by the pool and then stood with her hands on her hips, surveying the area as if it was hers, and it wasn't an exaggeration to say she'd seriously miss the place once this job was up. She'd spent almost an hour figuring out the sound system and now had a summer pop playlist filtering through the speakers Victor had installed outside. Ariana Grande was singing about her ninety-nine problems, and Amelia snorted a laugh.

"You're too young to understand real problems, Ari."

And then the dogs were barking, and Amelia's heart was pounding, and her lips were smiling because it was happening.

Kirby was there.

CHAPTER FOURTEEN

There was something different about Amelia that day. Kirby felt it the second Amelia opened the front door and smiled at her. She couldn't put her finger on exactly what it was—a shift in the air? a change in attitude?—but whatever it was, she liked it. It was good.

"Come on in," Amelia said as she stood aside and let Kirby enter. A cacophony of barking came from the back of the house.

"Dogs gated?" Kirby asked as she followed Amelia through the house, her tote bag on her shoulder and a cooler in her hand.

"Force of habit," Amelia said with a laugh. "I guess I don't have to do that on the weekends, do I?"

"They don't seem like runners," Kirby commented, setting down her things. "Or they're used to you now."

Amelia slid the gate away so the dogs could greet her. "I wonder what they think, you know?"

Kirby squatted down and let herself be bumped, kissed, pushed against. "What do you mean?"

"Well, like, their dad has disappeared, and I show up in his place. Feed them. Hang out in their house. Sleep in his bed. Do they think, *Where's Dad and who's this chick who's moved in?* Or do they just not care as long as they have food and water?"

"Excellent questions, my friend," Kirby said as she stood up and took in Amelia. She wore a cute pair of black and white Under Armour gym shorts and a white T-shirt, but it was clear there was a bathing suit underneath. The black one-piece, if what Kirby could make out was correct. Her feet were bare, her toenails now polished a glittering pink, and Kirby couldn't hide her surprise. Pointing to Amelia's feet, she said, "I would never have pegged you for pink."

"It's not my usual color, but I let Savannah talk me into it last time we got pedicures." She seemed to study her feet before adding, "It's grown on me." She wiggled her toes and then met Kirby's gaze. "What would you call it?"

"When I Pink of You," Kirby said, without missing a beat, and Amelia laughed, and the sound went right into Kirby's system and flooded it with warmth. Yeah, she needed that sound more. A lot more.

"Perfect. I love it." Amelia's eyes landed on the cooler. "What did you bring me?"

"Why, I'm so glad you asked." Kirby bent and gave each dog a kiss on the head, then stood back up and opened the cooler. She pulled out various Rubbermaid containers, lifting each as she announced their contents. "I made little finger sandwiches. Cucumber. With dill mayo." She lifted a different container. "This is fruit salad. Blueberries, strawberries, watermelon." She grabbed a round container. "This one has to go in the freezer for later. Ice cream."

Amelia's eyes had gone slightly wide, which was exactly the reaction she'd expected and hoped for. She took the bowl and put it in the freezer. "You made all this?"

"I am much more than just a pretty face," Kirby said, then gave her a wink.

"Clearly." Amelia looked up and smiled at her. "Wait. Did you make the ice cream, too?"

"I have many skills, chocolate almond ice cream being one of them."

"Wow." Amelia's grin widened, and those dimples were out in full force. Another thing Kirby wanted more of. "This is amazing. Thank you for bringing it all. I have some stuff, too. Follow me."

The spread outside was impressive, and Kirby took it in as Amelia lifted a bottle in question. At Kirby's nod, she poured the pink wine into glasses and handed one to her. They touched their glasses together, no words said, and sipped. The rosé was crisp and walked the line between sweet and dry beautifully. "Man, this is good," she said. Then she set her glass down, held her arms out to the sides, dropped her head back, closed her eyes, and filled her lungs to capacity. "What. A. Day." She opened her eyes and dropped her arms. "Thank you, Amelia. For having me over. There is honestly nowhere I'd rather be right now." She surprised herself with the words, but they were true, and once they were spoken, she wasn't sorry she'd said them. Amelia looked taken aback, but in a good way, and Kirby watched her face, watched various emotions play across it. The surprise morphed into a slight fear, then what looked like comfort, and maybe acceptance. She didn't know Amelia well enough yet to be sure she was reading her accurately, but over the past couple of weeks, she'd gotten pretty good.

"Is there an order to things?" Kirby asked finally, wanting to lighten things up a little.

"What do you mean?"

"Like, can I jump in the pool? Can I have my wine near the water? Are there rules? Victor rules? Amelia rules?"

The smile was back. The dimples were back. "Well, my mother would say if you're gonna eat, you have to wait half an hour to go in the water."

"If I get a cramp, I trust you to rescue me." Kirby pulled her shirt over her head, having put her bathing suit on under her clothes like Amelia had.

"Promise," Amelia said, but her voice sounded scratchy, and her eyes were on Kirby's bare stomach.

"I knew I could count on you." She stepped out of her shorts, kicked them aside, took the four steps to the pool, and dived in. The water was the perfect temperature—not too warm, still cool enough to be refreshing on a day that was already well into the eighties. She touched the bottom, then pushed herself to the surface and shook the hair out of her eyes.

Amelia hadn't moved.

Kirby began to tread water, then tipped her head to the side and squinted against the bright sun. She hoped her satisfaction wasn't super obvious as she asked, "You okay?"

As if the words released her, Amelia blinked rapidly and

nodded. "Oh. Yeah. Yes. Fine. I'm fine. I'm good." And then she lifted the glass to her lips and nearly drained it.

Kirby dived back under the water to hide her grin. God, she was enjoying this woman. All her sharp edges and soft curves. Her whiplash-inducing mood shifts. Nobody had interested her more. Not in years. She had no idea what made Amelia Martini tick, but she wanted to find out.

❖

"Jesus Christ, Amelia, why don't you stand there with your buggy eyes and your tongue hanging out like the creeper that you are?" Amelia muttered to herself as soon as Kirby dived underwater. "Very subtle. God." She closed her eyes and shook her head, but behind her eyelids, all she saw was Kirby's body in her bathing suit. Her athletic yet curvy, strong yet feminine, ridiculously hot body. An unexpected flare of hips. An even more unexpected chest—seriously, where the hell had *those* come from?—and an expanse of bare back that had Amelia's palms itching.

This was a terrible idea.

The thought ran through her head loudly until it bumped up against her original thought from yesterday.

I want to get to know her.

Which would mean this was a great idea. Right?

Why was this so damn hard?

"What is your brain struggling with?" Kirby's voice yanked her out of her own head, and she turned to find her at the edge of the pool, forearms on the concrete, chin on her hands, watching Amelia. Water glistened on her face, her hair was slicked back, her strong shoulders were visible, and Amelia almost cried with the wave of desire that shot through her. Her first in years. *Years.*

"How do you know my brain is struggling with anything?"

Kirby used her forefinger to point to her own face. "You get a divot right here at the top of your nose when you're thinking hard. And your eyebrows point down. It's not a scowl. Just your thinking face."

Amelia blinked at her.

"I surprised you." Kirby's grin said she liked that.

"You surprise me constantly."

"Not a bad thing." A beat went by. "Come join me in here."

"Oh, I don't think so."

"Why not?" Kirby asked the question in a tone that said she already knew the answer. But how could she? How could she have any idea how self-conscious Kirby's gorgeous body had her feeling about hers? How could somebody as young and confident and beautiful as Kirby Dupree ever understand what it was like to be uncomfortable in your own skin?

Amelia just shook her head, feeling sad.

"How about this?" Kirby swam to the end of the pool where steps led down into the water. Easy entry for people who didn't enjoy the shock of diving right in. "You come over here, leave your shorts and T-shirt on, and come down these steps into the water."

Amelia blinked. Thought about it. That could work. It was hot out, after all, and she *did* want to get in the pool.

"If we get it out of the way now, we can enjoy the rest of the day without you feeling weird about it."

Amelia headed to the steps. "Get what out of the way?"

Kirby merely shrugged and stood at the bottom of the steps, smiling and waiting, hand outstretched.

Even the dogs seemed to be holding their breath, Calvin from his spot under the table, Stevie in the corner under the shade of a small Japanese maple just outside the fence.

Amelia looked around. She took in the dogs, the pool, the deep summer-blue of the sky, the lighter blue of the water, the stunning woman who stood before her, a tender smile on her face and a hand held out for her to grab, and she was hit with a wave of—what the hell was it? Joy? Perfection? Luck? She didn't know and it didn't matter. All she knew was that this was a moment. A defining one. Somehow, this very second in her life was pivotal, and she knew it.

And damn if she was gonna let it slip by.

She took the steps down into the water, reached for Kirby's hand, and was shocked by the strength of it, the sturdiness, the security her grip offered. She stepped down all four steps without hesitation, right into Kirby's space and stopped when there was less than an inch between their noses, Kirby's head tipped up slightly to make up for the height difference. The water was just below her shoulders.

"Nicely done," Kirby whispered, and when her gaze dropped to Amelia's mouth, it was all over.

Amelia didn't know who moved first. Maybe she did. Maybe it was Kirby who leaned forward. It didn't really matter, though, because in the next second, they were kissing. It was tentative at first.

But tentative didn't last long because, oh my God in heaven, it felt good. The softness of Kirby's lips, the taste of her mouth—sweet and salty at the same time—the sexy sound of the catch in her breath. It all combined, and there really was no other course of action than to deepen that kiss. To open her mouth. To let her tongue do what it wanted to. And for the love of all that was holy, when was the last time Amelia'd been kissed like that? The first few months with Tammy? All the way back to her very first kiss from a girl her senior year in high school? When? She couldn't remember, couldn't grasp the details because honest to God there was nothing else that mattered. Only Kirby's mouth. Only Kirby's hands, which were suddenly gripping her waist. Then one slid up into her hair and behind her head and pulled her in tighter and then Amelia's hands were doing their own thing. Reaching for Kirby's waist. Except it wasn't the smooth nylon of a bathing suit under her palms. Oh no. It was skin. Glorious, warm, soft skin and it took everything in Amelia's power not to squeeze, to lightly scratch, to dive under the water and nibble it with her teeth.

Holy shit, she was in trouble.

They pulled apart when air became an issue, and Kirby's lazy smile did things low in Amelia's body.

"See?" Kirby said. "We got that part out of the way. Now"—her fingers toyed with the hem of Amelia's T-shirt—"you're safe under the water, so how about we get rid of this?" Amelia didn't protest as Kirby slowly pulled the shirt up and over her head, not as easy a feat as if it had been dry, but they managed it. Kirby tossed the wet shirt onto the cement, and then she slid one finger underneath the waistband of Amelia's gym shorts. This time, Kirby didn't say anything, simply raised an eyebrow in question.

It was as if Amelia had no choice, and her body knew it. Hands on Kirby's shoulders for balance, she stepped out of the shorts, and they followed the path of the T-shirt.

"There. And now we're both in the pool in our bathing suits." Kirby glanced down at Amelia's body. Amelia could almost feel her gaze as it roamed over her, over the black one-piece bathing suit, and she did her best not to squirm in discomfort. The water somehow acted as a buffer, even though it was clear, and that made it easier for her somehow, made her feel slightly less self-conscious about being looked at. But Kirby took her time. She made sure Amelia knew she was looking. She'd glance up and meet Amelia's eyes, then continue on her path along her body. Finally, her gaze caught Amelia's and held it as she said, "You're so beautiful. I don't know why you're so self-conscious. You have nothing to be self-conscious about. Not a thing."

And then there was more kissing.

And more kissing.

Kirby backed her up to the edge of the pool until her back hit, and she was trapped between the pool wall and Kirby's body, and she had absolutely zero desire to escape.

Zero.

It was in that very second that Amelia decided to stop fighting this. Stop fighting, stop questioning, just sink in.

And sink she did.

Right into Kirby's mouth. With her tongue and her teeth and a whimpered groan and the kiss went even deeper. Hands began to wander, and breathing became ragged and Jesus, Mary, and Joseph—

"Okay," Kirby said, completely breathless. When her gaze met Amelia's, it was dark. All pupil. Heavy lidded. "Wait." Another ragged breath. "Hang on."

A surge of power shot through Amelia at the sight. Had she done that? She felt a smile tug up one corner of her mouth. "You started it. Pretty sure."

Kirby's grin was wide. "I did. I totally did. And I knew it would be amazing, but damn, woman, you're gonna make me burst into flames." She looked around, slightly wild-eyed. "In a pool."

Amelia laughed. Felt it bubble up from deep in her body and burst from her lips. And then she reached her hand up and ran her fingertips along Kirby's cheek. Felt the warmth. The smoothness. Saw those greenish-hazel eyes soften. "Let's get something to drink and cool you off, yeah?"

Kirby kissed her quickly on the mouth. "Sounds perfect."

CHAPTER FIFTEEN

Monday was a holiday. July Fourth.

Which meant Kirby would not be painting that day, and when Amelia opened her eyes that morning, it was the first thought she had. No Kirby today.

Her level of disappointment was truly surprising.

They'd spent the rest of yesterday eating and drinking and talking. Occasionally kissing. It would've been easy—God, so fucking easy—to ask her to stay. To take Kirby to bed. To let *Kirby* take *her* to bed. But it felt too fast. Too soon. Kirby seemed to feel it, too, because she made no moves, offered no hints about wanting to spend the night. And when it was past dark, and they were still stretched out on lounges by the pool, after taking a sexy night swim, Kirby had gotten up and collected her things. Then, with her hands on the arms of Amelia's chair, she'd leaned down and kissed her. So slowly. So deeply. So thoroughly that Amelia knew all she had to do was run her fingers over the crotch of her own bathing suit, and she'd come harder than she had in ages.

But she'd tamped it down, walked Kirby to the door, and watched her drive away.

And now it was Monday, and it was a holiday, and Kirby wouldn't be coming over to paint today. Damn it.

She hated that she hated it.

She hauled herself out of Victor Renwick's king-size bed and headed down to the kitchen with sleepy canines at her heels to let them out. The sky was overcast and gray, and she thought about heading right back up and crawling back under the covers to sleep some more. The forecast called for thunderstorms, the perfect kind of weather for sleeping in and only getting up so she could make some coffee and curl up with a book.

But she had a few clients to see. And she really needed to sit down and work on her marketing. Dogz Rule was doing pretty well but could do better if she'd just put some time and effort into her online presence.

Her second cup of coffee in hand, she was showered and was just sitting down in front of her computer when her phone pinged a text. Expecting Vanessa, who texted her every morning, she was surprised to see a different name. Her heart did a little flip, and a throbbing started low in her body, astounding her at how quickly it showed up.

"Wow. Is that the effect she has now? Already?" Amelia shook her head, feeling both a little giddy and a little freaked.

Good morning, beautiful.

Well. How lovely was that greeting? She quickly typed back a hello.

Busy tonight? came Kirby's next text. And a crossed fingers emoji.

"Nope," Amelia said as she typed.

I'd like to take you to dinner.

Amelia blinked at her phone. A date? Kirby was asking her on a date, right? Warmth flooded through her, and the throbbing kicked up a notch or twelve. And in that moment, she wanted nothing more, nothing else in the entire world than to spend more time with Kirby. It wasn't something she wanted to dwell on or analyze—there was an entire day stretched out before her, and she'd have plenty of time to freak out during those many hours. But right then, right in that moment in time, she let herself feel what was most prominent: excitement, desire, wanted.

Okay. She sent her answer before she could second-guess herself.

Good! Pick u up at 7. Dress nice. And that was followed by a winking emoji.

Oh God, she was gonna need some help here. She quickly fired off another text, this time to Vanessa.

Need your help.

Vanessa was a teacher, so texting her during the day usually didn't get a response until later. But once it was summer and Vanessa was free, it was like she made up for lost time. Her response was instantaneous.

What happened? You ok?

She typed back quickly so Vanessa wouldn't worry. *Fashion 911.*

❖

Kirby's golf game had gotten cancelled. Which was a bummer. She'd been looking forward to whacking the ball around, getting some fresh air and a walk, chatting up her peeps. And the rain hadn't come, it just threatened to, but her foursome had decided to play it safe rather than risk getting caught while out on the course, apparently afraid of lightning while they walked around carrying metal clubs. Wimps.

The house needed to be cleaned anyway, so she guessed it was for the best, and she got right to it. As long as she could stay busy, she didn't mind being home. It was sitting still she had trouble with. So she did the floors and dusted and cleaned the bathroom and emptied the dishwasher, then filled it up again with the dishes she'd left in the sink for the past few days, eating on the run going from work to softball or Frisbee golf or hiking.

It was her father's house. She still thought of it that way, even though it was hers now. He'd been gone for nearly fifteen years, but she hadn't changed a whole lot about it. Same furniture, same wall colors. She ignored the irony of never updating her own house with a coat of paint. And it really could use it.

One of these days…

Keeping busy also took her mind off her date that night. Well, kind of. She was able to tuck Amelia into a back corner for a little while. Blasting music helped, and she sang along to Justin Bieber while she buffed the house to a worthy shine.

When she'd finished, though, Amelia came screaming right back into her head, and that's why she now sat in the Oakview

Cemetery, on the grass, legs crossed, talking to her father's gravestone.

She took good care of his grave. Fresh flowers, always. He was a rugged, hardworking guy who loved flowers. Not many people knew that about him, but Kirby did. She made sure to stop by at least once a week, had ever since he passed away. The grounds crew knew her well, always waved at her, and she was pretty sure they put a little extra care into keeping her dad's spot tidy.

"So, Pop, I'm a little confused," she said quietly. She always talked out loud to him. She found it helped her organize her thoughts. Sometimes, it helped her see from a different angle. "I really like this girl. I mean, I don't know her that well, and honestly, she makes it kind of hard to get to know her." She reached out toward the fresh daisies she'd put in his vase, rubbed the small petals between her fingers. "But I'm *drawn* to her. I don't know how else to describe it. She…pulls me. Like a damn tractor beam. I don't know why. I don't know how. I just know whenever I'm near her, I want to stay near her. It's really weird. Like, *super* weird."

And that was the thing, wasn't it? It was weird. Nothing like this had ever happened to her before. She'd had a couple of relationships in the past, significant ones in her life. Jen had been her high school sweetheart, and they'd lasted almost three years out of school as well. Then they'd drifted apart—grown up is actually what they'd done. Kirby had played the field for a few years, then dated Cori for almost four years. Again with the drifting, and she'd been single ever since, preferring it that way, liking her time and her space and her freedom.

No woman had ever made her sit up and take notice quite like Amelia Martini. Not one.

"She's got some issues, Pop." Kirby chuckled at her own words, raised her head as the wind picked up, and looked around the cemetery. She could hear her father's words as if he stood right behind her.

You're not taking on another project, are you, kid?

She felt the corners of her mouth tug up at the familiar words, the way they echoed through her head because, even though he was long gone, she still knew what he'd say.

"I mean, I hope not." She picked at the grass. "I'm taking her on a date tonight. We did some kissing yesterday, and I think we could've pretty easily gone to bed, but..." She stopped. Again, it was weird. She'd never redirected herself when sex was on the table. She'd always taken it if it was offered, but yesterday, she'd stopped herself. "I want to do this right. That's kind of a big thing, right?"

This time, no words from her dad appeared. She'd never been here before, in this spot in life, and it was messing with her head a little bit. A rumble of thunder began in the south, and she knew a storm was on its way.

"I gotta go get ready, Pop. Wish me luck, yeah?" She kissed her fingers, pressed them to his gravestone as she stood, and jogged back to her car. No solutions, but she felt a little bit lighter, which she always did after talking things through with her dad.

At six fifteen that evening, Kirby stood in front of her full-length mirror and scrutinized her reflection—a deep green dress, cut simply with capped sleeves and a V-neck, and hair carefully tousled. She was pretty sure she'd chosen well, though now she was wishing she'd asked Katie or Shelby for some help. Interestingly, she hadn't told either of them she'd asked Amelia out. And she hadn't told either of them about yesterday. The pool. The kissing.

Why not? Why wouldn't she have discussed something like that, something that big, with her closest friends?

"'Cause I don't want to jinx it," she whispered to her reflection. Then she grinned. "Plus, Katie would've tried to make me wear higher heels." The cute kitten heels were as high as she could go and still be able to walk with confidence. She stood still, studied, and finally gave one nod. "Okay. Good. Let's do this."

As she pulled into the driveway of Victor Renwick's house, she wondered if Amelia expected her to show up in her van. Most people didn't realize she had an actual car. A Mustang, to be precise. Black. Sleek. Her pride and joy and likely to get rained on soon. Oh, well. It looked great in the moment, thanks to the last-minute car wash she'd run through on her way. Impressing Amelia was a high priority, and also something she didn't want to allow her brain to dwell on right then.

She bopped up the front steps, shook out her arms, finger-combed her hair, then took a big, cleansing breath and rang the bell.

When it opened, her eyes went wide. "Wow."

That one word caused some major blushing for Amelia, who was nothing short of gorgeous. It was true that Kirby found her wildly attractive always, but right then? Standing in the doorway in a long black dress and strappy heels, her light hair down and wavy, wearing perfume that had her smelling deliciously like a mix of nature and sex?

How the hell am I supposed to get through dinner? was Kirby's first thought.

"You look stunning," she said quietly, almost reverently, because that's how she felt. Like Amelia was royalty and Kirby, merely her humble servant.

"Thank you," Amelia said, still blushing. "And might I say, you certainly clean up nice. I wasn't expecting a dress, but wow, what a terrific choice." And then she let her gaze roam over Kirby. And Kirby felt it. *She felt it.* Bringing her gaze back up, Amelia said, "The dogs are all set."

"Perfect." Kirby turned and held out her elbow like a gentleman. "Shall we?"

CHAPTER SIXTEEN

Between Vanessa and Grace, Amelia had fashion advice to spare. Thank freaking God, because she was so uncomfortable in her body that she was inches away from putting on leggings and an oversize T-shirt and calling it a day.

"The last thing in the world I want to do," Grace had said to her as she pulled an astonishingly large stack of clothing out of what Amelia had thought was a small duffel, "is invalidate the way you're feeling. I hated when Michael did that to me. I know it doesn't help you if I contradict what you're saying about yourself, so instead, we're gonna work with it. Yeah?"

Amelia had looked from Grace to Vanessa and back, and the relief that had swept through her had shocked her. "Yes, please. And thank you."

She and Grace were roughly the same size, and they'd spent the next two hours trying on outfits that Grace had pilfered from her closet, as well as a few things from Vanessa's.

They settled on a dress that was deceptively simple. Black. Long. Covered enough of Amelia's body to tell her insecurities to shut the hell up, but it also followed every line and every curve like it was made to. She'd initially been worried about it clinging, showing too many of what she considered her new imperfections, but when she stood in front of the enormous mirror in Victor's bedroom, she was left shockingly speechless. They added black strappy heels—not too high, but very sexy. A silver bracelet and matching earrings. She turned one way, then the other, then back, then spun around to look at her own ass.

"The thong is key for this kind of dress," Grace reminded her.

Amelia nodded. She didn't love wearing a thong, but she loved panty lines less, and the way she felt like every flaw she had was on display lately, panty lines would ruin the entire outfit for her. So she'd bitten the bullet, stepped into the thong, put on the dress, and stood very, very pleasantly surprised as she studied her reflection.

"You look beautiful," Vanessa had said quietly, and when Amelia met her gaze in the mirror, her cousin's smile had been soft and genuine. And honestly? Amelia couldn't remember the last time she'd looked in the mirror and hadn't been disappointed. This was new. And wonderful.

And empowering. She felt an unfamiliar surge of confidence.

That had been an hour ago, and she'd shooed Vanessa and Grace away quickly, so Kirby wouldn't run into them and realize two things—one, that Amelia had zero fashion sense, and two, that this date with Kirby was important enough to her to call in reinforcements to help her dress.

Judging by the way Kirby had stood on the front steps, eyes wide, mouth open, words absent, those reinforcements had been exactly the right decision. Points for her.

Now she slid her hand into the crook of the arm Kirby offered and let herself be led to—

"What is *this*?" she asked, feeling her own eyes go wide at the sight of the sleek black Mustang.

"This is my baby," Kirby said, her voice filled with pride. "Tell the truth—you thought I was going to pick you up in my van, didn't you?"

Amelia laughed. "I totally did."

"Well, I'm happy to surprise you." She opened the passenger door for Amelia and waved her in with a flourish.

"You're making it a habit," Amelia said, her voice soft as she sat. And it was true. Her eyes followed Kirby around the front of the car. She hadn't expected the Mustang. She hadn't expected the soft green dress or the sandals. She hadn't expected to want to forego dinner and drag Kirby directly upstairs to the bedroom.

She swallowed hard at that last thought as Kirby's door opened and she slid in. "Ready?"

Amelia gave one nod.

Gazes held.

Did the temperature in the car just go up by a few or fifty degrees?

Kirby leaned toward her then, kissed her softly, and pulled back with a grin. "Okay, can't be doing that anymore, or I won't stop." Kirby's gaze wandered over Amelia one more time—which Amelia *felt*—told her she looked incredible, and pointed the car toward dinner.

Forty-five minutes later, they were seated at a cozy table for two at Napoli's, an upscale restaurant on the lake with a gorgeous water view that Amelia could've sat and stared at for hours and hours.

"This is amazing, Kirby," she said as she watched the gentle lapping of the water, the sound coming in through the open windows. The smell on the breeze was fresh and summery, and Amelia was surprised to feel herself relax. Like, *really* relax. She was sure she could actually feel the tension drain right out of her body.

"If you want, we can get an after-dinner drink and wander down there." Kirby pointed with her chin at the smattering of people milling around a seating area with fire pits and Adirondack chairs. "I bet it's really great when it's dark. And I think we can order s'mores for dessert and make them ourselves."

"Oh yes, can we?" The words were out before Amelia could catch them. Or censor them. She sounded like an excited child.

"Like s'mores, do you?" Kirby asked with a grin.

"My parents used to take me camping when I was a kid. We had one of those pop-up camper things?" Her body filled with the warmth of memories.

Kirby propped her chin in her hand. "Just the three of you?"

A nod. "My mom was all about the food. There are so many gadgets now, but she loved to be able to cook things on the fire. I remember this one time, she made this gingerbread batter. Then we scooped out oranges with a spoon but left the peels round, so they were like empty oranges with a hole on top." She mimicked holding the roundness of the fruit. "And we put the batter in, then wrapped the whole thing up tightly in foil and just tossed it into the fire." She mimed the toss.

Kirby's eyes lit up. "And the batter cooked into cake inside the orange peel?" At Amelia's nod, her grin grew. "That sounds amazing! We should try it." At Amelia's surprised look, she said, "Why not? I have a fire pit at my house. Victor's got one at his. Let's promise to give it a shot sometime."

Amelia didn't let herself think about the assumption of a future. She just went with it and said, "I'm in."

They were interrupted by the waiter, who read them the specials, took their wine order, and left them alone again. They gazed out at the water, and Amelia was amazed by how easy it was to be with Kirby and not talk if she didn't want to. It didn't feel awkward. There was no urgency to fill the silent spaces. The waiter returned with the bottle of Malbec they'd ordered. He uncorked it, poured, let Kirby sample it, then filled their glasses, and left.

Kirby raised her glass, elbow on the table to brace as she seemed to be searching for the right toast. Amelia mirrored her and waited, studied her face, noticed the cuteness of light freckles across her nose for the first time.

"To the joys of summer—s'mores, pools, and being outside—to the joys of spending time together, and to the joys of being alive."

"I will definitely drink to that," Amelia said. "To those. To all three." And she grinned, and they touched their glasses together.

The waiter took their orders and left them. Kirby set down her glass and asked, "What made you decide to start Dogz Rule?"

Amelia couldn't hide her surprise. "You know the name of my business?"

Was Kirby blushing? She glanced down, and yeah, Amelia was pretty sure Kirby's face had tinted pink. "I *may* have done some googling…"

Amelia laughed and held up her glass. "I may have googled

you, too, Dupree Paint Design, established 1985." They clinked glasses again. "You've got some terrific reviews on Yelp."

"Why, thank you. I work hard for those suckers."

"Have you ever gotten bad ones?" Amelia asked.

Kirby made a show of thinking. Dusk was slowly arriving, and the candle on the table, which had gone almost unnoticed when they'd arrived, now flickered and reflected in her eyes. Definitely green today. "I'm sure we have. You can't please everybody. And people can be assholes."

"So true."

"You didn't answer my question."

"Right. Well." Amelia sipped her wine. "I was married for nearly ten years. I'd been lucky enough to land a government job right out of college, and once you put in twenty years, you become eligible for retirement. So our plan—mine and Tammy's—was that I'd retire at forty-five. She was older than me, and she'd retire at fifty-five, and we'd travel around and keep our house as a sort of base camp to come back to when we wanted."

Kirby was watching her intently. Amelia didn't tell this story often. Hated to, actually. Found it embarrassing. Was surprised at the way it was simply spilling out of her.

"So, I turned forty-five. Retired. From a really good job, FYI. And the next year, she told me she was no longer in love with me, that she'd fallen in love with somebody else, that she didn't mean to, it just happened. All those stupid clichés. And then she left."

"Wow," Kirby said, and when Amelia met her eyes, there was genuine sympathy there. "That sucks."

"It really did."

"How long ago was that?"

"Almost two years."

"What about your house?"

Amelia glanced out the window at the tiny sliver of sun left just peeking over the horizon. "She wanted to sell it. And I fought her at first, but...I decided I didn't want to stay in a house I bought with the person I thought I'd be with for the rest of my life. So I moved into my parents' house. My dad has a place in Florida, and he comes home less and less often, so I have it to myself. Our house is up for sale."

The waiter stopped by, refilled their glasses, and told them their dinners would be out soon. With a grin, Kirby held up her glass and said, "To living in our parents' houses."

Amelia raised her eyebrows in surprise. "That's right, you, too."

"Me, too."

"Well, look at that. Common ground." Amelia sipped.

"I think there's more than you think there is."

"With a fourteen-year age difference?" Amelia gave a little snort. "I don't know."

"You're kinda hung up on that, aren't you?" Kirby's tone held no accusation. If anything, she was amused.

"I mean, you have to admit it's significant."

Kirby shrugged.

"Amelia?" A voice interrupted them, and Amelia looked up into a face she hadn't seen in a while. "I thought that was you. Hi."

"Jessie. Hi. How are you?" She smiled, but she wasn't sure it reached her eyes. Jessie Reynolds, an old friend of hers and Tammy's, stood there in a pretty blue dress, surprise clear on her face.

"Good. I'm good. How are *you*?" The way she emphasized the *you* made it clear that if either of them wasn't doing well, it would be Amelia. Her dark eyes moved from Amelia to Kirby and back.

"I'm good." She cleared her throat. "Jessie Reynolds, this is Kirby Dupree. She's—"

"Her date," Kirby said as she stuck out her hand and they shook. "Nice to meet you."

"Same," Jessie said, her attention more on Kirby than Amelia now. She seemed to give herself a little shake. "Isn't this place gorgeous?" Her gaze moved to the front of the restaurant where a man stood, clearly waiting for her. Without waiting for Amelia's response, she reached out and squeezed her arm. "I've gotta run, but so good to see you. Text me. Let's get together. It's been too long." Then she bent, kissed the air next to Amelia's cheek, and hurried off.

Amelia followed her retreat, then reached for her wine and took a very large drink of it.

"Old friend?" Kirby asked.

"Haven't heard from her in almost two years." Amelia shrugged.

"Lost her in the divorce?"

"One of many people, yes."

"You should make sure to text her about lunch or something." There was a twinkle in Kirby's eye that made her grin, and just like that, any sadness or discomfort she might normally have felt over the meeting dissipated like morning fog in the sunshine.

"Yeah, I'll get right on that," she said with a snorted laugh.

The arrival of their dinners interrupted them and gave Amelia a moment to just breathe. She shoved Jessie aside and returned to the earlier conversation. Hung up? That's what Kirby had said, right? She didn't think she was hung up, but Kirby couldn't deny that she was a lot younger than Amelia. She felt her irritation start to simmer, and she turned to look out onto the water.

When she returned her attention to the table, Kirby was looking at her. Tenderly. Sweetly. No accusation. No annoyance.

And she smiled, and Amelia could feel it, as though it was the sun, holding her, warming her.

And just like that, her tension eased. Her shoulders relaxed. The fog in her head cleared, and her thoughts became easier to access. She blew out a breath and held Kirby's gaze.

"I know exactly what it is," she said, surprising herself with the admission. "I just don't know how to combat it."

Kirby cut into her filet mignon. "So, talk to me. We can battle it together."

Was it that simple? Of course it wasn't. Amelia knew that. Kirby was being naive, right? She was thirty-five. What could she possibly know about the things Amelia was going through at almost fifty?

But her expression was soft, and her eyes were kind, and

her face was open and waiting and so, so gentle, and Amelia just started talking. About all of it. About her moods and her body and her psyche and how perimenopause and then actual menopause affected all those things. It was like the floodgates had opened. The levy broke. The dam cracked and crumbled. It all came rushing out. She ate as she spoke. Kirby ate as she listened.

"It's about having so little control. Over your moods. Over your emotions and your feelings. And holy hell, over your body. I have never, ever felt so insecure." She stopped to take a breath and a sip of wine. "My God, it feels good to spill all of this." A laugh bubbled up from deep in her lungs. "I'm really, really sorry," she said.

Kirby grinned widely at her. "What are you sorry for? First of all, I asked. Second, you have nothing to be sorry for. I love listening to you talk, and this is the most I've gotten to know about you since we met." She held up her own glass. "I'm loving life over here on my side of the table."

"Where did you come from?" Amelia asked. The words were out before she could catch them, but that was okay because it was an honest question.

"Right here in Northwood. Born and raised."

"You know, I love Julia and Vanessa. They're the best. I'd do anything for them. But they're so sick of listening to me whine and complain that I just don't talk about this stuff at all anymore." She held up a hand. "It's not their fault. Really. I was a repetitive mess for a year, so I can't blame them for tuning me out."

Kirby studied her for a moment, and it stretched out until Amelia squirmed a bit.

"What?"

"I have comments," Kirby said, chewing some potato.

The way she said it made Amelia laugh through her nose. "I bet you do." And when Kirby tipped her head and arched an eyebrow, Amelia nodded. "Sorry. Go ahead."

"My first comment is this—damn, girl, you are *rough* on yourself."

Another snort from Amelia. "Not news."

"My second comment is this—I am more than happy to

listen to you *whine and complain*"—she made air quotes with her fingers—"anytime you need it."

Amelia pointed a fork at her. "You say that *now*…"

"My third comment is this—I don't think you're going through anything that isn't exactly normal. It sounds awful, yes, but in case you're thinking there's something wrong with you, there's not."

"Says the thirty-five year old who will likely still have her period for another fifteen or twenty years."

"Woo-hoo, lucky me." Kirby twirled a finger in a circle.

Amelia finished off the wine by dividing what was left in the bottle evenly into their glasses. "Well, I appreciate your comments."

"I'm not done."

Kirby's tone was…Amelia couldn't describe it, but it got her attention. It had gone fully dark now, and the candle flickering in the green of her eyes was suddenly mysterious and sexy. Amelia picked up her glass and sat back, then gestured with her hand. "Please, continue."

"My fourth and final comment is this." Kirby leaned forward, forearms on the table, and lowered her voice to just above a whisper so only Amelia could hear her. "I know you're feeling awful about your body lately, but I do not feel awful about it. In fact, I feel very, very terrific about it."

"Oh, really?" Amelia arched an eyebrow, suddenly feeling flirty and sexy and how in the hell did Kirby do that to her?

"Yes, really. I happen to find you very, very sexy." She sat back and took a sip of her wine. "Just so you know."

Well. That was unexpected. And bold. And hot as hell.

Amelia looked for words. Found none. Tried to stifle a grin and failed. Sipped her wine instead.

The rest of dinner was easy. Smooth. She felt more comfortable than she could remember in recent months. It was like Kirby had taken all her worries and insecurities and put them in her own pocket for safekeeping, so Amelia could relax. When they were finished, they put in an order of s'mores and headed toward the water and found a fire pit with an Adirondack chair with a double seat.

"I didn't know they made these in love seat form," Amelia said as Kirby pulled it closer to the fire and they sat.

The fire was fueled by an unseen propane tank, so the heat it gave off was minimal, but the ambiance was there, dim and romantic, and when their s'more makings arrived, they scooted to the edge of the seat.

"Okay," Kirby said, sliding a marshmallow onto the provided stick. "I'll do the marshmallows if you prepare the chocolate and graham crackers. Deal?"

"Deal."

"How do you like your marshmallow? Just warm, slightly golden, or burnt to a crisp?"

"I feel like this is an important question, given the way you're looking at me." Amelia squinted at Kirby.

"Might be the most important one I've asked all night," Kirby deadpanned.

"No pressure."

"None."

Amelia took a breath and said, "Burnt to a crisp, please. And then I will eat the burnt part, and if you could burn the rest of it again, I'd appreciate it." She winced, braced...

And Kirby laughed. Loudly. "Ladies and gentlemen, we have a winner." She shoved the marshmallow right into the flame. "Black and crispy, it is. Twice."

Only by feeling as comfortable and relaxed as she did was Amelia able to question how it was that she was so comfortable and relaxed. It was Kirby. She was the only difference in her life right now. How could it be that one woman—a woman fourteen years younger than her and in the prime of her life—could make Amelia forget the things weighing on her? Being single at her age, hell, just *being* her age, menopause and how it had wreaked havoc on her, body and spirit. Oh, those things weren't gone. Of course not. But somehow, it was as if Kirby had gathered them up, put them in a box with a tight lid, and set them up on a high, high shelf for the time being. They'd be back. Amelia knew this. But not here. Not now. Not tonight.

They closed the place.

Before she knew it, the waiter had informed them that it was nearing midnight, and when Amelia looked around, they were the only people left.

Kirby turned to her with sparkling eyes and said quietly, "Let's get out of here."

CHAPTER SEVENTEEN

The ride back to Victor's place was quiet. Quiet, but not silent, at least not in Amelia's head. Oh no, in Amelia's head, voices were screaming. Okay, not voices. One voice. Hers.

She knew what she wanted. That was easy. She wanted to take Kirby inside, upstairs, into the bedroom, and strip her naked. Take in her body, her skin, her shape. First with her eyes. Then with her hands. Then with her mouth.

Jesus God, when had she last felt this way? The early Tammy years? She did have a yearning then for Tammy, but she didn't remember it ever being this…intense. This *urgent*.

"I can almost hear the gears cranking over there," Kirby said, amusement clear in her voice. "You okay?"

Amelia nodded. "Yup."

A small laugh left Kirby's lips. "Sounds it."

Amelia swallowed. It was loud.

Kirby turned the car into Victor's driveway and shifted it into park but made no move to get out. Instead, she turned her body slightly so she was almost facing Amelia. Then she waited. Amelia could feel the eyes on her, and when she finally turned to look, Kirby had that gentle smile on her face. That goddamn gentle smile.

"Doesn't anything worry you?" Amelia asked, and if she sounded snippy or harsh, Kirby didn't show it.

"Sure. Lots of things worry me."

"This doesn't?" Amelia moved her finger back and forth between the two of them.

"Not even a little bit."

"But *why not?*" Yes, she whined it like an eight-year-old, and it made Kirby grin.

"Because I don't overthink everything the way you do." It could've come across insulting, but it didn't. Somehow, Kirby actually made it sound sweet and kind.

Amelia groaned and covered her face with her hands. "Oh my God, I'm such a mess. Why are you even interested in me?" She laughed, though. She couldn't help it. The stress had eased at Kirby's words.

"Because I happen to think you're interesting. And fun to talk to. And smart. And *insanely* sexy. And I am pretty hopelessly attracted to you." Kirby took one of Amelia's hands in both of hers, studied it, turned it over and looked at the palm as she said, "I wish you could see what I see when I look at you."

Amelia felt everything in her turn soft. "Oh, you are good." At Kirby's grin, Amelia squeezed her hand.

"Look." Kirby shifted again, so she was literally turned in her seat and fully facing Amelia. She still held her hand. "I will never put any pressure on you. I had a fantastic time with you tonight. I'd like to do it again." She paused for a beat, but her eyes held Amelia's.

"Me, too," Amelia said. And then something weird happened. Words left her mouth that should have freaked her the hell out. Asking Kirby not to leave should have sent her insecurities sprinting out into the open, screaming at the tops of their lungs *Here we are! We're back!* and waving their arms around madly. But that didn't happen. Instead, she got out of the car, went around to the driver's side, opened Kirby's door, and held out a hand. "Come inside with me."

The smile that bloomed across Kirby's face was glorious, worth every penny. It lit up everything—her eyes, her cheeks, the entire interior of the car, and Amelia couldn't not kiss her right then. She backed Kirby up against the car and kissed the hell out of her right there in the driveway until they were both breathless and Stevie could be heard howling from inside the house.

"We'd better get in there," Amelia said, and they kissed for a few more minutes before heading for the front door.

The dogs were happy to see them both, and they had to set aside their own agenda to take time to love on them. Petting and loving and making kissy faces at them took the next few minutes, but every time Amelia glanced up, Kirby was smiling at her, looking at her, and totally undressing her with her eyes.

"Stop that," Amelia said quietly, but with a grin.

"Nope," Kirby replied, obviously knowing exactly what she meant.

They stood at the back door while the dogs wandered the yard.

"I have an idea," Kirby said, her voice soft in the quiet of the night.

"Tell me."

"Let's go swimming."

It was the most perfect idea, and Amelia nodded her agreement instantly. "It's heated and has amazing lighting." She went to the box on the wall in the three season room that Victor had showed her. She flipped off the floodlights, then flipped on the pool lights.

It was like a damn movie. Blue lights lit the pool softly from down in the depths of the water, while tiny twinkle lights hidden in various spots around the pool lit things up just enough for them to see where they were going. The privacy fence was tall, and Amelia knew the neighbors couldn't see a thing because she'd scanned every angle the first time she lay out in her bathing suit.

"I might have an extra suit you can wear," she said, but her voice began to trail off when her eyes met Kirby's, and the sheer sensuality in them hit her square in the chest. "Or shorts and a tank. Something…"

Kirby leaned close to her and whispered, "I don't think we need any suits. Do you?"

They were kissing again. Softly. Unhurriedly. It was as if Kirby had decided to take her time and slowly explore every single part of Amelia's mouth. Good God, the woman knew how to kiss.

She felt Kirby's hand slide down her arm and link her fingers. Then the kiss ended, and Kirby was leading her to the end of the pool with the steps. Amelia didn't have a chance to let any stress or worry in because there was more kissing.

God. Kissing was *so* often underrated. Seriously, she loved sex, but a good make-out session was so satisfying. She let herself sink into Kirby's mouth, to taste the remnants of chocolate and wine, to savor the soft warmth. And when she had banished just about every thought that didn't have to do with this kiss, she felt Kirby's fingers at the sides of her thighs, gently scraping, bunching up the fabric of her dress.

Kirby pulled back from the kiss just slightly, enough to meet Amelia's gaze. She held it as she continued to bunch up the dress until the hem was in her hands and Amelia's legs were bare.

Amelia didn't look away.

She held Kirby's gaze as Kirby lifted the dress higher, higher, and Amelia lifted her arms. The dress was up and off, and Amelia was in her underwear. And doing pretty well being on display, if she did say so herself.

Kirby's eyes stayed on her until Amelia broke the tether and glanced down. "Can we get in the water?" she asked quietly, as she brought her arms up to cover her stomach.

Kirby took her hands and tugged them away. "You are so beautiful," she said, and the sincerity in her tone, in her green eyes, brought tears to Amelia's, and she swallowed. "But yes," Kirby added, "we can get in the water."

Amelia took the first step down, then turned to her and pointed a finger, waved it around in front of Kirby. "Um, the dress comes off."

Zero hesitation. That's what Kirby had as she whipped her dress off and tossed it to the concrete, and Amelia wondered if her own eyes actually bugged out the way they felt like they did at the sight. Kirby was lean and fit, with surprisingly round hips and surprisingly ample breasts. "Wow." It was out before Amelia could catch it.

Kirby splashed into the water in her bikinis and bra. "Right back atcha," she said as she took Amelia's hand and led her down the steps.

The water was warm and felt sensual against her skin, and

they waded until the water was chest level, and then Amelia felt hands on her bare skin. Kirby grasped her sides, turned her so they were face to face again, and this kiss was not soft. It was not gentle or tender or tentative. It was hard and demanding and such an incredible turn-on that Amelia's knees went weak, and she was thankful to feel the side of the pool at her back.

The water had been a fantastic idea, and Amelia felt her insecurities slink away into their corner. The blue light held an erotic quality, and sexy wasn't something Amelia had felt in longer than she could remember. But the water, the dimness, and Kirby's tongue in her mouth all combined into one huge sensual experience that shot through her body like a steady dose of electricity.

Kirby was shorter than her, but in the water, it didn't matter. Kirby's hands grasped her thighs and pulled them, so she wrapped them around Kirby's waist, locked her ankles around her back, and held on.

And then her bra was off.

She didn't feel it happening, but suddenly, the cool water caressed her nipples, and Kirby tossed the bra onto the side of the pool. "Come here," she whispered in Amelia's ear as she half led, half carried her back toward the steps and set her ass down about halfway down them. Now the water reached just above her belly button, and the cool air on her breasts brought her nipples to attention. Kirby muttered a curse under her breath, and then Amelia's breast was in her mouth, and holy hell, the pleasure that shot through her at the feel of it, the combination of the cool night air, the warm water, and Kirby's mouth…Amelia thought she might pass out from the overload. In the very best of ways.

Kirby was going to have marks on her back tomorrow. Amelia had the thought as she dug her fingers, her nails, into flesh, wanting her closer, closer, and she arched her back and pushed her breast farther into Kirby's mouth.

"God," she whispered, and when her fingers hit the clasp of Kirby's bra, she didn't think twice about unfastening it, sending the fabric flying behind her and then her hands had both Kirby's breasts, and Kirby's eyes went wide in surprise.

Eye contact. Hot, intense eye contact.

"You are so fucking sexy," Kirby whispered to her.

"Look who's talking," Amelia responded and squeezed the flesh in her hands, which caused Kirby's eyes to flutter closed and a super sexy moan to emanate from her throat. Oh, man, she liked that sound and squeezed again. Kirby dropped her forehead to Amelia's shoulder and swore again as Amelia's thumbs ran over her nipples, stroking them, circling them.

Kirby seemed to drift on a wave of pleasure for another moment or two before she lifted her head, and there was a flash of...something...in her eyes. Arousal? No. It was more primal than that. Raw. Amelia no sooner had that thought then Kirby had scooped her up off the steps again and they were back in deeper water.

"Stand up for a sec," Kirby commanded. And that's what it was, a command. And Amelia obeyed it, letting her feet settle on the pool floor. The whimper that escaped her at the feel of Kirby's hands tugging her thong down was out of her control. "Also, a thong? Jesus, woman, are you trying to kill me?" Before Amelia could answer, Kirby's mouth captured hers, and there was nothing at all but kissing.

God, the kissing.

Deep. Thorough. Sexier than any kissing Amelia had ever done. Ever. In her entire life.

"And now," Kirby ordered, walking her backward into deeper water, her lips against Amelia's, "wrap your legs around me again."

Amelia obeyed, but this time, Kirby's hands weren't on her thighs. They cupped her ass, and her fingers slid down, around, and through what Amelia knew was copious wetness that had nothing at all to do with being in the pool. She gasped Kirby's name in surprise, and without missing a beat, Kirby slipped her fingers into Amelia. Slowly but confidently, and Amelia cried out. And then her hips started moving on their own—she swore to God, she had no control. Her body took over, took the steering wheel away from her brain, and she crushed her mouth to Kirby's.

Everything blurred then, mixed and ran together until it was all one big wave of pleasure, arousal, desire. She no longer felt Kirby's fingers stroking her or Kirby's shoulders under her hands or Kirby's mouth on hers. She simply felt *Kirby*, with no idea where her body ended and Kirby's began. They were like watercolors that bled together to make a new hue. All Amelia knew was that she hadn't felt this confident, this sexy, this *wanted* in longer than she could remember, and there was something about that. It fueled her. Pushed everything else out of her mind. All of it fell into the pool water and drifted away on the ripples their bodies created as she simply let herself feel.

And then none of that mattered because an orgasm ripped through her with such an intensity, she was surprised she didn't just disintegrate into ash right there in a puff of gray smoke. A cry tore from her throat, and she held on to Kirby's body for dear life, sure that if she let go, she'd drift off into oblivion.

How much time passed?

She had zero idea. A minute? Ten minutes? A year? Who the hell knew? But her legs felt like weightless jelly, even in the pool, and Kirby's skin was slick and warm under her hands. At some point, she must've laid her head back against the concrete side of the pool, and when she opened her eyes, a blanket of dark night filled with a million twinkling stars was spread overhead and, *Oh my God, is this even real*, she wondered, feeling like the heroine of some romance novel.

But then she lifted her head. Her eyes met deep green ones and they were inviting and warm and kind and loving.

And then Kirby said, "Hey, you." And she smiled. Her cheeks were rosy, the roundness of her cheekbones pronounced. Kirby lifted a wet hand out of the pool and brushed some hair off Amelia's forehead, and Amelia realized she still had her legs wrapped around Kirby's waist, leaving herself exposed and open, but again, her body took the decision-making away from her brain, and instead of releasing Kirby's frame, her legs tightened and brought her closer. Kirby's expression brightened, the smile grew wider, and she spoke again. "Just for the record, that was fucking amazing." Cupping her chin, Kirby kissed her mouth with a tender softness that brought tears to Amelia's eyes. "You okay?" Kirby asked when Amelia hadn't spoken.

A nod. She wet her lips. Cleared her throat. "Trying to find my voice. And basking. I'm literally basking over here."

"Basking is allowed and encouraged."

"And I wanted to thank you."

"For the orgasm?" Kirby said with a wink. "Hey, anytime. And I mean that. Any. Time." She bumped Amelia's forehead gently with hers.

"Well, yeah, for that, but for…" She studied Kirby's face and accepted the realization she'd been toying with. Gave voice to it. "For the pool. I know what you did and why." Her throat seemed like it was about to close up. "Thank you for that."

Kirby looked down at the water for a moment, the first time Amelia had seen anything remotely resembling shyness since they'd met. It was cute, honestly. "You don't ever have to be self-conscious with me, Amelia. I think I've made it pretty clear how attractive I think you are."

She nodded. "I know." She gave her temple a tap with her finger. "It's up here."

Kirby nodded and she got it. Amelia could tell. She didn't understand how somebody in their midthirties could understand, but Kirby did, and Amelia was suddenly so thankful, her eyes welled up. Kirby must've noticed because she pulled her into a hug. "You are seriously one of the most beautiful women I've ever met." She pulled back so she could look Amelia in the eye. "I feel…privileged to be here with you. Seriously. It's an honor."

Amelia gave her a playful shove and a little splash because, yeah, that was too much for right now, not if she didn't want to burst into tears. "Well, maybe we should go upstairs, and I can show you what a privilege it is for *me*."

Kirby's surprise was clear on her face. Eyebrows went up. Eyes got slightly wider.

"What? You don't want to stay?" Amelia asked.

"Oh God, no, I absolutely do. I just…" Kirby seemed to

search the star-filled sky for the right words. "Wasn't sure you'd want that."

"I want that." Amelia tugged her closer again, wrapped her arms and legs tightly around her naked body, and squeezed. With her lips brushing Kirby's, she said, "I very much want that."

CHAPTER EIGHTEEN

Three fifty-seven.

That's what time Amelia's phone told her it was as she lay in Victor's bed, staring at the ceiling, eyes wide open, sleep playing hide and seek with her and doing a stellar job of hiding.

And yes, Victor's bed was huge, but she'd never have known it because Kirby was wrapped around her like a creeping vine of ivy. Legs intertwined with hers. Arm thrown over her middle. Face tucked into her neck, so she could feel the gentle breeze of Kirby's breath on her skin. Every now and then, a little snorfling sound would occur, and Amelia would smile and tighten her grip and stare at the ceiling some more.

She'd had sex.

For the first time in nearly four years. She and Tammy had been in a drought for almost two years before they split and after that, she just…had no desire, no opportunity, no, no, no.

But now? *Yes.*

She'd had sex.

Like, really great sex. Really hot, really great sex. With a younger woman. A much younger woman. A much younger, crazy super hot woman. Holy crap. Her mind tossed her images, memories, of Kirby underneath her, responding to her touch, her hands, her mouth. Amelia had never been with somebody so strong and so curvy at the same time. Kirby was a living, breathing dichotomy, all muscle and strength, but also soft and beautiful. Her body was…*God.* Her breasts were perfect. Her ass was perfect. Her hips, her back, God, her mouth.

And don't get her started on the sounds. Kirby wasn't loud in bed, but she hummed and moaned and whimpered, and every sound she made turned Amelia on more.

She swallowed hard and could hear it in the quiet of the early morning. A slight turn of her head allowed her to press a kiss to Kirby's forehead. When she felt warm lips on her neck, she knew she wasn't the only one awake.

Kirby's hand moved across her stomach and down, fingers slipping between her legs, and Amelia didn't bother to protest. She simply moved her legs apart and let Kirby in. Something that surprised her now, how easily she did that—let Kirby in. She was already soaked, and Kirby let out a quiet moan when her fingers reached Amelia's center. Less than a minute later, Amelia's entire body tensed, her hips lifted off the bed as her orgasm hit, and Kirby slid inside her, rode out the climax from there, moving easily in and out, drawing things out for Amelia, who was once again shocked by how quickly she came for Kirby.

No words were spoken. Kirby simply gave a little chuckle, kissed Amelia's neck again, then snuggled back in, her fingers still inside.

The throbbing eased, then subsided, Amelia's legs feeling rubbery. She let her eyes drift closed, and sleep finally let itself be found.

❖

Kirby loved the early mornings.

Even when she'd gotten barely three hours of sleep.

It was a little after six, and she'd gotten up, quietly let the dogs out so as not to disturb Amelia, made coffee, and headed back upstairs with two mugs. When she'd arrived at the doorway to the bedroom, she'd stopped, leaned a shoulder against the jamb, and just looked.

Amelia was still sleeping. And still naked, which surprised her. Between the water in the pool and the covers on the bed, she'd managed to keep her body fairly obscured. It bothered Kirby a bit, but not because she was mad about it. Because she felt bad for Amelia. It had to be hard to be so self-conscious of your appearance that part of your existence involved finding various ways to hide your body from others. And she had nothing to be self-conscious about. Nothing. She was beautiful, every line and curve and expanse of skin. Just gorgeous.

She stood there, a coffee in each hand, and let herself get lost in the sense memory of the previous night. Hell, two hours ago. Touching Amelia was something she didn't think she'd ever get enough of, and she was toying with the idea of crawling back under the covers with her, when she started to stir, that big inhale the body takes as it wakes up. Her eyes blinked open and she gazed around the room before settling on Kirby.

"Hi," she said, her voice sexily hoarse, which reminded Kirby of all the sounds she'd coaxed from Amelia, and just like that, her brain was off again, diving right back into sense memory.

"Hey there, sleepyhead." Kirby held up a mug. "Brought you a present."

Amelia pushed herself up, carefully keeping the covers over her naked breasts, and held out a hand, wiggling her fingers. "Gimme."

"Demanding in the morning," Kirby said, handing over the coffee. And then their eyes met and it was clear they'd both moved from the idea of demanding coffee to the idea of demanding other things.

"I mean, sometimes." Amelia sipped, but her eyes stayed focused on Kirby's over the rim.

"I'm telling you, if I didn't have two guys waiting on me to give them their work for the day, I'd be yanking those covers off you right now." She meant it. Every word. It was taking every ounce of strength she had not to do that very thing. "Because holy crap. You in the morning? All rumpled and relaxed? Yeah, super enticing."

"Enticing, huh?" Amelia asked, then continued to grin at her, dimples on display, and sip her coffee.

"You have no idea. If I didn't have to work, we wouldn't be leaving this bed."

"Except maybe to get in the pool again?"

"Except maybe to get in the pool again."

Their gazes held, and Kirby could swear she felt the sizzle of electricity flowing between them.

"So," Amelia said. "Don't you have to work…here? Today?"

Kirby nodded slowly, smiling back at her. "First, I have to get the guys all set on a new job. Then I have two estimates to do."

"But then you'll be back?"

"This afternoon, yeah."

"Oh, good." And Amelia left it at that, which Kirby had to admit she kinda loved.

They sipped their coffee in silence, and somehow, it wasn't awkward. At all. It felt perfectly normal to be quiet with Amelia, and Kirby didn't think she'd ever experienced that before. She hated to disturb the peace she felt, but time wasn't stopping just for them.

"Hey, can I borrow some clothes to wear home, so I don't have to put my dress back on?"

Amelia nodded and pointed to her giant pile of clothes on the floor of the open walk-in closet. "Help yourself. It's a mess, but it's all clean."

Kirby went into the closet, which was almost as big as her childhood bedroom, and riffled through Amelia's clothes. Once she'd found a pair of leggings and a T-shirt, she announced, "I am now coming out of the closet. Again."

"Hilarious," Amelia said, still in the same position in the bed, covers up over her breasts, coffee held in both hands. Her eyes raked over Kirby and then she said, "I like you in my clothes."

"Yeah? Well, I like being in your clothes. They smell like you."

Amelia made a face. "I hope that's a good thing."

"Oh, it's a very good thing." Kirby crossed to the foot of the bed and crawled up to Amelia carefully, so as not to spill the coffee. "I'll be back this afternoon around one," she said and kissed Amelia softly.

"I'll make sure I'm here," Amelia whispered back.

"Excellent."

Kirby kissed her again but kept it quick because she knew

if she allowed herself to sink into Amelia, she'd definitely end up late. Forcing herself away from the bed, she said, "I hope you know how hard it is for me to leave you while you're sitting there in a huge bed, all naked and stuff."

"Well, maybe we'll get naked and stuff later." And there was an edge of confidence in Amelia's voice that Kirby hadn't heard before. She liked it. A lot. It made her smile.

"Deal."

An hour later, Kirby had gone home, showered, changed, and zipped through the Dunkin' drive-through for more coffee. There wasn't enough caffeine on earth to wake her up, but she was trying her best.

Krog and Coop were already at the job site when she arrived with coffee for both of them as well as a box of Munchkins. She tried to be a good boss and took care of her people when she could, grabbed them coffee or doughnuts or both when she had a chance.

"Breakfast is served," she said and presented her goods with a flourish.

"Man, I love me some doughnut holes," Coop said as he dug into the Munchkin box.

She went over the details of the job and made sure they were clear on the directions and had all the supplies they required.

Krog sipped his coffee and watched her over the rim of his cup.

"What?" she asked.

"You're in a good mood," he said, and there was a tint of accusation in his tone.

She squinted at him.

"She's always in a good mood," Coop chimed in before she could.

"Yeah, but this is extra." Krog narrowed his eyes like he was studying her.

"Okay, stop it. You're freaking me out." She waved him off, grabbed a Munchkin, and popped it into her mouth.

Krog's eyes went wide in realization. "You got laid!"

"What?" Coop asked.

"What?" Kirby said at the same time.

But Krog just nodded and grinned, clearly proud of himself.

"Oh, clever guy, figured out a puzzle, did you?" Kirby asked, but she couldn't stop the smile. And why should she? She was in a good mood.

"Who was it? That chick from the softball team with the crush?"

"Emma?" Kirby snorted. "God, no. She's, like, twelve."

"Well, who then?" Krog popped a Munchkin into his mouth and chewed slowly while he waited.

"You don't know her," Kirby said with a shrug. And it was true. "She's house-sitting at the job I'm doing."

"Ah, that one. I thought so," Krog said. At Kirby's nod, he said, "Sleeping with a client is ill-advised, Kirbs."

"Good thing she's not the client then, huh?" She winked at him, punched his shoulder, and headed back to her van before he could ask more questions. Because the truth was, she knew his next questions—was it a one-time thing? where's it going? what does it mean?—were things she didn't have answers to. She also knew she should probably think about asking Amelia a few of them, but she wasn't ready to do that yet.

And that was fine. She wasn't worried. She wasn't wondering. She was simply…basking. Basking in an amazing sexual connection with a person she really liked and hoped to get to know even better.

And that was good enough for her.

CHAPTER NINETEEN

A melia was trying hard not to freak the hell out, but she pretty much was, just silently. She'd crafted four different texts to Vanessa, but deleted them all without sending them because she wasn't sure she was ready to let somebody else in on this information.

Maybe she just wanted to savor it.

No mistake, the freak-out was lingering just below the surface, but it seemed to be staying there for the time being, and she sent her thanks up to the heavens for that.

Once she'd heard Kirby's car pull out of the driveway, Amelia had thrown off the covers and padded into the huge bath, dogs on her heels, coffee still in her hand—and how sweet was it that Kirby had taken the time to deliver her a cup before she left?—and stood naked in front of the enormous mirror.

She never enjoyed that.

Standing naked in front of a mirror was the best way to send her brain down the rabbit hole of insecurity. She would know—she did it all the time. Nakedness in a mirror was a sure way to spotlight every single flaw she had and reflect them back at her in magnified detail.

This morning was different, somehow.

She noticed a few new marks. Two parallel scratches on her shoulder. What looked like a light bruise on the inside of her thigh. Her brain tossed her a flashback of Kirby's mouth on that very spot, sucking firmly before moving upward, and Amelia swallowed hard at the memory, felt her body wake right up. She ran a hand over her stomach, her hips, her ass. All places that had grown or changed over the past year. All places that made her incredibly uncomfortable in her own body lately.

And yet...

Kirby had made her feel beautiful. How had she done that? She'd made her feel sexy and desired and Jesus, Mary, and Joseph, did she want that again. She wanted to feel that all the time. All. The. Time.

But wait.

Okay, back the truck up there, skippy.

This was one date. One night. There was nothing exclusive or promised or even hinted at. She had no idea how Kirby was feeling about things. Was this a one-and-done sort of thing? Was it more? Did it have parameters and rules, or was she getting way ahead of herself?

Oh yeah. She totally was. So far ahead she couldn't see anything in her rearview mirror but the horizon.

"Just breathe," she told her reflection. "Just breathe. That's all you have to do right now."

Stevie nudged her thigh with his nose, and she reached down and stroked his soft head.

"You agree with me, huh?"

He wagged his stump of a tail and gave a small woof, which she took as polite agreement.

"All right. You win. I'll do my best. I'll just breathe."

And she did as she got ready for her day. As she headed for Junebug Farms and walked some of the shelter dogs. As she made three client visits. As she chatted briefly with Victor Renwick, calling from Japan, asking after his dogs and his house. She just kept breathing.

It wasn't until she returned to Victor's and pulled into the driveway behind Kirby's van, it wasn't until she got a glimpse of Kirby leaning back against the bumper and tipping up a can of Coke as she drank from it, exposing the column of her throat, it wasn't until she got an eyeful of the lean, curved, strong body that she'd seen naked, had underneath her, tasted every inch of the night before, that her breath caught in her throat. And she stopped.

"Hey, you," Kirby said when their eyes met. "How has your day been?"

All rational thought was gone. Amelia had none, couldn't find it, had no idea where it had gone. She had only one singular focus, and her feet moved on their own, walking her right up to Kirby, ignoring her surprise as she took Kirby's face in both her hands and kissed her soundly on the mouth. When she finally pulled back and opened her eyes, Kirby was grinning like a fool.

"You look as surprised by that as I was," she said, then ran her thumb across Amelia's bottom lip and kissed her again.

"I'm not really sure what you've done to me," Amelia said quietly. Uncertainly. "This"—she waved her hand vaguely around the area of their mouths—"is not me. At all."

Kirby shrugged. "I mean, maybe it is, and you just didn't know it."

Weirdly wise words, those.

Amelia forced herself to take a step back away from Kirby and turned toward the house. "Don't you have some painting to do?" She kept her voice light, not wanting to insult Kirby, but knowing she needed to put some space between them.

"I do, yes. Sorry about that. I was distracted by a beautiful woman."

"Mm-hmm." Amelia couldn't stop the smile, even when she tried. What the hell was happening?

An hour later, Kirby was working diligently on the half bath on the first floor, and Amelia was outside at the table under the umbrella, attempting to work on her laptop and invoice clients and answer emails. She had to give Kirby credit. She was excellent at separating her personal and professional lives, getting right to work once they'd entered the house. Amelia, on the other hand, sat motionless in her chair more often than not, daydreaming about the previous night. Fantasizing about possible nights to come. Generally working herself up into a hot, turned-on, sexed-up version of herself that she seriously did not recognize.

She walked around in kind of a daze, which was weird and unfamiliar. She kept doing stupid things like putting the dish towel in the refrigerator and leaving the back door wide open. At one point, she could actually hear Uncle Vinnie—Julia's dad—shouting in her head, *I'm not paying to air-condition the entire neighborhood. Shut that door!*

The majority of the afternoon went by like that, and finally, she slammed her laptop shut in frustration. This was not her. She was not this person. She didn't daydream. Her mind didn't wander. She focused. She was a focuser—she got the job done. Any job. This was uncharted territory for her. And she did not like it. At all.

With a groan, she pushed herself to her feet and headed inside to grab a Diet Coke. It wasn't until she had her head in the fridge and heard a startled, "Oh shit!" coming from down the hallway—the direction of the half bath—that she looked down at the dogs standing near her as usual, their eyes filled with the hope of a bite of turkey or maybe a nibble of cheese…and saw the paw prints.

So many paw prints.

Stevie-sized paw prints.

Smaller Calvin-sized paw prints.

Lavender paw prints.

All over Victor's lovely dark hardwood floors.

Before a shriek could rip itself from her throat, Kirby came skidding into the room, lavender paint smeared on one cheek, eyes wide with horror.

"Oh my God, I thought they were gated in the three season room," she cried.

"They were," Amelia replied, her own voice just as panicked. "I must've forgotten to close the gate." She took in the paw prints and her eyes welled up. "Oh my God, the floors. *The floors.*" She grabbed paper towel off the roll, put it under the water, squeezed it out, and stood there, arms out to her sides. "What do I do?"

"It's okay," Kirby said, suddenly calm. "Don't panic. It's okay."

"How is this okay?" she shouted at her. Because seriously, how the fuck was she so calm? "These floors probably cost more than my entire house!"

And then Kirby's hands were on her shoulders, and she moved her head, following Amelia's darting gaze until it locked with hers. "Take the dogs outside and clean their paws. Leave the floors to me." Amelia felt her tears spill over, and Kirby wiped one away with a paint-stained finger. "I got this. Don't worry. Go."

Amelia took the entire roll of paper towels and shooed the dogs out the back door, making sure to close it behind her this time. She tried not to cry, but the idea that she might have ruined the floors in this gorgeous house because she wasn't paying attention to the *one thing* she was hired to pay attention to—Victor's dogs—was enough to give her an ulcer. How had she let this happen? How had she let her brain drift so far from its standard course. This was not her.

Her father would be so disappointed in her.

Good news and bad news—the paint on the dogs' paws was still fairly wet, and it washed off easily with paper towels and water, and soon they were chasing each other around the yard. The weather was cool for July—high sixties—but Amelia had sweated through her shirt, her armpits damp, sweat rolling down her torso from under her bra. She needed to change. She needed a shower.

God, she didn't want to go inside. She wanted to pretend none of this had happened and that the floors were fine. The house was fine. And Kirby was simply the painter…

Okay. Not really. That wasn't really what she wanted.

What the hell did she want?

With a deep breath, she pushed her way inside the house, being extra, extra careful to close all the doors behind her, leaving the dogs outside, and went into the kitchen to face the music.

The paw prints between the kitchen island and the fridge were gone.

The paw prints that ran in a circle through the rest of the kitchen were gone.

Kirby was on her hands and knees in the hallway, wiping up the last of the paw prints there.

"Oh my God," Amelia said, not bothering to hide her shock. She bent her knees and looked more closely at the floor, expecting to see outlines, some kind of remnants, remains of the prints that had been there just moments ago. There was nothing. "Oh my God," she said again, then looked at Kirby. "How the hell did you do that?"

Kirby glanced up at her and smiled. "You think I've been in this business since I was a teenager, and these are the first dogs to run through my paint?"

The reprieve Amelia felt was intense and took the strength right out of her legs. She reached out to grip the counter so she wouldn't melt to the ground in a puddle of sweet relief. "Oh my God," she said a third time, and then, "Apparently, that's all I can say. Oh my God." Laughter bubbled up out of her, and holy crap, Kirby was going to think she was losing it. Certifiable. She certainly sounded like it with her weird, giggly laughter, but she couldn't help it. It just rolled out of her.

Kirby watched her, clearly amused, and when she finished with the floor, she stood up, dusted her hands off on the outsides of her thighs, then parked her hands on her hips and just looked at Amelia. And then she grinned. And then she started to chuckle. And within moments, they were openly laughing, cracking up, until tears leaked from their eyes, and Amelia's throat ached.

When Amelia finally caught her breath, the question slipped out before she had a chance to edit her words. "How do you do that?"

"Do what?" Kirby asked, stepping farther into the room. She reached out and ran a hand down Amelia's upper arm.

"Just…make things better. You stop me from freaking out." She snorted a laugh. "Nobody's been able to do that for me in years. *Years*. 'Cause I'm good at it. I excel."

"At freaking out?"

"Yup."

"Yeah, you kinda do." But there was nothing but kindness and affection in Kirby's tone.

"I never used to." With a sigh, she opened the fridge and took out two cans of Diet Coke. "I was always very steady and controlled. Ask my cousins." She handed a can to Kirby and popped her own open with a loud crack.

"What changed?" Kirby asked, as they both headed back toward the half bath by unspoken agreement. Kirby set her soda on the vanity and grabbed her roller to pick up where she'd left off.

"Everything, that's what changed," Amelia said, leaning a

shoulder against the doorjamb to watch. "I retired early, so my work life changed. Tammy left me, so my marital status changed. I hit perimenopause, so my body changed."

Kirby looked at her and clenched her teeth. "All at once? Wow."

"I mean, within about a year and a half, yeah."

"That's crazy. No wonder you freaked out. How could you not?"

Amelia blinked at her, surprised. "Thank you for that. I didn't think you'd get it."

"No? Why not?" Kirby rolled paint onto the wall, a glistening lavender that brightened the room up so much, it instantly lightened the overall atmosphere.

"That color is amazing," Amelia said quietly, then moved on to the question. "Um, because you're not even forty yet?"

"There it is," Kirby said with a laugh.

"There what is?"

"The age thing. Told you you were hung up on it."

Amelia squinted at her. "You have to admit there's credence to it. Don't you think?"

Kirby inhaled, then let it out audibly and shrugged. "I mean, you don't really know, though, what my life has been like. Right?" Again, there was zero accusation in her tone, and Amelia wondered how she managed to do that—gently tell her that her thinking was flawed without insulting her or getting pissed off about it. It was a talent, definitely.

"True," she admitted. She watched as Kirby poured more paint into her tray, then rolled the roller through it. As she returned to the wall, Amelia's eyes were glued to her shoulders, the muscles working there as she moved.

"So while I have not reached perimenopause yet, maybe I have had crazy changes hit my life. You don't know."

"I can admit that."

"Good."

They were quiet, the only sound the rhythmic swishing of the roller.

"You're really good at your job," Amelia said after some time.

Kirby shot her a smile over her shoulder. "Thanks."

"Do you love it?"

"I do."

"That's amazing. Not a lot of people can say that."

"Did you love the job you retired from?" Kirby asked her, refilling her roller.

"Love it? No. I liked it fine, but I didn't love it. That's probably why I didn't try to unretire after my marriage fell apart."

"But the dog stuff. You love that."

"I do. Absolutely."

"See? We're the same."

Amelia's smile was one she could feel as it blossomed. "I guess we are."

She could've stood there all day and watched Kirby work. It would've been easy. And more than fun. To say Kirby was easy on the eyes was an understatement. But Stevie chose that moment to bark, and she remembered that her laptop was still outside and that she hadn't gotten much of her own work done, so she pushed off the doorjamb.

She didn't freak out for the rest of the afternoon.

CHAPTER TWENTY

Having Amelia sitting in the bleachers during her softball game had an effect on Kirby. A good effect on her in general, but a bad effect on her game. She hit three singles and struck out twice.

Kirby didn't strike out. Ever.

Yeah, her concentration was in the toilet when Amelia was watching. That was new. A little thrill zipped through her as they slapped hands with the other team after the game was over.

As she gathered her things she glanced up to catch Amelia wave good-bye to her. She was meeting with her cousins about wedding stuff. As thunder rumbled in the distance, Lark bumped her in the shoulder.

"She's still hot," she said, and when Kirby looked at her, Lark's eyes were following Amelia's retreat. "You guys hook up yet?"

Kirby feared the blush she felt would answer for her.

"Oh my God, you *have*. I didn't expect that to be your answer. Go you."

Kirby continued to smile as she loaded her stuff into her bag and zipped it closed.

"And it's more than hooking up," Lark went on. Kirby could feel her eyes boring into her like they were trying to read her brain through her skull. "Wow. This is unexpected."

"How come?"

"I mean…" Lark shrugged. "It's just been a while since…" Lark wrinkled her nose, then shook her head.

"I like her." Kirby said it matter-of-factly. Because it was a simple matter of fact. She liked Amelia. A lot. And yeah, maybe it had been a while since she'd felt more than sexual desire for somebody, but so what? It didn't mean she wasn't allowed to. It also didn't mean that what she felt for Amelia was anything beyond that.

"You're thinking really, really hard," Lark said, busting in on her train of thought and shoving it off the rails. "Are you guys a thing?"

Were they?

That was a damn good question.

They'd had sex after their date on Monday. They'd had sex last night—though Kirby had gone home after. Would she go back to Victor's with her later? Would they have sex tonight? She didn't know—they hadn't made plans. They hadn't really talked about anything beyond whatever day it was at the time. And there was an element of relief around that for Kirby.

At the same time, though, did she want some set parameters? She never had before, but for some reason she felt…She searched for the word. *Untethered.* That was it. She felt untethered all of a sudden. And she didn't like it.

Since she didn't have an answer for Lark, she smiled and shrugged and said nothing.

"Mm-hmm," was Lark's response to that.

Thankfully, she didn't push, and less than half an hour later, they were in Martini's, drinking beer and reliving the game, just like they did every week. The cool bartender with the pink streak served their drinks and laughed with them. Chloe? Cleo? Something like that. The team laughed and joked and tipped her well. Kirby'd been with the same team for five years now, knew them well, loved playing with them, loved drinking with them. Everything was as it had always been for her on softball night. Amelia wasn't there. Which was normal, really. That's how it had been up until last week, right?

So why did it feel weird without her there? Why did she feel her absence so strongly?

Yeah, this was a lot.

Kirby gave her head a shake and did her best to stuff those

thoughts away and focus on the conversation around her. Softball. Yes. The game they'd just played.

And before she even realized she was doing it, she slid her phone out of her pocket and sent a smiling emoji to Amelia. That was it. Just a smile.

For no apparent reason.

❖

Amelia slid her phone back into her pocket.

"What's that grin?" Vanessa asked, pointing at her from across the table.

They sat around the kitchen table—her, Vanessa, Grace, Julia, and Savannah—in the house Vanessa now shared with Grace and, half the time, Grace's son Oliver. Vanessa's dog, Delilah, lay crashed out under the table, her chin on Amelia's foot.

"What grin?" she asked, knowing she was calling more attention to it, but unable to just let it go. She'd been unaware she was smiling until Vanessa pointed it out.

"The grin caused by whatever you just looked at on your phone," Vanessa said. "Was it the painter?"

"She has a name, you know." *Good job, Amelia, just give it away, why don't you?*

"An odd one. I've never known a Kirby before," Vanessa said, then glanced around the table. "Have you guys?"

Heads were shaken.

"Not me," Julia said. "But I think it's cute."

"The only time I've ever heard the name was on a character in one of the *Scream* movies." Grace was flipping through a binder filled with tablescapes. "Ooh, I like this one."

"I like the name," Amelia said quietly as they all leaned to see what Grace was pointing at.

"Me, too," Savannah said softly from next to her and bumped her shoulder. "I think it's cute."

They all agreed Grace should mark the page with a Post-it, and they moved on to other things.

"So, what's going on with you two?" Julia asked, not looking up from her laptop where she was scanning a wedding website, and her eyes went wide. "Holy crap, how are we supposed to choose from this many options? Should we hire a wedding planner?"

Savannah leaned toward her. "Sweetie, we don't have to look at them all. We find a few we like and just choose from those."

"But what if there are better ones, but we stop looking and don't get to them?" Julia asked.

"Then we'll never know, will we?" Savannah kissed her cheek as Julia shook her head and the others grinned at her.

"The amount of options for stuff is ridiculous," Julia muttered. Then, as if remembering where she'd left off, she fixed her gaze on Amelia. "You didn't answer me."

"What did you ask?" Amelia knew exactly what she'd asked but was trying to buy time because she honestly wasn't sure of the answer.

"Are you dating Kirby?" Vanessa chimed in. "Are you a couple?" There was no teasing tone, no snark, and when Amelia met Vanessa's eyes, they were filled with simple curiosity.

Amelia took in a deep breath. "You know, I'm not sure, to be honest." She looked to Savannah and grimaced.

Savannah closed her hand over Amelia's forearm. "Do you want to be dating her?"

"You know, I'm not sure, to be honest." And then she grinned.

"There you go," Grace said with a chuckle. "You gotta stay laughing, right?"

"I don't really know what else to do. It's all so weird." Amelia shrugged and reached for her glass of the pinot grigio they were all drinking. She took a sip, and it occurred to her then that if ever she was going to talk through this thing, these were the people to do it with. And before she could even *think* about thinking about it, she blurted, "I slept with her." When the gasps went all around the table and eyes widened, she held up two fingers and added, "Twice."

And then she couldn't contain her smile and tried to stuff it into the wineglass as she brought it to her lips and sipped and basked in the combination of laughter, surprise, and congrats that circled around the table.

"You're just now telling us?" Vanessa cried, trying to act insulted but laughing. "I can't believe it."

Amelia lifted one shoulder. "I needed to sit with it for a bit."

"And when did this event occur?" Julia asked, completely abandoning the website and focusing all her attention on Amelia.

"Monday. After our date."

"I knew that was the right dress," Grace said, clearly pleased with herself.

"It really was," Amelia agreed and stood to reach her glass across the table and touch it to Grace's. "Thank you for that."

"Anytime I can help you get laid by a cute girl, you just let me know," Grace said with a grin, and they sipped.

"And the second time was...?" Vanessa asked.

"Last night. After we had to clean paint off Victor's what I can only assume are crazy expensive hardwood floors."

More surprised gasps and wide eyes were all around the table, so Amelia told the story of the renegade dogs with paint on their paws. And found herself laughing. Not stressing. Not having heart palpitations as she relived it. But laughing. Her family noticed right away because who knew her better than they did?

"Look at you," Savannah said, pointing at her. "I haven't seen you this relaxed in a really long time."

"Agreed," Julia said with a nod. "And I'm still reeling over the fact that you got naked in front of somebody. I know you haven't exactly been feeling confident lately." Her tone was firm, but her eyes were soft, and Amelia knew she was stating facts, not trying to be an ass.

"It's really weird," Amelia said and tipped her head to the side. "But...she kinda gets it."

"What do you mean?" Grace asked.

"I mean, our first time was in the pool. At night."

"Oh my God, that's so sexy." Savannah slid down in her chair and sighed, making the others laugh.

"It was her suggestion," Amelia explained. "'Cause she knows I hate my body right now."

"She's heard your whining, too?" Julia asked, then winked to take the sting out.

"She has." And again, Amelia laughed.

"And the second time?" Vanessa asked.

"In the dark, under the covers. She hasn't actually *seen* me, really." Amelia shrugged.

"Yet," Vanessa said.

"To baby steps," Grace said and, again, reached her glass across the table to cheers with Amelia.

"I will so drink to that." Amelia touched her glass to Grace's.

"So, what happens tonight?" Vanessa asked. "I assume that text was from her?"

"It was. And I don't know. She had softball, and now she's at the bar, and she sent a smiley, and it was nice." She looked at her wine for a beat, then back up. "I don't know. We have no plans. That's okay, right?"

"Totally," Vanessa said. "Who says you have to have plans?"

"Have you met me?" Amelia said, and she laughed, but it held concern.

Savannah grabbed her forearm again. "Sweetie, you don't have to *do* anything. You know that, right?" When Amelia met her eyes, she went on. "You can just go from day to day and do whatever you want. You're a grown-ass woman. You don't have to label anything. You don't have to plan anything."

"Yeah, just relax and go with the flow," Julia added, opening her laptop back up.

"Oh, you mean like you did when you freaked out because Savannah was taking your focus off the bar?" Amelia turned to Vanessa. "Or the way you did when you freaked out because you fell for the mom of one of your students? That kind of relaxing and going with the flow?"

Silence reigned for a moment as the women around the table looked from one to another. Then, as if on cue, they all burst into laughter, which Amelia watched for exactly three seconds before joining in.

Then, like she was privy to the entire conversation, Kirby sent another text.

Can I see you tonight?

Amelia didn't hesitate and typed back immediately.

Victor's in an hour. And then she tacked on a smiley to mirror hers.

CHAPTER TWENTY-ONE

How had the weeks gone by so fast?

Kirby tried not to dwell on that as she painted the final room in Victor Renwick's house. The dogs were sleeping in the three season room, after making it very clear how unhappy they were that they couldn't be with her and help her paint. Amelia was working and was expected back before Kirby finished for the day.

This room was another one where she got to use her artistry. It was the front living room in Victor's house, and she wondered if he used it much. There was a chair rail on one wall, which he liked, but the wallpaper was hideous. She'd spent two days steaming it off, and then, instead of painting the wall all one color or putting up new wallpaper, she painted the bottom a solid color and painted a pattern on the top. So it looked like wallpaper but wasn't. Not diamonds this time, but big, thick stripes. Subtle colors. Champagne and just a shade lighter, so the stripes drew the eye because you weren't sure if you were actually seeing them or if they were a trick of the light. It was one of Kirby's favorite effects, though she rarely had a chance to create it.

As she rolled the opposite wall with the darker shade of champagne, her brain traveled, as it often did when she rolled. It was a task that was easy, and she'd done it so often, it was almost mindless for her. Which meant her brain could wander off to other things.

Lately, the only other thing on her mind was Amelia.

They'd fallen into a bit of a routine. And it was comfortable. They'd work, each going wherever they needed to. Kirby would check in with Krog and Coop or get supplies or meet with a new client and do an estimate. Amelia would volunteer at the shelter or walk her clients' dogs or check in on those that needed meds. She'd even had to meet a few new clients and do some estimates herself because Dogz Rule was taking off. But each of them would end her afternoon at Victor Renwick's house before Kirby would scoot off to whatever activity she had. Amelia would often accompany her or meet her later. They inevitably ended up back at Victor's to take care of the dogs, to maybe eat or have cocktails, to make out, undress each other, have sex.

The joys of having their own private pool were countless. She'd lost track of how many orgasms had been had in it over the past few weeks. She was definitely going to miss it.

That flutter low in her body—the one that had started after her first kiss with Amelia and had remained constant ever since—increased in its intensity as her brain tossed her an image of Amelia's head thrown back, the quiet whimper as she squeezed her eyes shut, the way her fingers dug into Kirby's shoulders.

"Jesus Christ," she whispered to the empty room, and she put the roller in the paint tray and coated it once more. Kirby'd had a good amount of sex in her life. She'd had girlfriends. She'd had flings. She'd had one-night stands. None of them compared to Amelia. There was something about the way they fit sexually. Their bodies. Their minds. It was like they each had a handbook detailing exactly what to do to the other for maximum pleasure. Being with Amelia was goddamned explosive, and Kirby was always, *always* left wanting more.

She'd never had that before.

And now, here she was, painting the last room in Victor's house. She'd be done today. This was her last Friday in this house. And Victor was due home tomorrow evening, so it was Amelia's last night here. Kirby would miss it all. The house, the pool, the dogs, the fantasy she and Amelia had created. Together.

She'd been trying all day not to let herself get depressed. The end of a job was a good thing. Finishing on time and under budget was fantastic. Good for business. And aside from the one hiccup that involved dogs with paint on their paws running through the house, everything had gone smoothly. The job had been a damn delight. What she wouldn't give to have them all be so clean and easy.

Yet Kirby was bumming hard.

Which was stupid. She gave her head a shake. "Come on, Kirbs. Cut it out."

She succeeded in concentrating on her work for a good seven minutes before her mind wandered some more. Right back to Team Amelia.

Kirby's mother had been gone since Kirby was twelve, and while she missed her every day, she was used to the absence. Today, though, she wished she was here simply so she could talk to her about what Amelia was going through. Not that her mom had been through it before she died, but she was certainly more educated on it than Kirby was. Menopause wasn't something she knew a lot about. Seriously, what woman who wasn't in it knew anything about it other than your periods stopped and it messed with you a bit? She wanted to ask her mother how she could help Amelia, what she could do for her, say to her, to get her to understand how beautiful and sexy and *vital* she was. She thought she was pretty good at showing her, but they couldn't spend their entire day in bed.

"Which really is too bad," Kirby muttered, then grinned, and kept rolling. Maybe the couple of books she'd ordered would help.

Her phone pinged an incoming text and when she took a look, the grin grew wider. Amelia.

Ur ears burning? she typed, then sent a flame emoji. *Was just thnkng bout u.*

Amelia's response came immediately and made her laugh out loud in the empty house. *And here I thought that was just a hot flash.*

Not this time!

The little dots bounced and bounced. Then stopped. Then started bouncing again. Finally, the message came through. *Shelter asked me to come back later cuz they're shorthanded, so I won't be back before you leave.*

Well, hell.

It wasn't like Kirby could stick around and wait for her because she had Frisbee golf that night, which Amelia knew. *I can come by later*, she typed.

More bouncing and stopping and bouncing. Kirby started to wonder if Amelia was having trouble deciding what to say, and she wondered why. Something felt off.

If you want.

"You should try to be less enthusiastic," Kirby muttered. Then she typed simply, *I want.*

K. Lock the door when you leave.

"Again. Killing me with the enthusiasm." Kirby promised to let the dogs out and lock up, then told her she'd text when she finished with her game and was having a quick drink with her pals. *Don't wanna miss our last night in paradise*, was how she finished the text, and when no reply immediately came, she sighed and slid the phone back into her pocket.

She'd never waited for any woman. Ever. She was always in control. Always had the steering wheel firmly in her hands. Always knew where things were going, how fast, when they'd reach their final destination. But with Amelia, she was the passenger, she was clueless about where they were going, and she had no idea how the hell she'd let that happen.

With a groan and a shake of her head, she picked up her roller and got back to work, doing her best to push thoughts of Amelia into a corner for later.

She failed miserably.

❖

Little by little all week, Amelia had packed up some things and moved them home so that when she reached her last day at Victor's, she could simply pack her toiletries and a few leftover clothes and go without having to stuff her car the way her parents used to stuff her Christmas stocking.

"I'll miss this place," she said softly as she stood in the kitchen and popped the top on a can of Diet Coke. Stevie jolted awake at the sound and looked at her from where he was sprawled on the kitchen floor like a throw rug. It was hot today, and he'd decided in the AC was a better place to be than outside in the heat. Calvin did him one better and was lying on his stomach directly on top of the air vent. Panting. "I will miss you guys, too," she said with more conviction as she squatted down to love on Stevie.

Calvin watched her and looked honestly torn before finally pushing himself to his feet because getting love won out over keeping his belly cool.

She sat on the floor with the two of them for a long time, got herself comfortable and sat with her back against the cabinets.

"Your daddy will be home tomorrow," she told the dogs as their tails wagged and she petted them, fondled their ears, let them lick her face. "He's gonna be so happy to see you both. And I'm going to tell him what good boys you've been." The wagging tails were giving her life, and she felt her spirits lift a bit.

She didn't know how much time passed before she finally pushed herself to her feet. It was time to feed the boys. And herself. She'd barely eaten all day because, duh, a lot on her mind.

Okay, one thing on her mind. Kirby. Kirby on her mind.

Some people stress-ate. Amelia was a person who stress-starved. She carried all her nerves, stress, worry, and concern in her stomach, so when any of those things kicked up to high gear, she couldn't eat.

She'd had a banana all day. Oh, and coffee.

My stomach is eating itself, she thought. It was what Vanessa always said when she was overly hungry, and both Amelia and Julia had adopted it.

She took her last Lean Cuisine out of the freezer and popped it into the microwave. She hadn't heard from Kirby about timing, and part of her wondered if Kirby had decided not to come over after all. It wasn't like Amelia had been excited or even inviting. The truth was, she really, really wanted to see Kirby. But also, she was really bummed that this was all going to be over.

But all good things come to an end.

Wasn't that how the saying went? It was certainly true in Amelia's life. And at forty-nine years old, she'd learned not to hold on to anything wonderful too tightly because it was going to leave her sooner or later. It always did. Her mom. Her job. Her marriage. Her house. Soon, Kirby would be added to the list.

It was life.

It was inevitable.

The microwave beeped, and she moved her mac and cheese to a plate, then called the dogs to sit outside with her. It might have been hot, but it was her last evening of pretending she had a large, expensive house and a custom-designed pool, and she was going to take advantage of it, goddamn it. Finding a spot under the umbrella, she sat, both dogs parking themselves at her feet, and she looked out at the water while she ate.

The quiet was good. Peace was hard to come by, but Amelia felt a sliver of it as she ate her dinner and listened to the water lapping against the sides of the pool. Letting go always brought her peace, even though she often sucked at it.

Two hours later, she was in the water, and peace was the farthest thing from her mind because her entire brain was taken up by the toe-curling orgasm she was in the midst of. She held on to Kirby, dug her fingers into the flesh of Kirby's shoulder, buried her face in the crook of Kirby's neck as she whispered her name.

Coming back to herself, she lifted her head to find Kirby smiling at her, and God, those eyes, that face, the way Kirby held her. She felt safe, and she couldn't remember the last time she had.

But the fantasy had to end sometime.

"What time does Victor get back tomorrow?" Kirby asked, her voice soft, as if she was also thinking about the end.

"His flight comes in around five. I'll stick around until early afternoon and then head back to my place."

"It'll be weird not being here," Kirby said, her voice wistful, "acting like it's ours."

"I know." She continued to hold on to Kirby, even as her brain told her she should start to let go.

"But I'm looking forward to seeing your place and showing you mine."

Amelia blinked at her. "What?"

"I mean, my house is about a third the size of this one, but it's cute."

More blinking. And then Amelia grabbed Kirby's face with both hands and kissed her. Hard. Spun them around so Kirby was against the side of the pool, and Kirby let out a soft, "Oof," as Amelia pushed into her. She was suddenly rabid. Couldn't get enough. Hands everywhere, tongue deep in Kirby's mouth. She tugged at fabric, pulled, then yanked until Kirby was naked. The night had gone dark, and the blue lights of the pool were on, and Kirby was backlit and gorgeous and so fucking sexy, Amelia almost couldn't deal with it. She looked into those green eyes and mentally told Kirby exactly what she thought. And watched Kirby's eyes darken with desire.

She would do just about anything to see that happen. To be the cause of it. To have Kirby quietly beg her like she was now. To hear her whisper, "Please…"

Fingers sank into the warm wet of Kirby's body, and that little gasp she made just spurred Amelia on. She set up a rhythm, slowly, so slowly, in and out until Kirby's breathing was ragged and her head rolled from side to side. Her legs tightened around Amelia's waist, heels pressed into the small of her back, and Jesus, Mary, and Joseph, it was the most amazing feeling in the world.

Amelia picked up the pace. Just a little.

Kirby moaned loudly enough that Stevie lifted his head from under the table where he lay, and Amelia smiled at him before speeding up a little bit more.

Kirby was biting her bottom lip now, her eyes squeezed shut, and when she leaned her head back on the concrete, Amelia took advantage and ran her tongue from Kirby's collarbone to her chin.

"You're killing me, Amelia," she whispered, and then another moan. "Killing me. Please."

"Please what?" Amelia asked, stilling her fingers.

"God," Kirby cried out. "Finish me. *Please*."

"Your wish is my command," Amelia said on a whisper. This time, she didn't temper her pace. She pushed into Kirby, then pulled out, then pushed back in firmly, her rhythm quicker, and it only took a handful of seconds before Kirby's orgasm hit, tearing a super sexy cry from her throat. Amelia winced as she felt Kirby's nail break skin somewhere on her back, but she didn't care. She loved it. She loved that she'd have a physical mark tomorrow. Proof of what they'd done.

When Kirby came back to herself and opened her eyes, they said nothing to each other. Just stared. Held gazes and bodies and stood there, submerged in the shallow end of the pool in the dark of the night. There were so many words in Amelia's head then. So very many. She had a feeling there were things Kirby wanted to say, too, but they continued to half stand, half float, and held each other quietly.

Eventually, they got out of the pool and headed to bed where they made love into the wee hours of the morning.

The last time Amelia looked at the clock, it was 3:26. Her body was wrapped around Kirby, their legs a tangle of limbs, torsos pressed together, Amelia's head pillowed on Kirby's chest. The steady, even rise and fall of that chest told Amelia Kirby'd fallen asleep. She snuggled in. Burrowed close. Let herself get lost in the smell of Kirby. The feel of her. The warmth of her skin. The firmness of her arm around Amelia's back. Kirby was smaller than she was but definitely took on the role of protector when they slept, which Amelia found endearing and—once again—it made her feel safe. Secure. Looked after. The last time she'd felt that way was... When? Ever? Had she ever felt that way?

She angled her head slightly, just enough so she could see Kirby's profile as she slept. The small, straight nose, the sandy color of her hair, the whorls of her ear with the sparkling stud in it that was likely a small diamond. The strong chin with the dimple. The long column of neck. She was going to miss her.

Stop being stupid.

The voice was in her head, but it wasn't hers, and that made it even weirder. It was Vanessa's, and Amelia almost laughed out loud when she heard it. Didn't it figure that the voice of her subconscious would be one of her cousins'? Unbelievable.

Stop being stupid, it said again, and it was now 3:40, and she really, really needed to sleep.

Yeah, okay. She'd stop being stupid for now.

She snuggled back in.

CHAPTER TWENTY-TWO

When Amelia woke up Saturday morning, she was alone in the bed and Kirby was gone. She knew before she opened her eyes. The bed was huge and she could feel the empty expanse of it before she even looked. Of course. What did she expect? Forever? A marriage proposal? The fantasy was over. It had ended, as she knew it would, and that was okay. She'd deal.

She opened her eyes and rolled onto her back. Stared at the ceiling and sighed. This was expected. She wasn't surprised.

Was she?

She gave her head a literal shake because who was she kidding? This was how it was always going to go. Fine. She needed to pack up the rest of her stuff. She'd told Victor she'd hang around with the dogs until early afternoon before heading home.

The dogs.

She didn't hear them. They usually waited for her to get up before they left the bedroom—if they didn't wake her up first. But she sat up—whoops, still naked—and clutched the sheet to her chest as she scanned the room. No dogs.

She made a move to get out of the bed, and that's when Calvin came bounding in, all happy, tongue lolling. Wide awake as he jumped up onto the bed and lavished her with kisses. Not sleepy.

Not to be outdone, Stevie followed, and soon, she was being lovingly mauled by two canines, and her worries and disappointment were shoved aside, even if it was only for a few minutes.

"Well, that's quite a pile of love." It was Kirby's voice, and it was a surprise, and everything in Amelia's body tightened pleasantly at the sound of it. God, she had no faith, did she?

Peeking around furry bodies, she blurted exactly what was on her mind. "You're still here."

"Of course I am. Where did you think I was?"

"Gone. Somewhere else?" Amelia grimaced at the needy tone in her voice.

Kirby's brow furrowed adorably as she stepped all the way into the room, two mugs of coffee in her hands that Amelia could now smell. How had she not smelled it brewing? The scent was so strong and glorious right then. "Somewhere else? Why would I go somewhere else, you weirdo? What were you thinking?"

"I was thinking it was fun while it lasted." Amelia wrinkled her nose and took the mug Kirby handed her as she sat on the edge of the bed, then scooted closer to Amelia so her back was propped against the headboard.

"It can keep lasting, you know," Kirby said quietly.

Amelia swallowed. Looked at the ceiling. Tried to find words for her thoughts. A wave of her hand encompassed the enormous suite they occupied. "I don't have this and neither do you. I don't have a pool. Or a huge private yard. Or a gourmet kitchen. And I'm guessing you don't either. Don't you think it'd be like...going from fantasy to reality? Kind of a rude awakening?"

"You mean like on *The Bachelorette*?" Kirby's face held the traces of a grin. Why wasn't she taking this seriously?

"Yes! Exactly like that."

"I happen to like that show. Don't judge me."

Amelia gave her a look. "Of course you do. It never works. Those couples never survive."

Kirby held up a finger. "Not true. Some of them do." Her face did grow serious then. Finally. "Don't you want to see where this goes?" She waved a finger between them. "See what happens?" The serious face blossomed into a grin. "'Cause I sure do."

Oh God. She did. She absolutely did want to see. But the fear? The fear was so fucking real, she could feel it paralyzing her. She blinked, swallowed, but had trouble with words. And then her entire body began to heat up, like somebody flicked a switch in her chest, and the heat just bloomed out from there until her entire face was clammy, and she felt a bead of sweat running down her ribcage.

"I do." She nodded. "I do."

"Well, you're certainly glowing," Kirby said, reaching out a hand. She stroked her thumb over Amelia's cheek.

"Yeah, that's a hot flash. I'm having a hot flash right now."

"That must be super uncomfortable," Kirby said, and then she shocked Amelia silly by adding, "What about black cohosh? It's a supplement that I've read has helped a lot of women with their hot flashes."

Amelia blinked at her. It was all she could do. Kirby didn't make fun of her. Didn't roll her eyes. Her face didn't glaze over like she'd checked out. No. She offered a suggestion. She'd been reading up on it. Sweet baby Jesus, Amelia had never been more attracted to somebody in her entire freaking life.

"Come to my house for dinner," Kirby said before Amelia could jump on her and ravish her.

More blinking. A moment to think.

"I will, on one condition," Amelia said, arching an eyebrow.

Kirby tipped her head. "What's that?"

"That you take your clothes off. Right now."

❖

OMG, I can't believe ur doing this!

The text from Katie was followed by several heart emoji, which made Kirby grin.

It's just dinner, she typed back.

She was at her own house now, having left Victor's house later than planned due to Unexpected Orgasm. That's how she thought of it in her head. With capital letters. Amelia had requested she undress, and what was she going to do, say no? Kirby Dupree was a lot of things, but stupid wasn't one of them. She'd stripped in record time and found herself on her back in the enormous bed, Amelia's tongue doing terribly erotic things between her legs until her thighs quaked, and her fingers gripped a handful of Amelia's hair, and she begged her for release. *Begged.*

Amelia had obliged, and Kirby was pretty sure she'd blacked out for a few seconds, the climax was so intense.

This woman. Jesus Christ, this woman.

U nvr have women to ur place, Katie texted, and she wasn't wrong. Well, never might've been a slight exaggeration, but very slight. Kirby stayed busy. She liked to be out and about. Her home was her sanctuary. *Her* sanctuary. She didn't share it. With anybody.

Until now.

That's the effect Amelia Martini had on her. She wanted to be around her, yes. But she wanted more than that. She wanted to share things with her. Thoughts and dreams and she wanted her to be here, in her house. To know what it meant to her to have Amelia there.

But would that freak her out?

It might. That was the truth. It was a definite possibility. Amelia wasn't exactly on solid ground right now. Easily freaked would be an understatement.

Well, maybe it's time I did, she typed back to Katie.

Katie's response came back instantly. *MAYBE IT IS, KIRBY ANN.* The capital letters made Kirby laugh out loud. Then came, *Update me when you can. 2nite. Or maybe 2morro cuz ur gonna be busy n I don't want u texting me while ur n8kd.*

She signed off with Katie, still chuckling, glad she'd told her, but also a teeny bit worried about jinxing things. Which was stupid. She wasn't superstitious, but she also wasn't dumb, and she knew things with Amelia were…delicate. That was a good word. And delicate was not something Kirby usually ventured to explore. No, delicate was dicey. Delicate could be dangerous. Delicate was certainly not a sure thing.

But Amelia drew her.

That was the only way to explain it, and God, had Kirby tried. Because it was weird, right? The tug. The pull. Since the moment she'd laid eyes on Amelia the first time, way back last year when

Martini's had first opened and Amelia had been sitting at the bar alone, all Grumpy McGrumperson, criticizing the color choice, she drew her. It was a pull she couldn't figure out, so instead of fighting it, she'd decided maybe going the other way was the better choice. Embracing it. Letting herself be pulled.

And now here she was, cleaning like a tornado, polishing pieces of furniture that hadn't seen a dust cloth in weeks. Okay, that was a lie. Months. She hadn't dusted in months. But her living room practically sparkled now. There was chicken marinating in the fridge and a bottle of wine chilling in an ice bucket on the counter. She had the ingredients for strawberry fucking shortcake, for God's sake.

Because Amelia Martini was coming over for dinner.

"I have completely lost my fucking mind," she muttered as she stood in the middle of the living room with her hands on her hips. And then she smiled. Big.

Because Amelia Martini was coming over for dinner.

Two hours later, she was showered and dressed in a cute pair of denim shorts and a white tank, her feet bare, her hair air drying. She pulled the chicken from the fridge and took it out of the marinade, set it on the cutting board, then diced up potatoes, and coated two red peppers in olive oil. She was just sprinkling salt and pepper on them when her doorbell rang.

"She's here." She said the words aloud, then gave a full-body shake because the nerves! Oh my God, the nerves had kicked in so intensely, and she didn't get it. She'd slept with this woman many times already. This wasn't a first date. Wasn't even a fifth date. It had been weeks. They'd spent time together for weeks now.

The nerves didn't care. They cranked themselves up to eleven.

At the front door, she put her hand on the knob, inhaled, blew it out, and pulled the door open.

Amelia stood there in a mint-green sundress with spaghetti straps. Time at Victor's pool had deepened her tan, and Kirby only just now realized that. Her olive skin was glowing, smooth, and the sun had brought out freckles that were sprinkled across her shoulders. She had her light hair in a casual ponytail, and she carried two bottles of wine.

Quite simply put, she stole all the air from Kirby's lungs.

"Hi," Amelia said, then stepped inside and quickly kissed her on the mouth.

The peace that settled over Kirby was foreign. Totally foreign. In a way she couldn't even begin to comprehend, she felt like she was exactly where she was supposed to be, with exactly who she was supposed to be with.

And she wasn't about to question it.

❖

Amelia wasn't sure what she expected—a studio apartment? a dorm room? a frat house feel?—but it wasn't this adorable little Cape Cod on a quiet tree-lined street. It wasn't the pots of geraniums in reds and whites on the front steps. It wasn't the sheer tidy adorableness of the house. That was when she realized she'd been projecting her own opinions and expectations onto Kirby, and they didn't fit. At all.

The denim shorts and white tank? Yeah, *those* fit. Perfectly. Teasingly. They were simple and sexy and so very Kirby. The bare feet and the still-damp hair only added to the appeal. And don't get her started on how good Kirby smelled. Soft, like baby powder and the summer sun.

Once inside, she held up the wine. "I wasn't sure what we were having, so I brought a pinot noir and a sauvignon blanc."

"You didn't have to do that," Kirby said, taking both and heading toward what Amelia assumed was the kitchen. "Marinated chicken breast. I hope that's okay. I'm going to grill it."

"That sounds fantastic." Her eyes took in the chicken, and she watched Kirby's hands as she put them on a plate to take outside.

"Good." Kirby reached for a bottle of wine that was submerged in a bucket of ice. "I'm not super well-versed at wine and food pairing, but my friend Lindsay works at a wine bar, and she suggested this one."

"If it's in a glass next to my plate, it pairs with my food as far as I'm concerned," Amelia said, and it made Kirby laugh. Yeah, that was fun, making Kirby laugh.

Amelia looked around the kitchen, which had clearly been updated, as it had a deep farmhouse sink and brushed nickel hardware on the white cabinets. "This is beautiful."

"Thanks." Kirby looked around, too. "I remodeled it two years ago with the help of a couple of my buddies who are in construction. The house was built in the seventies, and the kitchen screamed that out loud." She poured the wine. "I'm talking dark cabinets and orange countertops. *Ugly.*" Sliding a glass to Amelia, she held hers up. "Wow, that's pretty. I'd name this color Here Comes the Sun, 'cause it looks like the rays of sunshine first thing in the morning."

"Perfect." She grinned. It really was a gorgeous color, not quite champagne, but not dark enough to be considered any kind of yellow. The label said it was a sauvignon blanc, and when Kirby lifted her glass to toast, she did, too.

"To reality and how wonderful it will be."

Amelia tipped her head and gave a slight squint, but touched her glass to Kirby's anyway.

"What, you don't think it will?" Kirby sipped and her focus moved to the wine. "Holy crap, that's good."

"I don't think what will what?"

"You don't think reality will be wonderful?"

"My reality hasn't been wonderful in quite a while," Amelia said. Without thinking, obviously, and when the flash of ouch zipped across Kirby's face, she held up her hand and did her best backpedaling dance. "No, I didn't mean us. Not at all. We've been great."

"Well, that's the reality I mean. Duh." Kirby set her wine down. She flipped a dish towel over her shoulder, grabbed a bowl of what looked like seasoned potatoes out of the fridge, and picked up the plate of meat. "Time to grill," she said, which Amelia took as an invitation to follow her, so she did.

If the front of Kirby's house was colorful and inviting, the backyard was a full-blown oasis. Not large by any means, but totally lush, relaxing, and private. The fence was high and that brown color that leaned almost toward rust, but not enough to think of it as any kind of orange. Flowers lined one side, bookended by a rosebush close to the deck and what looked to be a tall lilac bush in the back corner. The center rectangle of lawn was bright green, the grass clearly healthy and well-tended. The deck wasn't large, but it was made of two levels. Coming out of the house, to the right were three steps up to the grill and a small round table with four chairs and a green-and-white striped umbrella, closed now. To the left in the corner sat a small hot tub, steadily humming.

"Wow." It was the first thing that came to Amelia's mind, and it shot right out of her mouth. And it was perfect. "This is amazing."

Kirby looked up from the grill. "You like it? My dad was really particular about his yard." She gave a chuckle as she raised the lid to the grill. Amelia joined her on that level and peered over her shoulder at the metal frying pan filled with holes. Kirby poured the potatoes into it. There were also two glistening red peppers that went directly onto the grates. "Didn't matter how busy he was at work—he always found time to take care of the yard. I don't think it was work to him. I think it was how he decompressed. You know?"

Amelia did. "My uncle John decompresses by making homemade limoncello."

"That is a fun uncle," Kirby said with a laugh.

"He is. Vanessa's dad."

Kirby pointed with her tongs. "So, my dad put in the lilac bush and the rosebush for my mom. Those flowers in between? I plant those every year. Dad built the deck. I added the hot tub last year."

"Are we getting in that later?" Amelia asked, surprising herself.

"I mean, we're very good in water," Kirby said with a casual shrug. "I think we've proven that."

"About a dozen times."

Their gazes held, and just like that, the tension from earlier slipped away, evaporated like mist.

Kirby cleared her throat, slapped the chicken onto the grill, then set everything down and grabbed Amelia's face with both hands. She looked deep into her eyes for a moment, so deep that

Amelia felt like she was reading every private thought she'd ever had with no effort at all, as if she could see them all that clearly.

Then came the kissing.

Soft. Wet. Hot. So goddamn hot. Seriously, had Kirby gone to some kind of kissing school? Where they taught the ins and outs of perfect kissing? And if she had, did she graduate valedictorian? Because that would make total sense.

Thank God Kirby had to pull away in order to tend to the grill because if they kissed any longer, Amelia's legs weren't going to hold her. Weak in the knees was a real damn thing when it came to Kirby and kissing. As it was, she had to reach out a hand to steady herself on the nearby table. Jesus.

"I just needed to get that out of the way," Kirby whispered once she'd finally pulled back from Amelia's mouth. Had it been five minutes? A year? Amelia had no idea. All she could do was nod. Kirby turned back to the grill where she picked up her tongs and flipped the chicken.

Amelia sat on a nearby chair, that weak-in-the-knees feeling back in full force. Of course, not two minutes later, she felt the switch in the center of her chest flick, and suddenly, she was overheating. Sweat beaded on her upper lip, and the back of her neck became damp.

"I'd love to think my kissing made you all dewy," Kirby said with a smile, "but I'm guessing that's a—"

"Hot flash," Amelia said, nodding, before Kirby could finish.

"Thought so," Kirby said as she moved the peppers and then shook the pan of potatoes. "So...I've been reading up on menopause."

"Still?" Amelia's surprise was clear in her voice because really? "How come?"

Kirby looked at her, brow furrowed. "Because I want to understand how you're feeling," she said, and Amelia heard a very clear but unspoken *duh* at the end of that sentence.

"Oh." More surprise.

"So, what does it feel like?" Kirby closed the lid on the grill and turned to face Amelia, who picked up her wine and took a large sip.

"Are you gonna make fun of me?" Amelia asked. "Mock me? Tell me I'm crazy based on what you've learned?"

Kirby's eyes widened. "No, of course not. Why would you think that?"

"Because that's the most common response I've gotten anytime I try to talk about how I'm feeling." She felt her face heat up, ashamed that she sounded so whiney. More wine, please.

Kirby came to her then. Took three steps and spanned the distance between them and squatted down so they were eye level. She put warm hands on Amelia's knees. "I just want to understand," she said quietly, and the sincerity in her green eyes almost brought tears to Amelia's. "I want to understand how somebody I've grown to care very much about has been feeling, so I know what I can do to help her."

Wow. Amelia blinked at her. Took in her words. Then she cleared her throat and did her best to explain it to Kirby. "I have never felt so uncomfortable in my own skin," she said. "I don't feel like myself anymore." The more she spoke, the more she wanted to speak. She put both hands on her stomach. "I don't know where this came from. It just showed up one day, and it won't leave, no matter how much I exercise or how little I eat. I can't sleep because the hot flashes wake me up in the middle of the night." She looked back up at Kirby, who got points because she was actually listening. "I cry at the drop of a hat. I am *not* a crier. And I have zero patience. For anybody. Zero. Get out of my way and leave me alone. That's my attitude lately."

"Except for with me," Kirby said with a mischievous grin.

"Except for with you, it seems." Amelia smiled. She couldn't help it.

"Well." Kirby kissed her forehead as she pushed herself to standing. "That all sounds horrific, and I'm really sorry you're dealing with it." She opened the grill and took things off. "Are there things I can do?"

"What do you mean?"

"For you. Are there things I can do to help you when you feel bad?"

Amelia blinked at her again. Because holy crap, nobody had

ever offered that. Not Tammy. Certainly not Tammy. Not Julia. Not even Vanessa. And then, to her horror, but not her surprise, her eyes welled up. Kirby glanced at her and then dropped everything she was doing and squatted back down. Her hands returned to Amelia's knees.

"Oh, baby, what? I'm sorry. What did I say wrong?" And the clear apology in her voice made Amelia want to sob.

She shook her head and smiled through the threat of tears. "Nothing. You said nothing wrong. You said everything exactly right, which nobody has done since my body decided to start on this hellish journey."

Kirby wrapped her up then. Just put her arms around Amelia and held her tight. Amelia forced herself not to sob, but she wanted to. She wanted to cry in relief and sorrow and anger and gratitude, but that was so much to put on Kirby. So much.

But the hug? To be held? Cradled? Comforted the way Kirby was comforting her now? That was what she needed. When these inexplicable shots of emotion hit? A hug. Some understanding. Not to be mocked. That was what she needed. That was all she needed.

When she finally felt better and pulled back so she could look at Kirby, all she saw in her eyes was affection. "Thank you," she said quietly.

"For giving you a hug? Listen, that's as good for me as it is for you."

"Oh, I don't know about that." She noticed Kirby was still squatting and had to silently give props to Kirby's job. Amelia's legs would've been on fire by then. But Kirby simply pushed herself to her feet, and Amelia made sure to appreciate her quads as she did so.

"Hungry?" Kirby asked.

"God, yes."

Kirby's eyes honest-to-God twinkled, and she waggled her eyebrows, which made Amelia laugh. "Follow me then, sexy."

CHAPTER TWENTY-THREE

August was so fucking hot.

Amelia was walking Arnold, a West Highland white terrier, a new client's dog. And she adored him. He was sweet and playful and curious. Totally fun to walk, even if he did stop to sniff every single tree. Every. Single. Tree.

Except for days like today when it was eighty-nine degrees with eighty-seven percent humidity. Even now, well into the evening, it was like walking through water. Slogging was a better word for it. Poor Arnold was slow, looking up at her occasionally as if to ask, "Why are we doing this again?" as his pink tongue lolled out, attempting to cool his little tank of a body.

"I'm with you, buddy," Amelia said down to him as they turned the final corner on their jaunt and headed back to his house.

Business had steadily increased. She'd picked up three new clients just in the last three weeks, and they'd all come from word of mouth. Her father was always telling her that was the best advertising, that if somebody liked your work enough to recommend you to a friend, somebody who trusted them, that was the highest compliment you could get. She was now beginning to understand what he meant.

That being said, her business hadn't grown so much that she could support herself without her pension. And being in her father's house helped. The mortgage was paid off, and her father wouldn't take rent from her, but she was paying the utilities and such while he was down south. He wouldn't let her pay the taxes on it either, but if he was going to stay in Florida all year round and not come home for the summer anymore, which it was starting to look like, she'd need him to let her pay the taxes until she figured out what to do about her living situation.

They reached Arnold's house, and both of them breathed a sigh of relief to be back in the blessed air-conditioning. Arnold slurped down half a bowl of water, then fell over sideways on the kitchen's tile floor like he'd been shot. Amelia stared at him and had a moment of jealousy because that tile was probably super cool and felt good on his overheated skin, and the idea of lying down next to him was awfully tempting. Instead, she grinned, squatted down, and gave him pets on his little chubby belly. She left a note for Arnold's dad, a young gay guy who worked in IT who was a friend of her cousin Dante and was working late, and locked up the house. In her car, her phone pinged a text and her heart kicked at the name on her screen.

Tammy.

We got an offer! Call me asap!

Well, damn. It wasn't fast, but it still felt like it was. Realistically, Amelia knew the house would sell. It was in a great neighborhood, and the housing market was out of control. High demand, low supply. And yet, she was still caught off guard, which was her own stupid fault. She should've been ready for this the second the Realtor's sign went into the ground out front. Should have prepared herself adequately. Clearly, she hadn't, because her eyes welled up as she put the phone down and sat in her running car in Arnold's driveway. It took a few minutes to pull herself together, and then she called.

"Hey," Tammy said, and would there ever be a time when hearing that voice didn't make her heart swell and her head think of home? Amelia forced herself not to get sappy, not to fall back toward Tammy. "It's a great offer," Tammy went on, her voice annoyingly cheerful. "Finally! Isn't that fantastic news?"

Okay, that helped, because Amelia now wanted to punch her in the throat. "Yeah. Fantastic."

"You don't sound happy. I thought you would be, given your life now." She knew Tammy well enough to know the different tones of her voice. This one was *I'm attempting to sound supportive, but really, I'm just being a little snarky.*

"What does that mean, *given my life now?*"

"I mean having a whole house to yourself. Dating somebody *way* younger than you. Sounds like you're doing great." Again, her tone and words didn't exactly match. And what the hell? How did she know her dad wasn't home yet? How did she know about Kirby? As if reading her mind, Tammy added, "I saw Jessie the other day."

And then Amelia remembered Jessie running into her and Kirby at Napoli's over dinner. *I knew she seemed way too happy to see me.* Jessie had obviously been thrilled to have gossip to share.

"Anyway," Tammy went on, not waiting for a response. "I emailed you the offer. It's a great one, and I think we should accept it."

"I'm sure you do," Amelia said, not bothering to keep the edge out of her voice. "I'm on my way somewhere, so I'll take a look at it as soon as I can." Maybe she was being unnecessarily difficult, but too damn bad. Tammy certainly hadn't taken her feelings into consideration when she'd started seeing somebody else. Or when she'd decided to end their marriage. Or when she'd announced she thought they should sell the house. So now? Tammy could fucking wait. "I'll let you know." And then she did something she'd never done before to her ex-wife. She hung up on her while Tammy was speaking.

And *O-M-G* did it feel good.

If she hadn't already had plans to meet her cousins at The Bar Back, she'd have made some right then. She steered her car in the right direction, and within fifteen minutes, she was parked in the Martini's parking lot and knocking on the side door to the building.

"Hey," Vanessa said with a grin as she let her in and kissed her cheek as she passed.

"We got an offer on the house already." She wasted no time blurting it out. Julia was, as usual, behind the practice bar likely mixing up something new. Savannah was in her pink scrubs with panda bears on them, clearly coming directly off a shift at the pediatrician's office where she was a nurse. Grace was scrolling on her phone and looked up from the couch where she sat with her ankles crossed on the coffee table. The whole gang was there, and the relief at the sight of them made Amelia's eyes well up.

God, she was a fucking waterworks lately.

Also, she used the word *fucking* way more than she used to now. Even just in her head.

"Oh, sweetie, I'm sorry." Vanessa wrapped her arms around Amelia from behind. The others made similar sounds, spoke similar sentences, and they ended up a living, breathing blob of limbs in the center of the room, all five of them in a big group hug.

Once they disentangled themselves, Amelia gave a humorless laugh. "I don't know why I'm so upset. It's not like I didn't think it would sell."

"Is it at least a decent offer?" Savannah asked, her voice gentle as always.

With a sigh, Amelia told them, "I don't know. Tammy emailed it to me, but I hung up on her before she could tell me."

"Tammy can fucking wait," Julia muttered from back behind the bar, and Amelia had never loved her more.

Vanessa took her hand and led her to the bar where they each perched on a stool. "Maybe this is a good thing. The final closure you need, you know?" Her eyes were kind, and her voice was soft, and she was totally right. Amelia knew that. She even nodded, but it wasn't enough to keep the tears at bay.

They spilled over, and in the next moment, she was crying. Goddamn it.

Another group hug, but this one quiet, as if the girls were allowing her to let it out without interruption.

Closure. That's what it was. That's exactly what it was. It wasn't like she had any reason at all to ever think she and Tammy would get back together. And she didn't want that. She was no longer in love with Tammy—she didn't even love her as much anymore. But this was really, truly the end of the relationship. With the house gone, there would be nothing else tying her to Tammy. And while that was ultimately a good thing, the best thing, it was still a very bold period at the end of a very important chapter in her life.

It was done.

So she cried for that.

When the group hug broke for the second time, they all stayed quiet for a long moment. Julia slid a drink in front of Amelia, something red on the bottom and orange on the top. She looked up at her cousin, who lifted one shoulder and said simply, "Tequila sunrise. To mark the beginning of the next, most wonderful, stage in your life."

Amelia smiled in gratitude, not trusting herself to speak, 'cause enough tears already. She lifted the glass to Julia, then sipped. It was sweet and refreshing and delicious.

"Speaking of the next, most wonderful stage," Grace said, "how are things with the painter?"

They all knew Kirby's name, but referring to her as *the painter* had stuck. Which meant, of course, that she would forever and always be *the painter*, even if Amelia ended up with her forever and always.

Which was a thought that was starting to creep into her brain every now and then. Trying to set up camp until Amelia chased it away like a bear protecting its forest.

"Things are..." She searched for the right word as the others waited, all eyes on her. She sighed in defeat. "Things are really good." And they were. They were taking it slowly. Well, as slowly as two people who'd slept together almost immediately could take it. "She's playing golf right now."

"Well, I don't know about the rest of you," Vanessa said, looking around at each face, "but I think it's time you started bringing her here."

Amelia's eyes went wide. "Here? To The Bar Back?" This was a big deal. The Bar Back was like a club. Like a society where you had to be approved by all members in order to join. Were her cousins saying they'd approved Kirby? She hadn't even known there'd been an application.

Julia nodded her agreement, and when Amelia made eye

contact with Savannah and Grace in turn, it was clear they both agreed with Julia.

"It's time. You guys are seeming more and more like a couple," Grace said. Vanessa nodded.

"Which means, you bring her. Be a couple here. With us." Savannah smiled at her.

Having Julia and Vanessa ask her to bring Kirby was one thing. But having Savannah and Grace say it was quite another. They both knew how important this group was. How the only people allowed into what she'd taken to thinking of as the inner sanctum of the people who meant the most to her were people who were going to stay.

And that was the big question, wasn't it?

Was Kirby going to stay?

"Okay," Amelia agreed. "She has Frisbee golf on Friday, and I know she and her friends like to mix up the bars they go to afterward. I'll see if she can come by…?"

"Thursday," Julia said. "It's karaoke night, and I will not want to be out there." She pointed toward the door that led to the actual bar, then clenched her teeth and made a face.

They all laughed in agreement.

"Okay. Thursday. I'll tell her." She finished her drink, then blew out a breath. "Well, I guess I'd better read the email and then make the call. Get the details."

"Yeah, but maybe call your dad first," Vanessa said. "Run it all by him."

"Good idea," Amelia said and pulled out her phone. Another big breath, then she said quietly to herself, "Let's finish out this chapter."

CHAPTER TWENTY-FOUR

Krog hated when they had a job with cathedral ceilings. Though he'd never admit it to anybody else, Kirby knew heights terrified him. But Krog was tough, thought of himself as kind of a badass, so it was a little tidbit that she kept to herself.

That meant, though, that she had to help him whenever they had a job with super high ceilings because he did not want to be on the scaffolding. He took care of the bottom half, and Kirby did all the high work. A decent trade-off, as she kind of liked being up high. Classic rock played in the background from the boom box Krog brought to every job site. Kirby joked that it was likely older than she was.

"Things going good with dog-sitter?" Krog asked. It was an innocent enough question, but also a bit out of the blue, and Kirby paused before answering.

"Yeah." She nodded, eyes on the wall where she was spreading Sunshine Meadow, a yellow that she would've named Yellow, It's Me. "They are. Real good, actually."

"You've been in a good mood lately."

Kirby stopped rolling. "Um, that implies that I'm not in a good mood normally, and we both know that's not the case, sir."

Krog kept his eyes on his work as he chuckled. "Fair enough. You've been in a *better* mood then."

She took a moment to absorb that before nodding her agreement. "I have."

"'Cause you're gettin' laid." A statement, not a question.

"There is that," Kirby said, then waggled her eyebrows at him down below.

This time, he did look at her. She could feel it. "It's more than that, though." She didn't respond to that, just kept painting. "You seem different."

"I do?"

"Yep." He was quiet, and just when Kirby thought that was the end of the discussion, he continued, "You're content. More relaxed."

"Huh." She let herself think about that. Was she more relaxed? Did she feel content because she was dating Amelia? "Well, it's certainly not because *she's* content and relaxed," she said with a laugh. "She's the opposite. She's worried and nervous and…" Her roller stopped, simply sitting against the wall as Kirby looked out into the middle distance of the room. "And unassuming and beautiful and very, very kind. Though she doesn't let a lot of people see that side of her."

"How come?"

"She's gone through a rough patch for a couple years, and I think she's afraid to let her guard down." Kirby blinked in surprise once the words were out. It was a perfect assessment, and she hadn't even thought about it.

"Aren't we all," Krog said with a snort. "You seein' her soon? Been a few days, yeah?"

It had. Three, as a matter of fact. Now that they didn't have to be in the same place for work, they'd had to shuffle schedules and make more of an effort. "She wants me to hang with her cousins tonight."

"Why're you nervous?" Damn Krog and the way he knew her so well. He was the only father figure she had, and he knew it and took the role seriously. Also, he could read her like a friggin' book.

"'Cause these are her people. She doesn't have siblings, but these cousins are like her sisters. I've met them, but I've never hung out with them."

"Big step, meeting the family."

It was, and she knew it. She'd accepted the invitation easily and enthusiastically. At first. "Very big. It's like...kinda solidify-ing, if that makes sense."

"Solidifying...?" Krog glanced up at her. "Like, you guys as a couple?"

"I guess? We haven't really talked about it. But that's what it feels like."

"You good with that?"

"Being a couple? I hadn't really thought about it." Lies. She knew it and so did he. She'd thought about it more than anything else lately.

"Uh-huh," was all Krog said, clearly letting her know he thought her answer was bullshit.

"I like her. A lot."

"Love her?"

"Wow, you don't pull any punches."

"Nope."

"I'm on my way. I think I will. Soon."

"Then go hang out with her peeps."

"Is it that simple?"

"Unless you decide to complicate it, yup."

"All right. I'm gonna sub for Lark's Thursday night softball team, but I'll go after that." She heard Krog stop painting before she saw it.

"Why would you do that?"

"Do what?"

"Sub for a softball team when your girl has asked you to meet her family." At Kirby's no response, Krog shrugged. "That's what it is, idiot. She wants you to meet the folks that are important to her. And your response is, *Okay, but after I play a game*? Get your head outta your ass, girl."

She would've barked a laugh if his words hadn't surprised her so much. And if they didn't have the tiniest bit of an edge. He was annoyed with her, that much was clear. And when she heard his evaluation of her actions, she kind of got it.

"Put yourself in her place." Okay, clearly Krog wasn't finished. "She's become important enough to you that you want to introduce her to the most important person in your life." With a flourish, he indicated himself. "*Moi*. And she says, *Sure, okay, but I'm gonna do some shopping first.* How would that make you feel?"

Kirby blinked at him as his example struck home. "Hell, Krog, you sure you're not a girl?"

He scratched at his beard and adjusted the blue bandanna tied around his head. Then he shrugged and said, "I'm not ashamed to be in touch with my emotions, Kirb-side." He went back to painting, and Kirby wasn't sure if she'd hurt his feelings, if he was done talking because he'd made his point, both, or neither. She loaded her roller as his words set up camp in her mind. He was right. If Amelia had made it clear Kirby was less important than a shopping trip—or a softball game—she'd be stung. "I'm used to moving," she said, surprised when the words left her mouth.

"I know," was all Krog said.

"It's what I do."

"I know," he said again. "'Cause if you stop, you have to think about stuff."

She dropped her hands. "Jesus Christ, Krog, when did you get a psychology degree? You're freaking me out up here."

"Tell me I'm wrong and I'll shut up." He continued to paint as if he hadn't just dared her to look closely at herself and her life. Bon Jovi was singing in the background about Tommy and Gina, and Kirby did not envy their troubles. She was stalling, of course. Thinking about Gina waiting tables kept her from honestly pondering Krog's words, and she knew it. So did he. "That's what I thought."

"I mean, is that bad?" she asked, moving to the right to roll some more.

"That you don't stop and analyze your life once in a while? I mean, it ain't *good*." He gave a nonchalant shrug, and it was like they were talking about coffee or the weather. "But that's how you've been pretty much your whole adult life."

Code for *since your father died*, she knew. And he wasn't wrong. Moving meant survival. Back then, staying busy had equaled making it to the next day. So again, he wasn't wrong. "All right," she said. "What should I be analyzing?"

Krog dropped his paintbrush arm to his side and looked up at her with a clear expression of *duh* on his face, but she stared back at him until he sighed. It was the mighty sigh that only a father figure could heave in exhaustion over the denseness of his offspring. "Do you want something more with this girl? That's what you should be analyzing." He gave a grunt as he went back to his wall. "But you already know that."

"Something more than—?"

"Fucking, Kirby. Something more than fucking." His frustration with her was clear. And surprising. He might as well have slapped her.

"Why the hell are you snarking at me?" she asked.

He set his stuff down then. Put his paintbrush down, turned down the volume on the radio, and stepped out into the center of the room so she could clearly see him. Hands parked on his hips, he waited until he had her full attention.

Kirby was technically Krog's boss, but she respected him like she would a parent. She listened to him. He could scold her. He was the only person in the world who could. She valued his opinion, and she knew this moment was big. She set her own roller down and turned to look at him fully, then sat down on the scaffolding, her legs hanging over the side.

"I don't want you to be alone," he said quietly. Interesting place to start was her first thought, and when she opened her mouth to make a smart-ass comment, he held up a hand as if shoving the words right back in. She clamped her mouth shut. "I couldn't love you more if you were my own kid," he said, looking down at his scuffed work boots speckled with dozens of different colors of paint. Krog wasn't an emotional guy, and he certainly didn't talk about feelings, so Kirby straightened up and paid attention. Okay, important stuff on its way. "And I promised your dad I'd look out for you when he was gone. I think I do a good job of watching but not interfering."

"You do," she said softly. It was the truth.

"For the most part, I keep my opinions to myself, let you do you, answer if you ask me for advice, but I don't boss you."

She nodded.

"But the past month and a half, two months?" He shook his bearded head, a gentle smile on his face. "I've never seen you this happy. You've been…light. If that makes sense. You've been goddamn radiant."

Radiant. Now that was a word. She smiled big. She couldn't help it.

"And it's clear why. It's this girl."

Krog was batting a thousand, that was for sure. She nodded some more.

"Now, I've watched you date. I've seen a lot of girls come and go. I've seen you happy." He paused, scratched at his beard. "But not like this."

She didn't need to give that any time to sink in because he was right. "Amelia's…yeah. She's definitely not like anybody I've been with. She brings out things in me that I'm not familiar with." She looked at Krog in surprise, as if the words had come out on their own, without her conscious thought.

"Yeah? Like what?" He folded his arms. Waited.

Concentrating hard, Kirby forced herself to think about it. Krog was asking, and it was a good question, and it deserved an answer. *She* deserved an answer. "Like…nurturing?" Her voice rose in a question because she'd never considered herself a nurturing person, and she said so to Krog. "She makes me want to take care of her, to make sure she's okay, to give her whatever she needs and that's…new." A nervous laugh bubbled up then. Because it *was* new. Kirby wasn't selfish, but having lost both parents so young, she'd had to learn to take care of herself, to put herself first because nobody else was going to. And now here she was, and Amelia came first.

The realization hit her like a board to the head, and she looked at Krog in wonder.

"That's it," she said to him. "Amelia comes first."

"Yeah?" Krog's smile grew. "And how does that feel?"

"I kinda like it," she told him. "I really do. Yeah, I'm always wondering where she is, what she's doing, how she's feeling, what does she need, even as I'm moving through my day."

"At warp speed," Krog added with an eye roll.

Kirby laughed through her nose. "At warp speed, yeah."

"So slow the fuck down and take it in," he said, and this time, there was an edge to his voice. Extra emphasis. A pleading she'd never heard. "Don't let this one pass you by, okay? This one feels...right."

"How do you know? You haven't even met her."

Krog snorted. "Yeah, don't get me started on *that*, or we're gonna be here awhile. But *you* feel right. Since her. Like this." He waved a hand up and down. "I think this is how you're supposed to be. So hold the fuck on to it. On to her. Screw subbing for the game. This girl wants you to hang out with the most important people in her life. *Screw the game.* You just said she comes first. So put her first. That's what I'm saying." He turned back to his stuff, picked up his paintbrush and added, "Thanks for coming to my TED talk."

She laughed as the music turned back up. Another old eighties song, this one about building a city. Krog began painting again.

Kirby sat there for a few more minutes, swinging her legs and soaking in the conversation they'd just had.

Slow the fuck down.

Amelia comes first, so put her first.

It was so simple. So clear and clean and easy, Kirby was almost embarrassed that it took Krog to make her see it.

"Ugh. Who knew I was such a melon?" she said quietly as she pushed herself to her feet.

"I did," came Krog's voice from beneath her. "Bona fide member of the forty-watt club. That's you."

"Ha ha. Very funny. You're hilarious. And your hearing is creepily accurate."

"Don't you forget it."

Kirby slid her phone out of her pocket and unlocked it to text Amelia. Because Krog was exactly right.

Hey, beautiful. Just thinkin bout u. Gonna skip the game. Rather b w u.

And a heart emoji. Send.

Kirby's smile was wide, she could feel it, and it stayed even after she went back to painting.

CHAPTER TWENTY-FIVE

Amelia responded to Kirby's text from earlier and seemed to be happy Kirby'd decided to skip the game and come directly to The Bar Back. But she hadn't heard from Amelia since.

She and Krog finished up for the day, pretty sure they could finish completely tomorrow, a day early. That always made clients happy. Getting their space back sooner than expected always brought joy. She headed home, showered, and changed, hoping denim shorts and a black tank were appropriate attire for officially hanging with cousins. It was hot as hell out, and covering any more of her body with fabric just wasn't happening.

Gonna head to the bar, she texted, and she noted it had been four hours without contact from Amelia. They were in that weird early part of a relationship, the part where they hadn't discussed being a thing, so Kirby was unsure of her boundaries. Was she allowed to be irritated by the lack of contact, the lack of response to her texts? 'Cause she was getting there. Was she allowed to be worried when she hadn't heard from Amelia in a while? Because she was there, too.

Amelia had to know Kirby was nervous, right? Maybe she'd changed her mind. Maybe she actually *didn't* want Kirby to hang with her and her cousins and just didn't know how to tell her.

Well, that'd be some bullshit right there. Kirby shook her head and decided, screw that, she was going anyway, and if Amelia had changed her mind, she could damn well tell her to her face.

She had just shifted her car into reverse to back down the

driveway when her phone rang showing Amelia's number. "About fucking time," she muttered as she put the car back into park and answered the line. "Hey," she said in greeting.

"Kirby?" Not Amelia's voice. "Hi, it's Vanessa. Amelia's cousin?" Serious tone. No preamble. Kirby's stomach roiled.

"Vanessa, hey. What's wrong?" Because she knew something was. "Is Amelia okay?"

"Um, yes. I mean, no, but yes." Vanessa cleared her throat. "Her dad died. She got a call a little while ago."

"Oh no. Oh my God." Kirby's eyes filled because she knew— she knew—what that call was like. Horrendous. Heartbreaking. Unbelievable. She'd received one herself, and her emotions had run the gamut. "Where is she?"

"She's here, at her house—"

"I'm coming over." There was no question. She was going. And Vanessa could argue with her or try to keep her at arm's length because she wasn't fam—

"I was hoping you'd say that." Vanessa's relief was clear.

"Be there in ten," Kirby said and clicked off. It took almost twenty minutes to get from her house to Amelia's, but she didn't care. She'd run red lights if she had to. Amelia needed her, and she was going to be there, no matter what.

She pushed against her chest with her fingers, rubbing that familiar ache, the one she hadn't felt in years now showing back up with a vengeance. It wasn't her loss, but it was Amelia's, so it might as well have been hers. She thought about Amelia, sitting, absorbing the fact that she was never, ever going to talk to her father again. Yes, Amelia was almost middle-aged, and Kirby had barely been out of her teens. It didn't matter.

The pain was the same.

And Amelia was feeling that pain. Right now.

Kirby swiped at the hot tears tracking down her cheeks and pressed the gas pedal a little harder.

❖

She parked crookedly. Too quickly. Screeched her brakes as she stopped. Kirby didn't give a fuck. All she wanted was to get to Amelia.

The front door of Amelia's house opened before she'd reached the steps, and she bounded up them in one leap and was met by Vanessa, whose hair was mussed and whose eyes were puffy and red.

"Where is she?" Kirby asked.

Vanessa simply pointed to her right, indicating the living room.

Amelia sat on the couch. She wasn't crying. She wasn't crumpled. She didn't even look when the pretty blonde who'd been sitting next to her glanced up at Kirby with the kindest eyes she'd ever seen and stood, gesturing for Kirby to take her spot.

Kirby sat down next to Amelia, their thighs touching. "Hey, baby," she said quietly and brushed a strand of hair off Amelia's forehead, then tucked it behind her ear. "How're you doing?"

Amelia blinked a lot. There was that. She stared off into the middle distance, at nothing really. Kirby looked up at Julia, whose arms were folded as she leaned against the wall. Their eyes met and Julia grimaced.

"How long has she been like this?" Kirby asked.

"Since I got here," Vanessa said. "An hour, maybe?"

"Amelia?" Kirby said, keeping her voice soft. She put her arm gently around her, hand on her back, and rubbed small, gentle circles. "I'm right here, okay? You take all the time you need. I'm just gonna sit right here."

"I mean, should we call somebody?" Julia asked. "This isn't normal, is it?" The blonde was now standing next to Julia and ran a hand down her arm at her words.

"Everybody handles their grief differently," the blonde said, and Kirby met her gaze gratefully, as she said what Kirby was thinking. She gave Kirby a sad smile. "Hi, I'm Savannah."

Ah, Julia's girlfriend.

"It's nice to finally meet you," Savannah went on, "though I'd have preferred different circumstances."

"Same," Kirby said and instantly liked her. She was gentle and gave off an aura of tenderness and love that Kirby found uncommon in most. Savannah had a big heart and a huge capacity for caring about others. Kirby could feel it radiating from her.

Kirby continued to rub slow circles on Amelia's back as time went on. The cousins and their partners—Vanessa's girlfriend, Grace, showed up about half an hour after Kirby—came and went. And came. And went. At least one of the four was there at all times, and Kirby admired that. They really were more like sisters than cousins. Amelia's phone rang nonstop, and one of the cousins would answer, take the phone into the kitchen or outside, speak quietly to whomever was on the line, then return after a few moments. Kirby remembered Amelia talking about how large her family was, so she assumed a lot of them were calling.

Food appeared out of nowhere, it seemed. People came. Brought casseroles or pasta or salads or bread or pizza. Hugged Amelia. People left.

Amelia was alert enough to make eye contact, to nod, to accept hugs, to pretend to listen to whatever stories they told her about her father—who honestly sounded like the greatest guy in the world to Kirby. She heard every story because she never moved. She got a few puzzled looks. She did introduce herself to a few folks. But she stayed where she was. She sat next to Amelia and held her hand, rubbed her back, just stayed close. For hours.

It was after midnight when Julia came down from upstairs carrying an armload of blankets and pillows. She'd left for a while, presumably to check on her bar, and had returned about twenty minutes ago. The living room was dim, the TV the only light, as Savannah had turned off the main lamps before she left not long after Julia's arrival. They'd had a short, whispered conversation in the kitchen, then a kiss Kirby had seen in the shadows, and then Savannah had kissed Amelia on the head, given a small wave, and headed out. The local news had wrapped up a few minutes earlier, and now a rerun of *The Big Bang Theory* was on, its laughing audience sounding rude and out of place given the circumstances.

Amelia had fallen asleep about forty minutes ago, her head in Kirby's lap. Now, Julia covered her with a blanket that looked homemade. Crocheted? Knitted? Kirby didn't know the difference. But it was several shades of blue all blending together, and it was the softest yarn she'd ever felt.

"You can slip out from under her, you know," Julia whispered. "She sleeps like the dead." She winced. "Ugh. Terrible choice of words." Then she met Kirby's eyes and added with a small grin, "You probably know how she sleeps."

Kirby smiled back. "I do." And she rubbed her hand over Amelia's arm, careful not to disturb her. "I'm good here. Thanks." Julia nodded, handed her a pillow, then crossed the room and made herself a little bed on the recliner, clearly staying.

Kirby liked these people, Amelia's cousins. Her family. She'd met a few of them before, but most were new, and she liked that it was an unspoken thing that at least one of them would be there with Amelia for as long as she needed them. That kind of unconditional support was hard to find. It made Kirby relax a bit, knowing Amelia had that.

She shifted her position slightly so she could lean back a little better, lean her head against the couch. She wasn't terribly comfortable, but that was okay, because she was not leaving Amelia. No way. She would stay touching her, keeping some kind of physical contact, until Amelia let her know she was all right. Until then? She'd stay right where she was, taking occasional bathroom breaks, but returning as quickly as possible.

She didn't remember drifting off. Or even getting sleepy. She'd felt pretty wired the whole evening, and even after Julia had covered Amelia and snuggled in and fallen asleep across the room, Kirby stayed awake, mindlessly flipping channels. She had zero recollection of the last show she'd stopped on. All she knew was that she'd clearly fallen asleep because when Amelia cried out, Kirby bolted awake as if she'd been hit with a cattle prod.

"Hey," she said as she focused on Amelia.

And for what seemed like the first time since she'd arrived, Amelia actually focused on her. Looked her in the eye. Blinked. Swallowed audibly. And then she said, in the saddest voice Kirby had ever heard, "My dad's gone, Kirby. I don't have parents anymore. I'm an orphan now." Her eyes had welled up, and as if on cue from a movie director, they spilled over, tracking down her cheeks. She looked younger, shocked, and so very sad.

"I know, baby. I know. I'm so sorry." Kirby gathered her up in her arms. Held her close tightly. Rocked her gently as she cried. Her sobs were quiet, controlled but wrenching. Kirby could feel her body quake with them.

Over Amelia's shoulder, Kirby could see Julia, awake and watching, her tears shimmering in the blue light from the TV.

Kirby swallowed down her own emotion and simply held on. Time passed. Amelia's sobs died down. Kirby handed her a tissue from the box on the end table. Amelia shifted, winced, rubbed at her side.

"Hey," Kirby said softly. "How about we go up to your room? Get you into bed? It'd be more comfortable than the couch."

Amelia said nothing, just nodded.

Kirby glanced at Julia, who also nodded. "I'll stay here," Julia said and pulled the blanket up to her chin.

"Okay." Kirby held out her hand, and Amelia took it without question. They headed up to her room. Amelia shed her clothes without comment or self-consciousness and slid under the covers in a tank top and her panties. Kirby followed suit, borrowed a T-shirt, and got in next to her, first making sure there were tissues and a glass of water nearby. Then they resumed their earlier positions, as if somebody had picked them up from the couch and dropped them into the bed. Kirby wrapped Amelia up in her arms, and the crying came again.

It was going to be like this, Kirby knew. Probably all through the night.

She knew. She'd been there.

She tightened her hold, made sure the tissue box was within reach, and settled in.

❖

The thing about sleep was that yeah, it was restorative.

And it was also a tease. A mean one.

When Amelia opened her eyes the next morning, there were several seconds of Not Knowing. That's what she would call it from that moment on, she decided. Not Knowing. With a capital *N* and a capital *K*. Because when she first woke up, there was a moment, a few seconds, where her dad was still alive, just down south. A few seconds where she wasn't completely alone in the world. A few seconds where her heart wasn't sad because she wasn't an orphan.

She would give anything to live in the Not Knowing forever.

She was alone in bed. Of course. Not unexpected. Everybody left her, that was clear now, so why wouldn't Kirby? It was nice that she'd come yesterday, but what did Amelia expect? That she'd stay forever? She was a blubbering, sobbing, emotional wreck of a woman. Who wanted to hang around with that?

The pillow still smelled like Kirby, though. Amelia rolled over so her face was smooshed into it, and she inhaled the scent that was Kirby Dupree. A little woodsy, a little fruit, warm and comforting.

Her eyes filled with tears, and then she was crying, and goddamn it, how long was this going to go on?

Her face still in the pillow, she cried herself out and then lay there, probably looking like a corpse on an episode of *Law & Order* to anybody who walked in. Facedown. Half naked. Unmoving.

"You awake?"

The voice startled Amelia so much all her limbs jerked in surprise, and she lifted her face out of Kirby's pillow to find her—Kirby—standing in the doorway with two mugs of coffee. Amelia decided right then that this was the way she loved to see Kirby most—standing in her bedroom doorway first thing in the morning with coffee. Because she learned then that it meant two things—that she cared enough about Amelia to bring her coffee, and that she was still there. The thought went from her brain right out her mouth.

"You're still here." She said it before she knew she would.

"You always say that. Of course I'm still here. Where did you think I'd be?" Kirby took the few steps that would bring her to the bed where she took a seat and set the mugs on the nightstand. Then she tenderly brushed Amelia's hair out of her eyes. "How're you doing, kiddo?"

Amelia didn't care that the pet name was ridiculous given their age difference. It felt nice, the name and the care that came with it and the fingers against her skin. "I'm sad. Crushed. Devastated." Not hyperbole. Truth.

"I know." And Kirby did. That was the thing, right? She knew exactly what Amelia was going through, and while saying she was grateful for that felt horrifyingly selfish—because who would be glad somebody else went through something this awful?—she *was* grateful. She didn't have to explain how she was feeling because Kirby got it.

"Part of me still can't believe it." Amelia turned over. Pushed herself to a sitting position. "It's like part of my brain thinks this was all just a mistake, and somebody will tell me so very soon. They'll call and be all, *Whoops! Just kidding!* Isn't that stupid?"

Kirby shook her head. "It's not stupid at all. It's pretty normal. Denial is one of the five stages of grief."

Amelia held her gaze for a moment, then reached for her mug. The coffee was hot and strong, and she felt it course through her body as if she'd injected it directly into a vein.

"Julia's still here, but I think she's headed out soon and will be up to see you shortly. Vanessa's taking her place."

Amelia's eyes welled up. Again. "Jesus Christ, I'd like to stop crying now."

Kirby smiled and handed her a tissue. "Your cousins are pretty amazing."

"I know it." She blew her nose and wiped her tears. "God, I have so much to do today. I have calls to make." She groaned because the idea of telling people over and over that her father had died was more daunting than any other task she could think of.

"Actually, I think your family has you covered." At Amelia's raised brows, Kirby went on. "I think your aunts are taking care of that. Your uncle has made arrangements to fly your dad back here. Julia and Vanessa are calling your friends. And I took care of letting your clients on today's schedule know. You only had three, so it's not so bad."

The tears again.

"Goddamn it," she said as they flowed. And then she laughed because tears were ridiculous. And then she grimaced because, oh my God, was she laughing a day after her father died?

"It's okay," Kirby said, squeezing her forearm and leaning forward to look her in the eye. It was like she knew the exact train of thought Amelia's brain had just taken. "It's okay to laugh. It doesn't mean you're not grieving. Okay? Don't try to police your emotions. That just makes it all so much harder. Let them flow. Whatever they are—tears, laughter, screams. Let 'em flow." Kirby looked around and then reached for an extra pillow. "You wanna punch something?" She held up the pillow and braced herself. "Go ahead."

"I'm not gonna hit you," Amelia said, shaking her head.

"No, it's okay. Do it. I'm ready."

Okay. It was tempting, Amelia had to admit that. She looked at the pillow, then in Kirby's eyes and the look she found there made her pause.

"When my dad died," Kirby said, "I punched a wall and broke my hand. Trust me, this is way better. Go ahead."

Amelia moved her gaze back to the pillow. Kirby had a good grip on it, she could tell. And it was bunched enough that she was pretty sure she wouldn't hurt Kirby if she did punch it.

She swallowed hard.

Met Kirby's eyes.

Set her coffee down.

Looked at Kirby again.

Back to the pillow.

And punched it. Not terribly hard. Just an average punch.

"There ya go," Kirby said. "Again."

She hit it again, a little harder this time.

"Good. Again. Take out all your anger and frustration."

Whack!

Yeah, all right, that felt good. And her anger started to bubble.

And anger felt better than sorrow, so she did her best to embrace it, and she punched again.

"Yes! Again."

Whack!

"Again."

Whack!

"More."

Whack!

One more punch was all it took to crumble her. She vaguely wondered if that was what Kirby had expected because she was right there to wrap Amelia up in her arms while she sobbed. At one point, she was vaguely aware of Vanessa peeking in the room, and she and Kirby muttered some soft words Amelia couldn't make out. Between the pillow and Kirby's shoulder, she was completely insulated against the world, and there was an alarmingly large part of her that would've been happy staying right there forever.

But that was impossible, wasn't it? Not to mention childish. She was a grownup, and she had grown-up things to do.

Like call the funeral home and arrange to bury her father.

And the grief took her again.

CHAPTER TWENTY-SIX

The following week passed by in a blur of hugs and handshakes and kind words and tears and a church service with a full house and endless amounts of food, none of which Amelia ate. She was exhausted. Completely wrung out. If it hadn't been for her family—mainly her cousins and Kirby—she'd have curled up in a ball on the floor long ago and would still be there.

They were at Martini's, and it was Sunday. Her father had been dead for nine days now. It had taken some time to get him home from Florida, then arrange the wake, the Mass, the funeral. In order to hold a sort of celebration of her Uncle Tony, Julia had closed the bar to customers that day, but you'd never know it. The place was packed, and the fact that every person in the building knew and loved her father filled Amelia with a sense of pride that she was able to recognize, even through her grief.

"How're you doing, sweetheart?" Uncle Vinnie came and stood next to her, his arm protectively around her shoulders as he kissed her temple. He was Julia's dad, but all her aunts and uncles had been checking on her, quietly sliding into the parental spots her parents had left. It was comforting. And also hard. So very, very hard.

"I'm okay," she replied with one nod. It was her stock answer. Had been for every step of this process. Because, really, what was she going to say? Was she going to tell them the truth? No way. Somebody would come up to her, hug her, tell her what a wonderful man her dad was, and ask her how she was holding up.

She'd nod and smile and hold people who cried—God, that was the worst—and tell them all, "I'm okay."

Which was a lie. She wasn't okay. She was lost.

Uncle Vinnie stood next to her for a while. That's what he did. In fact, that's what all the men did. Her uncles, who were dealing with their own grief of losing a brother. Her male cousins. They'd hug her, kiss her, ask her how she was doing and then…stand there. Stand next to her. Stand behind her. Stand somewhere in her vicinity. And actually, it made her smile. Because she knew that's all they knew how to do for her. Be there. And it was enough.

The women, on the other hand, handled everything. *Everything.* The phone calls. The venues. The food—God, the food! Her clothes. Her rides. One of them was near her at all times. *All* times. Julia, Vanessa, Savannah, Grace, her aunts, her other female cousins. Somebody was always nearby to get her water or a tissue or remind her to try to eat something. They headed off people who were too chatty. Or too huggy. Or too emotional. Amelia would be forever grateful, and she had zero idea how she'd ever thank them all for keeping things moving and keeping her from completely drowning in her own grief.

Above all of that, though, was Kirby. Kirby kept her afloat, like her own personal living, breathing life preserver. She'd barely left her side all week. She'd scooted home once or twice to grab clean clothes for herself, but that was it. She'd taken the week off, left her jobs to be handled by her two employees. Just like that. It wasn't even a question. There was zero hesitation. It just was. She'd stayed at Amelia's house, made sure she slept in her bed and not on the couch or, Lord help her, the floor, which had been a distinct possibility more than once. And when Amelia cried, Kirby let her cry. She never told her to pull herself together. She just held her and told her that, while her pain and the missing of her father would never go away, it would ease up as time went on, that she could cry as much as she needed to. That she should. That she'd be right there.

Even now, she stood behind Amelia, never interrupting her

conversations, just checking in every so often, letting her know she was there, asking if she needed food, making sure she drank water.

"You know what I'm ready for?" Amelia said to her after they'd been in Martini's for over an hour.

"Alcohol?"

Amelia turned to her. "Yes! How'd you know?"

Kirby shrugged and smiled. "Lucky guess. What would you like? Go easy. You haven't eaten much."

"Good point. Maybe just a beer for now."

"You got it."

Amelia watched her leave the table where she'd sort of parked herself for the time being, so new arrivals could easily find her. She'd make the rounds again soon. She watched as Kirby stopped next to Julia and spoke in her ear. Julia made eye contact with Amelia, grinned and gave her a thumbs-up, and they went off, presumably to fetch a beer for her.

"Amelia."

The voice skittered up her spine and sat on her shoulders. She knew full well who it was before she even turned around, having heard that voice every day for many years. She turned to meet her, and before she could say a word, Tammy wrapped her in a huge hug, the feel so achingly familiar, her heart squeezed in her chest.

"Oh my God," she said next to Amelia's ear. "I'm so sorry, sweetie. I didn't know. I was out of town for work, and I just got back last night, and Sheri called and told me."

Amelia blinked as Tammy went on and on, telling her how she'd learned about her former father-in-law's death from a *friend* that Amelia had apparently lost in the split, given she hadn't heard a thing from Sheri in almost two years. The hug, though, honest to God, it was so familiar and warm, and Amelia could feel herself sinking into it, remembering how that used to be her favorite place. It was *Tammy*, for God's sake. The woman she'd married. The woman she'd planned to spend her life with. And here she was. Back again. Holding her.

Amelia's eyes filled, and a small sob escaped before she could catch it.

"Oh, honey." Tammy's arms tightened. "I'm so sorry."

"I can't believe he's gone," she said through tears. "It's not supposed to happen this soon."

"I know, sweetie. I know."

"I'm so glad you came."

"Of course. I wouldn't have missed it. I had Nina bring me right over as soon as I heard."

If they'd been in the middle of a movie and there had been a soundtrack to that scene, the shock of a needle scratching across a record would've been next. Because…Nina. *Fucking Nina.* That bitch that had helped ruin her life. That bitch Tammy had left her for. That bitch.

"Hey, Amelia? You okay?"

Amelia heard Kirby before she saw her, before she felt her. She heard her, and Kirby's voice slid into her ear and through her body and wrapped around her heart and held it so warmly and so tenderly that it somehow gave her strength. She pulled back from Tammy, then gently extricated herself from the embrace. A nod. "Yeah. I'm okay." That stock answer again, and she smiled over it.

"Here's your beer." And Kirby handed her a bottle. Frosty cold. Their fingers touched as she took it. Warm. Their eyes met and held, and when Amelia turned back to Tammy, it was written all over her face that she'd seen. That she'd understood. That this was likely the person who, as she'd said on the phone, was *way* too young. A shadow floated across Tammy's face as she turned to Kirby.

"Hi, I don't think we've met. I'm Tammy." She stuck her hand out toward Kirby.

"Tammy, Tammy, where have I heard your name before?" Kirby asked, squinting as she gripped Tammy's hand and seemed to feign thinking really hard. "Oh! You're the ex. The one who left Amelia for somebody else. After she retired early for you. Right?" Her smile was wide, and her eyes were friendly, and if Amelia didn't know any better, she'd think that Kirby was honestly saying these things without any ill will. "Hi, I'm Kirby. Nice to meet you."

Tammy also knew better, and her eyes zipped back over to Amelia. Her brows rose.

Kirby chose that moment to interlace her fingers with Amelia's, and they stood there, holding hands.

It was at that moment that Tammy seemed to realize maybe she wasn't all that welcome, after all. She glanced around the bar, which made Amelia do the same. To her shock, Julia and Vanessa were both looking their way, but from different sides of the bar. It was like they'd gotten a signal and homed in and just…stared.

It shouldn't have given Amelia such satisfaction to see Tammy swallow hard, but it did. She watched as Tammy's throat moved while she was looking from one cousin to the other, and Amelia smiled. Just like that. Swallow, smile. So weird. And felt so good. She was still smiling when Tammy turned back to her and blinked in surprise.

"I guess…maybe I should go?" Tammy asked it as a question instead of stating it like a fact. It was a habit of hers, something she did when she wanted somebody else to make the decision she wanted. As if posing it as a question would cause somebody else to jump in, all *Oh no, don't go.* But Amelia knew this, and for the first time in all the years they'd been together, she neatly sidestepped the trap.

"Maybe you should." She said it quietly. Simply. Unemotionally. And she didn't let her gaze skitter away. She held Tammy's, making it clear exactly who was running the show now, and that it wasn't Tammy.

"Well. Okay. I just…" Tammy took a deep breath, then blew it out like she'd worked very hard on the past ten minutes. "I wanted you to know how sorry I am."

"I appreciate that." Amelia had so many more things she could've said. But right then? In that moment? With Kirby holding her hand? She stood tall and realized she didn't need to say any of them.

"Okay." Tammy looked down at her shoes, then back up, then gave a nod. "Take care of yourself, Amelia."

"I will."

And Tammy left.

Amelia watched her exit, followed her out with her eyes.

"You okay?" Kirby asked softly and gave her hand a squeeze.

Amelia turned to her. "You know what? I am. It's so weird."

Kirby's smile seemed a bit hesitant, and Amelia couldn't really blame her. She'd kind of jumped into what might've been a hornet's nest.

She lifted their hands and kissed Kirby's knuckles. "You're amazing."

"Listen, I just brought you a beer." But her eyes softened, and she knew. Amelia could tell. "I was a little nervous there for a minute."

"You were? How come?"

"The ex showing up when the heroine is emotionally vulnerable? I've seen many a rom-com. That could've gone a very different way. I saw you sink into that hug and…" This time, Kirby was the one who swallowed hard.

"Muscle memory. That's all it was. A momentary lapse."

"Yeah?"

"Yeah." Amelia held her gaze, looked deeply into those greenish-hazel eyes that were favoring the green today, and the words just came. "I've got some things to tell you, I think." And Kirby's cheeks turned pink, and it was adorable, and Amelia wrapped her in a hug. Kissed the top of her head.

"Oh, Amelia, we're so sorry."

She let go of Kirby and turned to see an old friend of the family, and it was back to regularly scheduled programming. At least for a few more hours.

Kirby slid into the background again, close enough to reach for, but out of the way for hugs and discussions from friends and family. But she was there. Amelia knew it, she could feel it, and it meant everything. Every so often, she'd turn and meet Kirby's eyes and draw strength from them. Strength that helped her plow forward. All she had to do was get through this day, and then she could get back to normal life.

As normal as her life could be with no parents.

And just when that thought would press on her, just when she thought she couldn't take the weight any longer, she'd glance over her shoulder, and it was the same. Kirby was still there, and she'd smile at her. And Amelia would find the energy to push on. Every single time, it was the same.

Kirby was still there.

CHAPTER TWENTY-SEVEN

September came along on a wave of rain and wind. The Labor Day weekend had been a complete washout. School had started up in drizzle. The sun hadn't been seen in nearly six days.

It was the second Friday of the month, and Kirby was over the fucking rain. The damp air made for less than ideal circumstances for painting. It was fine. She could work around it, and did, but extra effort had to be taken and certain exterior jobs needed to be rescheduled. Still, work was crazy busy, and for that, she was grateful. Victor Renwick had been so happy with her work, he'd recommended her to half a dozen of his friends and colleagues, and because of that, Dupree Paint Design was booked up through the rest of the year, and Kirby'd had to hire two more employees.

No complaints about that.

She was painting a bathroom that was in the midst of a remodel, the contractor giving her two days to get her stuff done so he could come back and install the new vanity and tub. The cutting in was tight, but she had small hands—as Krog was always telling her—so she was taking her time and getting all the corners and crevices while she had the chance. The room wasn't large, and there were two other jobs on the schedule, so she was on her own with this one, painting the room a robin's-egg blue that she would've called How *You* Bluein'? That would've made Amelia laugh, and just the idea of making her girlfriend laugh made her smile, all by herself on the floor on her stomach, painting behind a toilet.

Her girlfriend.

Yeah, that's what she called Amelia now. At least in her head. They were exclusive, even though they hadn't talked about it. It had been a month since the funeral for Amelia's dad. Since the moment with the ex. Since life had gone back to *normal*. Her head put air quotes around the word because she knew from experience there would be no normal for Amelia again. Just life without her father. Nothing normal about that. She wondered if Amelia thought of her as her girlfriend. She should probably ask, but she was afraid to.

Which was silly. She knew it. Talking was key. Communication was the most important aspect of a relationship. She knew this, yet she didn't want to pull the focus from something as life-altering as Amelia learning to navigate life without parents to her little petty insecurities about where they stood. Because the truth was, she was in love with Amelia. Fully. Deeply. Irrevocably in love. And she wanted to tell her, but she was scared, of so many things. That Amelia wasn't ready. That she'd scare Amelia away. That Amelia didn't feel the same way.

She sighed. She was doing that a lot lately, and she shook her head in irritation when her phone in the back pocket of her jeans alerted her to a text. She finished the last of behind the toilet, slid her way out, and stood.

Hi. Bar Back 2nite?

Well, that was a surprise. It was usually Kirby making the plans and Amelia nodding and smiling and showing up.

Sure! Time?

Kirby had grown to love Amelia's cousins like they were her own family, so hanging with them for the evening sounded like fun, even if she did wish for some alone time with Amelia. She was feeling a little restless, but it was fine. It could wait. It would have to.

A few hours later, she was knocking on the back door of Martini's, feeling a little bit like she was entering a secret clubhouse, which she kind of was, really.

"Hey," Vanessa said as she let her in, then wrapped her in a hug. It was a thing that had taken a little getting used to for

Kirby—the Martinis were very physically affectionate people. Always with the hugs and kisses. But Vanessa was sweet, and her hug was warm, and Kirby hugged her back.

"How's the first week of school?" she asked as she entered.

Vanessa groaned and dropped her head backward toward her shoulder blades and did a pretty good impression of dying a slow, painful death, which made Kirby laugh. "I'll be right back. Gotta help Julia with something," she said vaguely, then left through the door that led out to the bar.

Amelia was the only other person in the room, sitting on the couch, a glass of wine in her hand, almost empty by the looks of it, and Kirby wondered how long she'd been there. She bent over and kissed her lips.

"Hi, beautiful," she said and sat next to her. "Where's the rest of the girl gang?"

Amelia's eyes darted and she seemed...off. Nervous? Kirby studied her for a moment. Unsettled. Uncomfortable. Uncertain. All those *un* words zipped through Kirby's head, and her heart sped up.

"What's going on?" she asked, not sure if she actually wanted the answer. "What's wrong?"

Amelia wet her lips. Cleared her throat. Slugged the rest of her wine and set the glass on the coffee table in front of them. Wiped her hands down her thighs. Cleared her throat again. "So. I wanted to talk to you."

Oh, damn. Kirby looked down at her lap, and if she was being honest, part of her had been waiting for exactly this. For Amelia to be done with her. It was true that Kirby thought they'd been doing so great, but losing a parent could mess with you, change your perspective and the way you feel things. She knew this from experience, so while she didn't want this, wanted to scream and shout and fight it, she mentally told herself she would take the breakup quietly. With dignity. For Amelia. She wouldn't make it harder. And then, when she got home, she'd figure out how to deal with her own feelings. She'd been thinking about her love for Amelia, and Amelia was about to dump her. Fuck, this was going to hurt more than Kirby cared to admit.

"You know how this"—Amelia gestured between them—"has been hard for me from the beginning. The age difference. My own insecurities." Then she stopped and sighed, and in a matter of seconds, there was a sheen of sweat on her forehead.

"Hot flash?"

"Of course." Together, they'd learned some of Amelia's triggers: exertion, nerves, humidity. All of them could send her temperature skyrocketing, causing her to break out in a sweat that could last anywhere from a few seconds to a few minutes.

Kirby got up and went behind the practice bar, where she opened the freezer and took out one of the shoulder wrap things that Amelia kept in her freezer. She brought it to Amelia and laid it over her shoulders as Amelia looked at her, wide-eyed.

"When did that get put in there?"

Kirby shrugged. "I picked one up last week and asked Julia if we could keep it here."

Amelia just stared at her, then slowly shook her head, like she couldn't believe her luck. Which poked Kirby right in the heart. Painfully.

Kirby took a deep breath. "Listen, I'm all for letting you do this the way you need to, but I'm not sure how long I can hold it together, so if you could speed up the dumping part, I'd appreciate it."

This time, Amelia's eyes didn't go wide, they went *wide*, and she leaned back, like Kirby had just said something so ridiculous, she wasn't sure if she'd heard her correctly, and then gave her a shove. "The dumping part?" Amelia asked, clearly baffled. "What does that mean?"

Kirby blinked at her. "It means…isn't that what you're doing? This whole *It's been hard from the beginning* thing?"

Amelia gasped and covered her mouth with a hand and just looked at her for a good ten or fifteen seconds before a sound burst out of her.

A laugh.

A laugh? What?

"You think I'm breaking up with you?" Amelia asked, and the smile that suddenly spread across her face was so wide and so joyous that Kirby could only look at her, completely confused, and blink. Like, a lot of blinking.

"You're not?" she finally asked.

"Breaking up with you? God, no. I brought you here to tell you I'm in love with you, you idiot!"

"What?" More blinking, because apparently, Kirby's brain had completely short-circuited, and that was all she was able to do now. Blink. And stare. Blinking and staring. And then there was brow furrowing. Because seriously, what the fuck was happening right now?

And suddenly, there was Vanessa, hurrying in from the bar, shaking her head. "Mother Mary on a baguette, you two are a ridiculous mess. Seriously. What the hell?" She came around and sat on the coffee table so she was between them, her knees bumping both of theirs. That's when Kirby looked up and saw Julia, Savannah, and Grace, all crammed in the doorway like children eavesdropping on the adults.

Vanessa took one of Amelia's hands and one of Kirby's and pulled both into her lap, so Amelia and Kirby were leaning awkwardly toward her.

"Kirby? Amelia loves you. She's hopelessly in love with you. She's been afraid to tell you because, to be honest, she's a fucking wimp. And we're all sick of watching her lovesick face moping around here."

"Thanks for that," Amelia muttered, looking utterly mortified as she covered her eyes with her other hand, which was actually pretty adorable.

Vanessa didn't miss a beat. "So we said if she didn't finally tell you, we would have no choice but to do it for her. And here we are."

Kirby looked from her to Amelia and back. Speechless, which she never was. She opened her mouth, but no sound came out.

"I see you're having trouble with speech," Vanessa said. "So lemme help. Are you happy with this new knowledge?"

Kirby nodded.

"And it is new knowledge, yes?"

More nodding, which made Vanessa shoot Amelia a look. Amelia grimaced appropriately.

"And now the biggie." Vanessa looked her directly in the eye, her blue ones seemingly searching Kirby's before she looked satisfied and asked her question. "Do you love Amelia?"

"Yes," Kirby said immediately, her nodding increasing in enthusiasm.

"And you're in love with her?"

"Truly, madly, deeply," Kirby said, her voice soft. "I have been for a while now. I was just—"

"Afraid to say it out loud," Amelia concluded, smiling.

"Yeah," Kirby agreed.

Amelia looked happy. Relieved. She turned to Vanessa. "Go away now."

"Yes, ma'am," Vanessa said and stood. "My work here is done. You're welcome. I'll bill you."

"You, too," Amelia said, shooting a look at the doorway. "All of you. Go away. We need a minute."

When the door shut, Amelia shook her head slowly, then turned to Kirby, held her gaze, gathered her hands in her own. Amelia inhaled slowly, then let it out.

"This is going to sound stupidly cliché, but I'm going to say it anyway." A peek of tongue as she wet her lips. "After Tammy left, I didn't think I'd ever find love again."

"You're right," Kirby said with a grin. "That's a line right out of a bad rom-com."

"Hey, I warned you." They laughed softly, then Amelia continued, "But I'm serious. I didn't even know if I would want to find love. And then you came along. All exuberant, always moving, fourteen-years-younger-than-me of you. And I rolled my eyes and scoffed and refused to see just exactly what you are."

"Which is?" Kirby was holding her breath and had no control over the fact.

"Perfect for me. You're my opposite in many ways, but in many more ways, you're not. You get me. You support me." Amelia's hazel eyes welled up. "When my dad died, you did the most perfect impression of a rock, which was exactly what I needed then. You took care of me, and I've never really had that before."

"No?"

Amelia shook her head, and her grip on Kirby's hands tightened. "I'm so grateful for you, and to you. I want to be for you what you've become for me. And I love you. So very much. I think we can make this work, but I'd like to know if you're on the same page."

Kirby barked a laugh. "Am I on the same page? Are you kidding? We're not only on the same page, we're on the same paragraph. The same sentence. Hell, I kinda think we're writing it. Together." She brought Amelia's hands up, kissed the knuckles. "You ground me. Do you know that?"

Amelia shook her head.

"It's what I need most in the world. I have a tendency to run myself ragged."

A snort. "Yeah, I noticed."

"I do that because if I sit still, I have to think. I have to feel my feet on the earth, and I have to acknowledge my life. Alone. Without family. And who wants to deal with that? So I keep moving." Kirby felt her eyes fill, and suddenly, there was a lump she had to swallow down. "But with you, I *want* to sit still. I *want* to look around and see what I have. Because if I have you, everything else makes sense. I actually think I've loved you since the first time I saw you."

Amelia's laugh was like a gunshot, and she pointed toward the bar. "Out there? When I mocked your color choice?"

"Yeah. You challenged me." Kirby grinned. "Pretty fucking sexy, if I'm being honest."

"Well. Who knew?"

"I did!" Julia shouted from the other side of the door.

Then Vanessa added, "Can we come in now? The wait is killing us!"

Kirby and Amelia burst out laughing, and Amelia called, "Yes, fine, you weirdos. Come in."

The door burst open and the four women flooded in, straight for them, hugs and kisses and celebration all around.

Kirby's smile was huge and she couldn't help it. All the others seemed to be talking at once, and the topics shifted so quickly, she nearly got whiplash trying to follow. From how they all knew she and Amelia would end up together to where would they sleep more often, Kirby's place or Amelia's place, to how Julia never had Savannah at her apartment to how Vanessa and Grace had to sneak around so Grace's son didn't know his mom was sleeping with his teacher. And the whole time these shifts happened, the whole time there was no break at all in conversation, Kirby just smiled and wondered how the hell she'd gotten so lucky as to end up with this instant family. Because that's what they were, and she knew it immediately. She and Amelia might be orphans, but they weren't without family. Amelia and her cousins were a package deal, and Kirby felt like she'd hit the jackpot.

Grace was talking about the night she and Vanessa were making out on her couch when her now-ex-husband walked in, and Kirby slid a glance toward Amelia, only to find her looking right back. Their hands were still clasped, and Kirby marveled at how natural it felt. Holding Amelia's hand was simply like an extension of her own. Part of her. She squeezed it and brought it up to her lips again. Kissed the knuckles. Silently mouthed, "I love you."

Amelia blushed a pretty pink. "I love you back," she mouthed in return, and then Amelia scooched closer, and Kirby lifted her arm, and Amelia snuggled into her as they listened to the stories that went on for the rest of the evening. They even contributed their own, mostly lamenting how much they missed Victor Renwick's pool.

"I think you either need to have a pool installed at one of your places or buy a new house that has a pool." Savannah took the glass of red wine Julia poured her. "Seems like it should be a requirement." Then she winked and sipped.

Everybody laughed, and as the topic shifted again, Kirby stayed on that one. Because yeah, she wanted to live with Amelia. She could see it. Not tomorrow. Not next month. But soon. Amelia was her home. She'd never felt anything more deeply or thoroughly.

She looked at Amelia as she piped in with her two cents about the benefits of pools, oblivious to Kirby's train of thought. She looked around at the five women.

Oh yes.

This was her family now. She felt it. Deep in her heart. Racing in her blood. Attached to every fiber within her. This was her family now.

And Amelia was her home.

EPILOGUE

February 14

"I can't believe it's today." Amelia said it more to herself than out loud. She wasn't looking for a response. She was standing in front of the full-length mirror in one of the little dressing rooms off the main gathering space in the Unitarian Church.

"I bet." Kirby was right there and peeked around her to meet her eyes in the glass. "Not so much for me, but you've been there since the beginning of...them."

Amelia nodded. She had been there since the beginning of *them*, and she nodded as she tugged at the sleeve of her dress. "I remember the first time I saw Savannah in the bar, sitting with her friends. The way she'd looked at Julia even before she'd known her."

"Yeah?" Kirby asked. "How?"

"Intensely. With curiosity. With wonder. She still looks at her that way, but now..." She turned to face Kirby. "It's like all those things are wrapped in a cocoon of deep respect and love."

"I can see that," Kirby agreed. Then she turned Amelia back around so they both faced the mirror, Kirby standing behind her, peeking over her shoulder. And Kirby was looking at her in exactly the same way. With intense and wondrous curiosity all wrapped up in love. "You look so fucking beautiful, I can hardly breathe." She said it on a whisper, and while it made Amelia feel wonderful, it also turned her the hell on. She lifted her hand and laid it against Kirby's warm cheek.

"Yeah, don't be saying things like that to me in your sexy voice, missy, or we're gonna have issues."

"Issues like, say, grabbing a quickie before the ceremony?"

The door opened just as Kirby was finishing her sentence. "No, ma'am." Teddi Baker, Julia's wedding planner, hurried into the room like she was in charge, the same way she hurried into every room and every space, or so Amelia had learned very quickly. Because she was. "No time for quickies. Sorry. Everybody is in place in the church, and we've got about five minutes before I need you out there."

Amelia blushed at being caught. Kirby laughed because, as she'd said more than once to Amelia, she liked Teddi.

Julia and Savannah had hired Teddi at the last minute because planning a wedding was goddamn overwhelming when you both had full-time jobs and demanding families, no matter how many cousins you had helping out. Luckily, Grace knew her from supplying flowers to dozens of weddings and called in a favor. It had been a brilliant decision. Teddi had taken over, took everything out of Julia's and Savannah's hands, and for the first time in a year, Amelia saw them sigh in relief. Sit back and relax. Actually enjoy the idea of their upcoming wedding instead of looking endlessly stressed out about it.

And now it was here.

"Are you ready, maid of honor number one?" Teddi asked her. "You look gorgeous, by the way."

Amelia took a last look in the mirror and had to admit, she looked damn good. Today, she would set aside that critical view of her body that she worried had become permanent. She picked it up, ignoring the slight bulge in her middle, set it in a corner, and allowed herself to see—*really see*—what Teddi meant. Her dress was red. Simple. Elegant. High-low and long-sleeved with a lacy overlay and a scooped neckline. Her hair was up, freshly highlighted, ringlets strategically dangling by her ears. Her makeup was on point, thanks to Savannah's friend the cosmetologist. Her heels had been dyed to match the dress. Kirby handed over her flowers, a small bouquet of white daisies,

Savannah's favorite flower. Both bridesmaids' bouquets had been handmade by Grace.

"She's not wrong. You're stunning," Kirby said softly in her ear, then kissed her on the cheek and turned back to Teddi with one nod. "She's ready." Back to Amelia. "I'll see you out there." Another gentle kiss, this one to her lips, and Kirby headed out to take a seat, leaving Amelia no time to stop and admire how unbelievably sexy her girlfriend looked in the emerald-green dress she'd chosen, the one that made her eyes pop.

"Vanessa's in the foyer waiting for you," Teddi told her, and not for the first time, Amelia was shocked by the calm expression on Teddi's face. No worry. No urgency. Just calm patience, despite the fact that she very likely wanted to grab Amelia by the arm and haul her poky ass out there. Yes, Teddi did this all the time, it was her job, but still. Admirable.

"Let's do this," Amelia said with a determined nod and followed Teddi out. The foyer was empty, save for Vanessa, wearing a dress that matched Amelia's and carrying a duplicate bouquet. Her eyes were already welling up, and Amelia smiled at her. "You can't cry yet, Ness, you'll ruin your makeup," she said, but gently. Tenderly. She reached out and ran her thumb over Vanessa's cheek. "You're beautiful," she said, and she meant it.

"Right back atcha, you gorgeous thing," Vanessa said. Then she swallowed audibly and took a deep breath. "Can you believe this is it? Our Julia. Married!"

"I can't...but I can." And convoluted as it sounded, nothing was closer to the truth.

"I can't either," came Julia's voice from behind them.

"Me neither," said Savannah.

Amelia turned, and there stood the brides. Breathtaking. Resplendent in their beauty. Their dresses simple. Ivory. Julia's hair was mostly down, talked into that by both her cousins as well as her fiancée. Because, let's face it, nobody had hair like Julia's, and she should showcase it every chance she got. Which was what they told her. Insisted on.

Savannah had never looked more beautiful to Amelia in the

more-than-a-year she'd known her. Her hair was up, her dress was formfitting, and her face was colored with such love for Julia, it brought tears to Amelia's eyes. Vanessa's spilled over.

"Ness, you're gonna ruin your makeup," Savannah said, reiterating Amelia's warning, but she laughed quietly as she pulled out a tissue like a magician, Amelia having no idea where it had come from, and dabbed gently at Vanessa's cheeks.

"I can't help it," Vanessa said. "You guys look so beautiful, and this is such an amazing day, and I'm just *so happy*."

"Exactly," Amelia said, pointing at Vanessa while looking at Julia and Savannah. "What she said."

And then Teddi was there. "Ready?" she asked, her hands on the handles of the closed doors. And there was no more time for anything but quick hugs and smiles.

"I love you guys," Amelia said quietly. Vanessa nodded. Savannah grinned, her eyes watery.

"I don't know what I'd do without you weirdos," Julia said, then held out her hand to Savannah, who placed her hand in Julia's. Julia lifted it to her lips and kissed the knuckles. "My family."

"Okay," Teddi said. "Maid of honor one, count of five, maid of honor two, count of ten, brides. Got it?"

Nods all around.

The doors opened.

❖

"Holy shit." Julia flopped down onto the couch in The Bar Back like she no longer possessed a skeleton, like she was just skin and tissue and had no way of staying upright. "That was the longest day ever and also went so fast, I think I missed a bunch of it." She let her body slide sideways, and she ended up with her head in Savannah's lap.

"Right?" Savannah said. "How is that even possible? It shouldn't be. I mean, scientifically, it's not."

"I'm exhausted, and it wasn't even my wedding," Vanessa said from her spot on the floor where she'd sprawled out upon arrival and hadn't moved since.

"That's because you danced like the world was ending," Grace reminded her with a laugh from her barstool.

"That's the only way to dance," Kirby said from her barstool, then leaned down and fist-bumped Vanessa.

Amelia watched from her seat in Julia's desk chair, and she smiled at the new bond that had formed between her cousin and her girlfriend. As if reading her mind, Julia waved a finger between Vanessa and Kirby and said, "Meels, I'd keep an eye on this. Trouble in the making, right here."

"Way ahead of you," Amelia said and squinted hard at the two and then laughed. Then she shifted the subject to what was foremost in her brain right then. "I can't believe you guys are married. It's surreal."

"Right?" Grace said, then stood and went behind the bar. "Anybody want water?" Five hands shot up, and Grace laughed. "Dehydration all around, then, I see."

"Listen, it was a wedding," Kirby said. "We *drank*."

"We did," Amelia said and took the bottle of water Grace handed her. They were quiet as bottles cracked open and sips were taken. Everybody had changed out of their wedding clothes and into more comfortable outfits for the reception, which was held, of course, at Martini's.

"That was the most amazing party," Grace said. "I think everybody had a blast." She looked at Julia. "And your parents!"

Vanessa barked a laugh. "Speaking of dancing like the world is ending."

Julia's smile was wide, and the relief there was clear as could be. Amelia knew she'd worried about not getting married in a Catholic Church or by a priest and how her parents would be about it. But to almost everybody's shock, Uncle Vinnie and Aunt Anna were totally fine and had a blast at the party. "My dad came up to me at one point and told me he was proud of me, and he couldn't have chosen a better partner for me if he'd been assigned to." Her eyes welled up, and she kissed Savannah's hand, entwined with hers.

"You guys," Vanessa whined as her own eyes filled.

"Oh my God, you cannot possibly have any tears left to cry,"

Grace said, but her affection was clear. "You've been a waterworks since the second you put your dress on this morning."

"I know!" was Vanessa's wailed response, which had the room dissolving in laughter. As it died down, Kirby cleared her throat.

"Can I say something?" Kirby asked and looked around at each of them.

"You're new here," Savannah said, "so we won't mock you—yet—because you may not quite get how Italians work. They don't ask to speak. They just jump in and raise their voi—"

"Hey! We do not," Julia jumped in, then clamped her mouth shut when she realized she'd just proven her wife's point. As Savannah smiled down at her, she said, "Um. Never mind. Continue."

Savannah bent down and kissed her. "Thank you, my love. As I was saying, you don't have to ask to speak. There. Done. Go ahead."

Silence fell, and Kirby cleared her throat again, then glanced at Amelia, whose heart swelled with love, something that never stopped surprising her. "I just wanted to say thank you. For including me. For welcoming me into this little group of yours. It's been a long time since I've felt like I had any family, and I had no idea that when I fell for Amelia, I'd be getting all of you guys as well." Her face flushed a deep pink, and Amelia's heart squeezed. She put a hand over it and tipped her head to the side, smiling at Kirby, who looked at her in that moment with such joy and love that the room seemed to get brighter with it. "I love you so much, Amelia. I can't believe my luck. And I want to say, right here and now, in front of the people who love you most in the world, that I will always be here for you. That I will make it my mission to make you the happiest woman around for as long as I draw breath."

Amelia didn't even try to stop the tears that suddenly filled her eyes and spilled over. "You know, I was thinking about this yesterday, about the past two years for me. I feel like my life was on pause, waiting for you to arrive. And now that you're here, it's like it's playing again. Moving forward. Full of color and music and laughter. And I'm so glad to have you as my family now. Because you are."

"Excuse me," Julia interrupted. "Are you two hijacking my fucking wedding day?"

Amelia held up a hand like a traffic cop and didn't even look at her. "Your day's over, bitch. Shh."

And that was it. The room dissolved into laughter as they cracked the hell up together. And through it, Kirby crossed the room to Amelia, sat in her lap, and wrapped her arms around her.

"I love you, baby," Amelia whispered in Kirby's ear, even as the others continued laughing.

"I love you back," Kirby said. "You're my family now. This"—she waved an arm around the room—"is family."

"Family," Amelia agreed and kissed her with her whole heart.

About the Author

Georgia Beers lives in Upstate New York and has written more than thirty novels of women-loving-women romance. In her off-hours, she can usually be found searching for a scary movie, lifting all the weights, sipping a good Pinot, or trying to keep up with little big man Archie, her mix of many tiny dogs. Find out more at georgiabeers.com.

Books Available From Bold Strokes Books

The Business of Pleasure by Ronica Black. Editor in chief Valerie Raffield is quickly becoming smitten by Lennox, the graphic artist she's hired to work remotely. But when Lennox doesn't show for their first face-to-face meeting, Valerie's heart and her business may be in jeopardy. (978-1-63679-134-0)

Cold Blood by Genevieve McCluer. Maybe together, Kalila and Dorenia have a chance of taking down the vampires who have eluded them all these years. And maybe, in each other, they can find a love worth living for. (978-1-63679-195-1)

Greener Pastures by Aurora Rey. When city girl and CPA Audrey Adams finds herself tending her aunt's farm, will Rowan Marshall—the charming cider maker next door—turn out to be her saving grace or the bane of her existence? (978-1-63679-116-6)

Grounded by Amanda Radley. For a second chance, Olivia and Emily will need to accept their mistakes, learn to communicate properly, and with a little help from five-year-old Henry, fall madly in love all over again. Sequel to Flight SQA016. (978-1-63679-241-5)

The Hummingbird Sanctuary by Erin Zak. The Hummingbird Sanctuary, Colorado's hottest resort destination: Come for the mountains, stay for the charm, and enjoy the drama as Olive, Eleanor, and Harriet figure out the meaning of true friendship. (978-1-63679-163-0)

Journey's End by Amanda Radley. In this heartwarming conclusion to the Flight series, Olivia and Emily must finally decide what they want, what they need, and how to follow the dreams of their hearts. (978-1-63679-233-0)

Secret Agent by Michelle Larkin. CIA agent Peyton North embarks on a global chase to apprehend rogue agent Zoey Blackwood, but her commitment to the mission is tested as the sparks between them ignite and their sizzling attraction approaches a point of no return. (978-1-63555-753-4)

Something Between Us by Krystina Rivers. A decade after her heart was broken under Don't Ask, Don't Tell, Kirby runs into her first love and has to decide if what's still between them is enough to heal her broken heart. (978-1-63679-135-7)

Sugar Girl by Emma L McGeown. Having traded in traditional romance for the perks of Sugar Dating, Ciara Reilly not only enjoys the no-strings-attached arrangement, she's also a hit with her clients. That is, until she meets the beautiful entrepreneur Charlie Keller, who makes her want to go sugar-free. (978-1-63679-156-2)

With a Twist by Georgia Beers. Starting over isn't easy for Amelia Martini. When the irritatingly cheerful Kirby Dupress comes into her life, will Amelia be brave enough to go after the love she really wants? (978-1-63555-987-3)

The Witch Queen's Mate by Jennifer Karter. Barra and Silvi must overcome their ingrained hatred and prejudice to use Barra's magic and save both their peoples from not just slavery, but destruction. (978-1-63679-202-6)

Business of the Heart by Claire Forsythe. When a hopeless romantic meets a tough-as-nails cynic, they'll need to overcome the wounds of the past to discover that their hearts are the most important business of all. (978-1-63679-167-8)

Dying for You by Jenny Frame. Can Victorija Dred keep an age-old vow and fight the need to take blood from Daisy Macdougall? (978-1-63679-073-2)

Exclusive by Melissa Brayden. Skylar Ruiz lands the TV reporting job of a lifetime, but is she willing to sacrifice it all for the love of her longtime crush, anchorwoman Carolyn McNamara? (978-1-63679-112-8)

Her Duchess to Desire by Jane Walsh. An up-and-coming interior designer seeks to create a happily ever after with an intriguing duchess, proving that love never goes out of fashion. (978-1-63679-065-7)

Take Her Down by Lauren Emily Whalen. Stakes are cutthroat, scheming is creative, and loyalty is ever-changing in this queer, female-driven YA retelling of Shakespeare's Julius Caesar. (978-1-63679-089-3)